RESCUING GRACELYNN (SPECIAL FORCES: OPERATION ALPHA)

BRAVO SERIES BOOK 1

ANNA BLAKELY

Cover by Lori Jackson Design
Content Editing by Trenda London
Copy Editing by Tracy Roelle

Dear Readers,

Welcome to the Special Forces: Operation Alpha Fan-Fiction world!

If you are new to this amazing world, in a nutshell the author wrote a story using one or more of my characters in it. Sometimes that character has a major role in the story, and other times they are only mentioned briefly. This is perfectly legal and allowable because they are going through Aces Press to publish the story.

This book is entirely the work of the author who wrote it. While I might have assisted with brainstorming and other ideas about which of my characters to use, I didn't have any part in the process or writing or editing the story.

I'm proud and excited that so many authors loved my characters enough that they wanted to write them into their own story. Thank you for supporting them, and me!

READ ON!
    Xoxo
    Susan Stoker

First and foremost, I have to thank the incredibly generous Susan Stoker for allowing me to write in her Special Forces World. To be able to include her amazing characters in my stories is an opportunity I never dreamed I'd be given. I've been a huge fan of Susan's for years, and like so many of you, I fell in love with her characters the instant I met them. So, thank you, Susan. For creating a world with such incredible characters and stories and for allowing me to be a small part of it.

Next, I want to give a shout out to Caitlyn O'Leary and Riley Edwards. From the beginning, you both had more faith in me than I had in myself. You've been such good friends throughout this crazy journey of mine, and if it weren't for the two of you making me believe I could do this, I never would have written in this amazing world. Thank you both...for everything!

Last, but definitely not least, I'd also like to thank each and every one of you, the readers, who took a chance on me. Of all the books you could have chosen, you picked mine, and I can't even begin to tell you what that means to me. From the bottom of my heart, I thank you!

PROLOGUE

"At the risk of sounding like a cheesy American film, I find myself compelled to say it," Edric Yavuz, the most powerful man in Turkey, remarked. He looked down at his prisoner and smirked. "This will go much easier on you if you simply tell us where it is."

Using his one good eye, the tortured man glared back at him from the chair to which he was cuffed. With sweat running down his forehead and drops of blood and saliva spewing from his mouth, he muttered, "Fuck...you."

The comment should have pissed Edric off. This man had the power to singlehandedly destroy everything he had spent years building. Yet, he couldn't help but feel a twinge of respect for the former American soldier.

The poor bastard had taken one hell of a beating by Achim—Edric's enforcer—in an attempt to retrieve the location of the file Edric knew he'd hidden. A broken nose, several cracked ribs, and two amputated digits later and the man still wasn't talking.

Moving closer, Edric was careful not to step into the pool of blood slowly growing beneath the metal chair. After all, he couldn't risk the soon-to-be-dead soldier's DNA being discovered on his expensive, black Oxfords.

"You are much stronger than I gave you credit for, Mr. Wyatt. I had assumed this"—Edric bent over and tapped his prisoner's metal, prosthetic leg—"would have weakened you long ago. I was wrong. You have been trained better than I anticipated."

Struggling to talk through the pain, the man took him off guard with a smile. "That was your first...mistake. You should never...underestimate...the strength of...Americans."

Edric threw his head back and laughed. "Ah, yes. There's the arrogance I have come to recognize from the people of your country. Americans always think they are smarter than everyone else and can do better in all things. You actually believe you *are* better than the rest of us." He turned and walked across the dark, musty room. "But, you know..." He faced the man again. "Simply thinking something does not make it so."

The former Navy SEAL glared up at him but remained silent. With all traces of humor gone, Edric inwardly prayed he would get what he wanted before leaving here.

"I do, however, believe you are a smart man. You wouldn't have survived this long if you were not. Which means you must understand that you will die today. Here, in this small, pitiful room. Tell me." He took a step closer. "How much longer are you going to put off the inevitable? How much more pain and suffering is your body able to endure?"

His prisoner narrowed his eyes once more. "Why don't you...save us both...some time and...kill me now."

Losing some of his tightly-reigned control, Edric fisted his hands at his sides and yelled, *"Tell me where it is!"*

But the other man simply let out a half-laugh, half-cough, spitting the blood from his mouth onto the floor beside him.

He smiled at Edric again. "Like I said...before, Yavuz. Fuck. You."

In that moment, Edric knew this man was never going to give up the file's location. With an angry nod, he gave the unspoken order to Achim.

Understanding what his boss wanted, Achim pulled out his knife, its blade already stained with the soldier's blood.

The once-formidable SEAL steeled himself for what was about to come. Rather than beg and cry for his mother as so many other men had, the American actually sat up taller. Straighter. Then, he lifted his chin and looked Edric square in the eye.

This was a man who was ready to die.

Craig Wyatt was willing to give his life to protect the one thing that would destroy Edric if it were ever discovered. Ironically, it was the same type of loyalty and strength Edric, himself, expected from his own men.

The man's one good eye remained locked with his. Even when Achim shoved all eight inches of the knife's blade into his gut.

A loud grunting sound escaped from the back of the wounded man's throat. Blood began to pour out over his swollen and split lips, streams of it stretching down like thin bands of elastic before breaking off and falling onto his lap.

Achim twisted the knife before shoving it upward, the tearing of flesh and muscle a sound Edric had never quite gotten used to.

Yanking the blade free, Achim stabbed the man again. And again.

Edric spoke calmly as the ill-fated soldier began choking on his own blood. "You're a fool, Mr. Wyatt. I could have made your death quick. Painless. This"—Edric waved his hands across the man's shriveling form—"was all for nothing."

He could tell from the bulging artery in the guy's neck that his pulse was rapidly decreasing as a result of massive internal bleeding.

"Your death will not stop me. I *will* find that file." Edric took a step toward the bloody, broken man. "And now, you will die knowing this is nothing compared to what I will do to the person who has it."

In a weak, almost indiscernible move, the man's eyes widened, and he shook his head before choking out what sounded a lot like 'no'. Wyatt's chin fell to his chest, the muscles in his neck no longer having the strength to keep it up.

Using his final breath, the American whispered something. It was too low for Edric to make out, but Achim was standing much closer, still hovering over his kill.

"What was that?" Edric asked excitedly. "What did he say?" His cold heart pumped harder, certain it was a clue of some sort. A name, perhaps? *Something* that would lead him to what he desperately needed.

Achim turned to his boss. "I can't be certain, but it sounded as though he said 'forgive me'."

Edric saw red. Pressure throbbed beneath his skull, and his nostrils flared with pure and utter hatred. Turning, he started for the door but stopped before exiting the room.

He smacked the palm of his hand against the frame's rough and worn wood as a stream of Turkish curses flew from his mouth. He faced Achim once more.

The other man's eyes had widened slightly, the emotional outburst clearly taking him by surprise. Filled with rage, Edric at looked down at the dead man.

"We are both as good as dead if we do not find that file." His twisted mind raced. "Did you see his expression when I told him what would happen to the person who has it? And after, he said 'forgive me'?"

4

"Yes. So?"

Edric lifted his gaze to Achim's. "So, someone he cared about has it. A friend or relative he trusted. Someone he did not want to see get hurt."

Achim scoffed. "That could be any number of people."

A moment of thought passed before Edric spoke again. "It would be someone he was close to. We need to look into every aspect of his life. Find out who he saw on a regular basis. Everyone he had contact with."

"That could take me weeks to do alone. Months, even. I'll need to bring someone else in to help."

This made Edric nervous. "Another person means more liability. We cannot afford to take that chance."

Achim glanced down at the dead man, then back to him. "We can't afford not to. Trust me, Edric. I know a man who will do this for us. For a hefty price of course."

His employee's words did nothing to appease Edric's paranoia. "You're certain he can be trusted with something of this magnitude?"

"He's good. Better than good. His reputation for both skill and discretion far exceeds others like him."

With no other choice, Edric begrudgingly gave Achim a sharp nod. "Fine. I'll pay whatever it takes as long as this man is swift. I do not have to tell you how imperative it is that this be taken care of as soon as possible."

"No, you do not."

More than ready to be away from the stench of blood and death, Edric turned to leave but paused once more to ask, "This man you speak of. He will need to talk to people who knew Craig Walker. How do you know he will not stand out and raise suspicion?"

Achim gave him a slow grin. "Because he is American."

CHAPTER 1

"So, let me get this straight. You walked away from a sure thing, just because she asked you to spout off some BS line while she sucked you off? Dude, that girl was hot…and *naked*. What the hell were you thinking?"

Nathan Carter looked at the man sitting to his left as if he'd lost his damn mind. Before becoming Bravo Team's medic, Matthew Turner had served as a Navy Corpsman, working in the field with both the Navy and Marines during high-risk ops.

Nate had to admit, Matt was a total badass. Though the team had only recently been formed, he was glad the other man was on their side.

When it came to women, however, Turner's revolving door spun faster than a windmill in a hurricane.

"Fuck, yeah, I walked away," Nate admitted. "Ain't no blow job worth falling into *that* trap."

"Oh, I doubt you walked." Kole Jameson, Nate's best friend and one of Bravo Team's two snipers, piped in. "I bet you looked like Scooby-Doo trying to outrun a ghost."

Nate lifted his beer bottle to his lips and took a swig,

giving his teammates plenty of time to laugh at his expense. Didn't bother him in the least.

Waiting until the chuckles died down, Nate tried his best to educate the men around him. "You fuckers think it's funny, but I've seen the kind of trouble those three little words can cause."

"Man, I'd have told her I loved her in a *heartbeat* to get a piece of that action."

"Sorry, Turner," Nate told Matt. "I guess my standards are a little higher than yours. I'm sure it's hard for you to understand, but some of us actually look for more than just a pulse when deciding whether or not to sleep with a woman."

"Fuck you, Carter," Matt shot back. "You're just jealous 'cause I can catch more ass in a month than you can in an entire year."

"I'd be more concerned about what *else* you've caught," Zade King, the team's other sniper, muttered. The former Marine didn't crack a smile, making his comment even more amusing.

The other men laughed, including Turner. "Don't have to worry about that with me, King. I wrap my shit up tighter than the Pentagon's secrets. I'm clean as a whistle. Got the test results to prove it."

"Do what you want"—Nate took another swig— "but there's no fucking way I'm uttering *those* words to any woman. Ever."

Kole slapped a hand to his chest, a feigned look of devastation crossing his face. "This coming from the guy who's supposed to be my best man in a few weeks?"

Kole and his fiancée, Sarah, were getting married in two months. The couple had just bought their first house, which was why Nate and the others were sitting around Kole's back yard drinking beer and hanging out. Sarah had invited the team over for a housewarming-slash-belated engagement party.

"What's the matter, Carter? Not a believer in true love?"

Nate didn't have to turn around to recognize the deep, gravelly voice coming from behind him. Gabe Dawson was a former SEAL and had been chosen as Bravo Team's leader.

"For guys like Kole? Sure." Nate tilted his head back as Gabe walked past him. "For Me? Not a chance."

"What makes Kole so special?" Gabe asked as he snapped open his camping chair and sat down in the space between Matt and Zade.

The six-four, two hundred sixty pound beast of a man looked as though he was sitting in a kiddie chair.

Putting his free hand to his chin, Nate pretended to ponder the question for a moment. "Kole's like an Amur leopard, Dawson. They exist, but are critically endangered and very rarely seen in the wild."

This time everyone laughed, including Kole. "Speaking of rare, I'm going to go find my amazing fiancée and see if the food is ready for the grill."

As Kole walked past Nate, he tipped the bill of Nate's ball cap, nearly knocking it off his head. After smacking his friend's leg and readjusting the hat, Nate took another long draw from his bottle.

They were constantly giving each other shit, but Nate had to admit, Kole was like the brother he never had.

He glanced around at the other men. They were all members of R.I.S.C.'s recently formed Bravo Team. As private security contractors, they worked under the leadership of former Delta Force operator, Jake McQueen.

The jobs they took were a lot like the ops they'd been on in the past, just without all the red tape bullshit.

In addition to owning the company, Jake also served as Alpha Team's leader. Alpha Team was R.I.S.C.'s original team and was well-known and highly respected throughout the military and U.S. intelligence communities.

Along with private jobs, the five man, one woman Alpha Team took on a lot of high-risk, under-the-radar jobs for Homeland Security.

But, with all the evil in the world, R.I.S.C.'s services were in high demand, so McQueen decided they needed to expand.

Enter Nate and the rest of Bravo.

Each member had been hand-picked by McQueen based on their former military experience and area of expertise. Nate was Bravo's technical analyst, which meant if it involved computers and finding intel, he was your guy.

Nate swallowed the rest of his beer as the Texas sun beat down on his face, neck, and forearms. There was just enough bite to its heat to let him know summer had officially begun.

Thankfully, the melt-your-face heat Mother Nature bestowed upon their great state each year had yet to arrive. It was only a matter of time.

Not that he didn't love living here. It was just that, having grown up near Richmond, Virginia—where the highest average summer temp was eighty-seven degrees—the Texas heat still took some getting used to.

Reaching down into the small cooler he'd brought with him, Nate's fingers met ice cold water as he pulled out his second beer of the day. After flicking the water from his hand, he twisted off its metal cap and looked around at the other men sitting nearby.

Less than a year ago, they didn't know each other existed. Now, they were his teammates. His brothers. There wasn't one man here Nate wouldn't lay his life down for, if necessary.

"So, what do y'all think about that new treaty agreement

President Russell's talking about signing?" Zade asked the group.

"The one with Turkey?" Matt asked. When Zade nodded, Matt shrugged a shoulder. "Sounds like it'll be good for both countries. If it happens."

"What are your thoughts, Boss?" Zade looked at Gabe.

"I think they're both politicians," the surly man grumbled.

"Meaning?" Nate asked.

Their team leader scooted forward as far as he could in the tight seat and rested his elbows on his thighs. "Meaning, at the end of the day, they're working to do what's best for themselves and their careers."

"Well, I think it's great." Zade relaxed back into his own chair a little more. "From everything I've seen so far, President Russell seems like the real deal."

"As real as any politician can be, you mean," Matt mumbled.

Tipping his beer bottle toward Matt, Zade raised a brow. "Good point."

As the three men continued their discussion on the players of politics, Nate's focus shifted from that conversation to the voices suddenly coming from the house.

From behind his sunglasses, he watched as Kole stepped outside the sliding glass door and onto the patio where they were all currently sitting. Held securely between both hands was a large tray filled with several raw hamburger patties and other assorted meats.

About fucking time. Nate had skipped breakfast and it was after twelve. He was starving.

As Kole walked over to the large smoker he'd just purchased, Sarah also came outside and made her way to Kole's side. Her long, blonde hair was pulled up into a messy bun, and her white shorts and black T-shirt showed off her great figure.

Not that he was looking at her like *that*. Sure, Sarah was attractive, but the young lawyer was like a sister to him.

Nate smiled. He may give Kole shit about being tied down, but the truth was, he couldn't be happier for his friends. After everything those two had been through, they deserved to get their happily ever after.

A strange twinge fluttered through his chest. It felt a lot like jealousy, but that couldn't be right. Nate didn't do relationships, and he sure as hell had no intention of doing the whole picket fence bullshit.

With Kole and Sarah, it was practically love at first sight. Even after Kole's shocking diagnosis and Sarah's near-death experience at the hands of a psychopathic stalker, the couple had managed to stick together.

Nate had to admit, the love his friends had for each other was almost inspiring. And a little nauseating.

Nate had zero desire to settle down. That was Kole's thing. Not his.

About to take another sip of his beer, Nate stopped just before the glass rim touched his lips. Frozen mid-motion, he suddenly and inexplicably found it hard to breathe.

A beautiful, vibrant-looking woman had just stepped outside and onto the patio. Nate knew from a couple pictures he'd seen, she had to be Gracelynn, Sarah's half-sister who'd just moved here from Maryland.

In the pics, both she and Sarah had been a good distance from the camera. They'd gone hiking somewhere, and Gracelynn had been wearing a baseball cap and sunglasses, so it was hard to gauge how she really looked.

Staring at her now, though, Nate knew without a doubt she was the most beautiful woman he'd ever seen.

Even from behind his dark lenses, he could tell her eyes were the same large, round shape as her sister's. But instead of being blue like Sarah's, Gracelynn's were golden brown.

They lit up when she smiled at something Kole said, and Nate found himself wanting to drink in every drop of the light he saw shining behind them.

It wasn't just her eyes that drew him in. Everything about this woman was captivating.

Gracelynn's long hair fell in waves to the middle of her back. Its golden, almost caramel color reminded him of a warm, fall day.

The thin straps of the yellow sundress she was wearing stood out against the naturally sun-kissed skin of her bare shoulders. And then there was her smile.

Nate could actually feel its warmth spreading over him as he sat there, staring like an idiot.

When the three of them began walking toward him, Nate shook himself out of the trance, and took a big gulp to regroup. *What the hell just happened?*

"Guys, I'd like you to meet Gracelynn, Sarah's sister."

The other men all said hello, standing to shake her hand and introduce themselves. Rather than the polite greeting he should've given, Nate remained seated and took another swig.

"It's nice to finally meet you all. And please, call me Gracie."

Hearing her voice for the first time was such a shock to Nate's system he had to catch his breath, again.

Unfortunately, he still had beer in his mouth when he did.

Coughing and sputtering, Nate spit most of it out onto the concrete in front of him, which also happened to be close to where Gracelynn—Gracie—was standing.

Jumping back to avoid the shower of beer, Nate continued to cough as though he were trying to hack up a lung.

"Are you okay?" Gracie asked at the exact same time Kole reprimanded him.

"What the hell, man?"

"Sorry," Nate managed to choke out. "Beer went down... the wrong tube."

After a few more seconds of the embarrassing coughing fit, he cleared his throat and apologized to Gracie again. "Sorry about that. I didn't get any on you, did I?"

"Nope," She smiled back, almost making Nate feel like he was choking again. "Pretty sure my catlike reflexes kicked in just in time."

Nate chuckled, her sense of humor making his already half-hard dick twitch inside his cargo shorts.

Down there, fella. Can't go sporting wood in front of the entire team.

"You must be Nate." Gracie held her hand out to him. "Sarah's told me a lot about you."

He stared at her outstretched hand, mesmerized by how small and delicate it was. Her nails were on the shorter side but were manicured and painted red to match her toes.

Nate could feel the crotch of his shorts becoming tighter and tighter, and fuck-all if he could do anything to stop it. He sure as hell couldn't stand up to greet Gracie in this condition, which meant he had to improvise.

Scooting forward in his chair, Nate reached out and took her hand in his. Ignoring the zing of electricity shooting through him, he shook her hand and smiled. "Whatever your sister told you about me, I can assure you it's all lies."

Just before she laughed, Nate could have sworn he heard a small intake of air. Almost like a tiny gasp. Satisfaction rolled through him as he realized she'd felt it, too.

Felt what? Jesus, man. Get a grip.

"Oh, it was all good things." She laughed nervously. "Don't worry."

Nate forced a smile. "See? Lies."

Gracie laughed again, and when she released his hand,

Nate immediately felt a strange void from the loss of her touch.

The two continued to stare at each other for what felt like several minutes. In reality, it was probably no more than a couple seconds before Sarah broke the awkward silence.

"Well, the burgers will be done shortly, so I'm going to go in and set the rest of the food out onto the kitchen island. Is everyone good on drinks? We have beer, wine, soda, and water if anyone needs anything."

The guys all nodded except Turner, who stood and walked toward Sarah and the other two.

"I wouldn't mind a beer. The invite said drinks provided, so I didn't bring any." He lifted his chin toward Nate's cooler and rolled his eyes. "Apparently not everyone here took the time to read it."

Forgetting the company he was in, Nate said, "I read it, asshole. I'm just particular on the kind of beer I drink. Plus, I'm not a fucking mooch, like you."

Matt flipped him off as he walked by, giving Nate the sudden urge to trip the bastard.

"It's not mooching if you're told in a formal invitation that drinks will be provided for you."

Nate snorted. "If you consider a hand-written note that's been Xeroxed a formal invitation, I'd hate to see what other events you bless with your presence."

"Eat a dick, Carter."

"No, thanks. I've seen some of the places yours has been."

"Aaaand, we've come full-circle, ladies and gentlemen," Zade said dryly. "Back to talking about Matt's sexual history."

Nate gave him a smirk, and the two men clinked their beers together.

"No fighting, boys." Kole raised his brows. "Sarah's only rule for today."

"Only one? I'm sure there are plenty of other ways we could cause a ruckus."

Kole shook his head at Nate. "You do, you're gonna have to deal with my fiancée."

Nate considered this a moment, then sat back and relaxed. "No, thanks. I've seen her when she gets pissed."

"Right? That woman is a force to be reckoned with, for sure. Luckily, I don't usually see that side of her unless I'm watching her try a case in court." With a wink, Kole walked back over to flip the burgers and brats.

Nate smiled back at him, but his eyes soon became glued on the woman on the other side of the glass door. He could see Gracie moving gracefully around the kitchen as she helped Sarah get everything ready. Matt, the fucker, had just said something that made her laugh.

The same, unfamiliar feeling returned from before, only this time it was stronger. Wilder.

The longer Nate continued to watch Matt talking and laughing Gracie, the less he could deny what it was.

He was jealous.

Out of nowhere, Nate pictured himself standing up, storming into the kitchen, and pounding the shit out of his teammate.

Whoa. Where the fuck did that come from?

Nate shook his head and looked away from the door. Maybe Matt was right. Maybe he just needed to get laid.

After the thing here was over, Nate decided he'd go back to Bucky's—the country bar and dance hall they'd all gone to the night before. He'd see if he could find the woman from last night and try to sweet talk his way back into her bedroom.

If that didn't work, he'd surely find *someone* half-way decent who'd be willing to take him home for the night. Or at least to his truck for a quick one-off.

For the rest of the afternoon, Nate and the others ate and shared a few drinks. When it began to get dark, the temperature dropped and a cool breeze came rolling through. They all moved their chairs around the stone fire pit Nate had helped Kole build a few weeks back.

There was a lot of laughing when the guys began telling Sarah and Gracie a few funny stories. They talked about their time spent training together when Bravo was first formed and some jobs they'd been on since.

They didn't share details, of course. Their jobs—especially those they did for Homeland Security—were highly classified. Only those with a certain level of government clearance could be read in on the specifics.

Thanks to her former position with the NSA, Gracie held almost as high a clearance as Nate and the rest of Bravo Team. He was still shocked she'd given up a job like that for what basically amounted to an office manager's position in their company.

"I can't believe you left a job with the NSA to come work for R.I.S.C.," Matt said bluntly, mimicking Nate's most recent thoughts.

Gracie simply shrugged. "Trust me, my job in Maryland wasn't very exciting. Plus, I wanted to be closer to Sarah and Kole. I love what R.I.S.C. does, and even though it's only been a week, I can already tell Mr. McQueen is a much better boss to work for than my last one."

"Yeah, Jake's awesome," Matt agreed. The other men all nodded their heads, as well.

"The entire Alpha Team is, really," Zade added in his thoughts.

"They're right, Gracie," Nate joined in on the conversation. "You won't find a more supportive, respectable boss. As long as you show up and do your job to the best of your ability, McQueen will have your back one hundred percent."

Gracie's perfect, bow-shaped lips turned upward. "That's the impression I got when I spoke to him on the phone that first time. And he was so nice when Sarah introduced us in person my first day in Dallas last week. Your team was in Mexico then, right? Working a human trafficking case?"

"We were," Nate answered, not surprised she'd been apprised of what the team was working on at the time.

Gracie's brown brows turned inward. "It's so scary how easily young girls and women can find themselves caught up in all that."

"Not just girls, either."

They all turned to Gabe, who'd been sitting quietly and listening for most of the evening.

"The number of young boys who are taken and sold gets higher and higher every day." He shook his head, a muscle in his jaw bulging. "Sick bastards."

"Sick is right," Matt chimed in. "The things these monsters do...seeing shit like that almost makes you lose your faith in humanity.

"Ain't that the fucking truth," Zade agreed.

"That's why the world needs people like you," Gracie said sincerely. She looked around at each of the men. "What you do is amazing, and I'm thrilled to know I'll be playing a small part in it all." She laughed at herself, then, added, "Even if it is mostly just setting up meetings with clients or answering the phone. The NSA literally has tens of thousands of employees. To them, I was just a number with hundreds of applicants waiting in line to take my place. I doubt anyone even noticed when I left."

I'd notice.

Clearing both his throat and his thoughts, Nate offered her a warm smile. "Well, from what Kole has said, we're lucky to have you."

Gracie gave him a bubbly, "Thanks, Nate." Her words

were immediately followed by a large yawn. "And on that note, I think I'm going to call it a night." She stood and began to fold her chair.

She's leaving?

Nate's heart pounded in his chest. He didn't want her to leave. Not yet. Keeping his voice as casual as possible, he asked, "Already? It's still early."

"Yeah, I know." She sounded regretful. "But I still have a few things to finish up around the apartment tomorrow, and I need to go grocery shopping. I know it's only Saturday, but Monday always comes before we know it." Looking around at the group once more, she said, "It was really nice to meet you all. I look forward to working with you."

Goodbyes were said, and Sarah walked Gracie inside. Nate didn't understand it, but he felt as though he were going to crawl out of his skin with the need to talk to her one more time before she left.

Standing swiftly, he announced to the guys, "I need to use the head." He walked inside just as Sarah was stepping back out.

"Are you leaving, too?" she asked, sounding disappointed.

"Nah, not yet. Just need to use the bathroom."

"Good." Patting his arm, she squeezed by him and walked over to the group.

Nate practically ran through the kitchen and living room to the front door, relieved when he caught a glimpse of Gracie just starting to close it.

"Hey, Gracie! Wait up." He reached for the door to keep it from shutting all the way.

She swung her head around. "Yeah?"

"Sorry. I know you want to go home, but I wanted to talk to you about something real quick before you leave."

"Okay."

"Kole told me the other day he and Sarah wanted to do

their bachelor and bachelorette parties together."

"Sarah told me the same thing. Between you and me, I don't get it, but whatever." She shrugged and rolled her eyes at the pair. "I mean, those two are practically joined at the hip anyway, so I guess it shouldn't come as a big surprise."

Nate laughed. "Right? So, listen. I was thinking, since you are the maid of honor and I'm the best man, the duty to plan said evening falls on us." He wanted to give himself a high-five for coming up with such a great excuse to talk to her on the fly like that.

"Okay..." Gracie let the word drag out, clearly wondering where Nate was going with this whole thing.

"Well, I thought...if you wanted...we could get together soon so we can iron out all the details. Figured since they're doing a joint thing, you and I should probably plan it all together, too."

"Makes sense to me. When do you want to meet up?"

"You doing anything tomorrow night?"

She frowned. "Yeah, sorry," she said sincerely. "I have a date with this really hot guy. He's going to take me to dinner, then we're going dancing. After that, who knows what the night will bring."

Her voice sounded all low and sultry when she said that last part, making Nate want to hack into her phone and find out who the hell this guy was.

"Oh, uh...okay. We can do it another night, then."

Gracie snickered. "I'm just kidding, Nate. A hot date? Please. I've barely been in town a week, and most of that time has been spent either unpacking, hanging out with Sarah and Kole, or at work."

Ignoring the insurmountable relief he felt, Nate narrowed his eyes playfully. "Funny girl."

Still chuckling, she shook her head. "I can't believe you actually bought that."

"Why wouldn't I? You're a beautiful, single woman. Not that hard to imagine someone wanting to take you out for dinner and"—he made his voice low and sultry when he said — "whatever the night may bring."

That last part made her laugh even harder. "Sarah told me you were the class clown of the group."

"I wear the red nose with pride."

Rolling her beautiful eyes again, this time at him, Gracie said, "Okay, so seriously. When and where would you like to meet tomorrow night?"

"You like Chinese? There's this little restaurant called Chu's around the corner from my place. It's not fancy, but the food is really good. If I remember correctly, Kole said your apartment is only a few minutes from mine."

"That's what Sarah said, too. And Chinese is my favorite. What time?"

"How about seven? That way you have plenty of time to get everything on your to-do list done."

"Sounds perfect. I'll see you then, Nate."

"See you tomorrow, Gracie."

She turned and walked down the sidewalk. Nate waited at the door until she got into her car, giving her one last wave as she drove off.

He went back inside and shut the door, nearly running into Kole when he turned back around.

"Jesus, man. The fuck are you doing, sneaking up on people like that?"

"I wasn't sneaking, just checking to make sure you hadn't fallen in."

"What?" *Oh, right. Bathroom.* "I was just walking Gracie out."

"That was mighty nice of you."

Nate had been around Kole long enough to recognize when he was saying one thing but meaning something else.

"What? We were talking about the wedding."

"Uh, huh."

"We were, jackass. We're meeting up tomorrow night to figure out this whole joint bachelor-bachelorette nonsense."

"It's not nonsense. Sarah thought it would be fun to celebrate together, and I agree."

"That's what the wedding reception is for, dickhead." Crossing his arms in front of his chest, he added, "And by the way, you do realize you're totally cheating the rest of us out of a hell of a good time, right?"

Kole's brows turned inward. "How do you figure that?"

With a deadpan expression, Nate said, "One word. Strippers."

Laughing, Kole shook his head. "Dude, there weren't going to be any strippers even if we *didn't* have a joint thing."

"Why the hell not?"

Kole put a hand on Nate's shoulder. "I know this is hard for someone like you to believe, but when you find the one, your interest in all that other shit goes away. Like immediately."

Nate shrugged out of Kole's grip. "What the hell do you mean, 'someone like me'?"

"Um...someone who's afraid of commitment and doesn't believe in true love. A guy who's last, serious relationship was in the second grade with a girl named Becky who wore a pink and purple polka dotted bow in her hair."

"It was pink and white, asshole, and Becky was a very nice girl until that fucker Max Brumwell moved into town. Bastard brings her one rose and suddenly I'm out of the picture."

Both men stared each other down for all of three seconds before simultaneously busting up laughing. Mainly because there was no Becky from Nate's past, nor was there a Max Brumwell.

"Look," Kole said with a smile. "I'm sorry you and the guys don't get to spend the night shoving your hard-earned dollars into some random woman's G-string, but this is what Sarah wants."

"And what about you? What do you want?"

Kole grinned. "To make her happy."

Nate released an exaggerated sigh. "Fine. No strippers. But I do intend to talk your future sister-in-law into having a penis cake made for Sarah."

With a silent shake of his shoulders, Kole agreed to the compromise. "Penis cake, it is." Then, erasing all humor from his face, he looked intently at Nate and said, "You know I love you like a brother, right?"

"Sure." Nate was taken off guard by his friend's sudden words of affection. "I feel the same about you, although I'm wondering why you're telling me this *now*."

Kole ran a hand through his sandy blonde hair. "I saw the way you were looking at Gracie today."

Nate's heart rate kicked up a notch. "How was I looking at her?"

"Trust me, man. I get it. She's easy on the eyes. But..."

"But, what? What exactly are you trying to say, Kole?"

"Part of what I said is true, and you know it. You *are* afraid of commitment. You meet a girl, take her out, and have your fun with her. But after a few weeks when it looks like there's a chance it could turn into something more, you high-tail it out of there."

With a shake of his head, Nate adamantly disagreed. "Just because I haven't wanted to get serious with anyone doesn't mean I've been running away."

"Scooby-Doo, man." Kole raised a brow, but said nothing more.

Shit. Nate hated it when Kole was right. If he knew anything, it was that numbers don't lie.

Why bother letting someone in, only to lose them later on? Statistically, that's what would happen, so why put himself or anyone else through that?

Nate had decided a long time ago to avoid the whole mess before it even started. Was that so wrong?

"I'm not afraid of commitment. I'm just not *interested* in it. There's a difference."

"Which is why I'm asking you to steer clear of Gracie."

What the fuck? "You're warning me away from your sister-in-law?"

"Future sister-in-law. And yeah. I guess I am."

Nate could tell Kole was serious, which pissed him off even more. "Not that I have to explain myself to you or anyone else, but I have no interest in dating, or doing anything else, with Sarah's sister. So, why don't you go give this big-brother speech to Turner. *He* was the one laying on the charm with Gracie earlier, and we both know his reputation with women is way the fuck worse than mine."

Rolling his eyes, Kole shoved his hands in his pockets. "Quit being such a drama queen. I'm not trying to be an asshole."

"Could've fooled me. But don't worry. I got the message loud and clear."

Digging into his pocket, Nate pulled out the keys to his truck and turned for the door. "Give Sarah a kiss goodbye for me."

"Seriously? You're leaving?"

"Yeah. I'm leaving."

"You okay to drive?"

"I'm fine."

"You sure?"

The guy's Mother Hen bit was getting really old, really fucking fast.

"I had three beers over four hours and then switched to

water." Nate glanced at his watch. "That was two hours ago. I'm fine."

"What about your cooler?"

"Keep it."

"Nate—"

With that, Nate walked out the door, slamming it shut behind him. He was still steaming about his and Kole's conversation two hours later while sitting on the bar stool at Bucky's, sipping on a beer he'd paid to damn much for.

To his surprise, the woman from last night was at the bar when he'd first walked in. Less surprising was the fact that she'd gotten up without saying a word and walked out the door the second she saw his face.

Since then, Nate had been scouring the room, looking for someone who caught his eye enough to approach. It was ladies' night, which meant there were plenty of hot women to choose from. Some had even come on to him.

They'd flirted, and he'd reciprocated. Normally, that would have led to them going back to the woman's place—he never brought them to his apartment. For some reason, though, the idea of meaningless sex wasn't quite as appealing as it had been last night.

He didn't want a relationship. That most *definitely* wasn't the issue. The problem was Nate didn't know what he wanted anymore. Whatever it was, it was pretty clear he wouldn't find it in this bar tonight.

To hell with this. He stood, threw a ten down to cover the one drink he never finished, and left.

Once back at his apartment, he took a quick shower, not wanting the smell of smoke from Kole's fire on his sheets. When he got to bed, he lay there for what felt like hours.

Nate tossed and turned, trying to think of anything other than golden eyes and honey-colored hair. Eventually, he gave up the fight.

"Fuck it."

Knowing he'd never get to sleep if he didn't find a way to relax, Nate decided to take matters into his own hand. Shoving the elastic waist of his boxers down below his balls, for better access, he wrapped a hand around his hot, pulsating cock and began to stroke.

Starting out slowly, he thought of Gracie's beautiful, smiling face. Laying back on his pillow, Nate closed his eyes and smiled back, imagining what it would feel like to run his fingers through her long, silky hair.

Before long, he saw himself leaning in and tasting her lips with his tongue. He began pumping his swollen shaft more forcefully as he fantasized what it would be like to feel her naked body beneath his. To slide into her delectable heat.

Nate's dick jumped beneath his palm. His breathing picked up and sweat began to bead on his forehead as he imagined them in a different position. He moved his fist up and down with more urgency as he envisioned Gracie lying on her back with her legs lifted and spread, his face nestled between her thighs.

Then, in his mind's eye, he dove in. The essence he knew would be sweet coated the tip of his tongue as he licked her body's most sensitive flesh.

"Ah, shit," he panted out, the familiar tingling in his spine telling him he was close.

Nate's balls tightened and his cock became impossibly full. His entire body shook with the need for release and a loud grunt escaped his throat as he jerked himself into blessed oblivion.

Despite his earlier convictions, it was Gracie's name that fell from his growling lips as he came. And after he cleaned himself up, Gracie's smiling face was the last thing he pictured before finally falling asleep.

CHAPTER 2

Gracie stood in the middle of her living room and smiled. She really liked how everything had come together.

She'd been a little skeptical at first. After all, who signs a lease agreement for an apartment they'd never actually seen in person? But, living across the country in Maryland, Gracie hadn't had a lot of options.

Kole and Sarah had offered to let her stay in their spare room until she found a place, but they'd just bought their first house and were busy with work and planning a wedding. The last thing they needed was her getting in the way.

So, she'd done some online searching and found a few places that fit her needs, wants, and budget. After closely inspecting the pictures from the ones she liked, Gracie had chosen this place. And she loved it.

The open floor plan made it appear even bigger than it actually was. The kitchen was sleek and modern and the living room's floor-to-ceiling windows offered a great view of the spacious balcony, which overlooked downtown Dallas.

Speaking of downtown...

Gracie glanced at the large clock she'd hung behind her couch less than an hour ago. Crap. She needed to leave now in order to be on time for her date.

Giving herself a mental smack on the head, she reminded herself this was not a date. She and Nate were meeting to discuss the plans for her sister's and Kole's party. Period.

Then, why does the thought of seeing him again make your heart race?

Ignoring that annoying little voice, Gracie grabbed her purse and keys from the coffee table and gave herself a once-over in the small mirror hanging next to her front door. Since this *wasn't* a date, she'd gone with her favorite jeans, a white V-neck, and her high-top Converse.

The white was a bit risky, since they'd be eating. She'd just have to be extra careful, especially since it was going to be Chinese.

Fluffing her hair with her fingertips one last time, Gracie opened the door and left. On the way to her car, she used her phone to pull up directions to the restaurant where they'd be meeting. The GPS told her it was an eleven-minute drive from her place.

Ten minutes and thirty-two seconds later, Gracie pulled into the establishment's parking lot. Creeping across the pavement, she carefully avoided the multitude of potholes and loose asphalt, finally finding a solid place to park at the far-end near a large dumpster. He was right when he said the place wasn't fancy.

Double-checking her doors to make sure they were locked, Gracie made her way across the lot and around the side of the brick building. She spotted Nate immediately through the business's large glass window facing the street.

He was at the end of the long counter where people were placing their orders. His head was bowed, and he was leaning on his elbows, casually scrolling through something on his phone.

When she walked in, a tiny bell above her jingled to alert the employees another customer had arrived. Hearing this, Nate's head swiveled in her direction, his eyes locking with hers.

Gracie's lungs seized inside her chest. *Lord, have mercy, he's gorgeous.*

Ignoring her heart's overactive imagination, she began looking for the best path to take to get to him. It wouldn't be easy since the place was packed. As in, shoulder-to-shoulder, standing-room-only packed.

Thankfully, Nate pushed himself off the counter and began squeezing his way over to her. She waited, watching as he politely asked someone to move before smiling back at her.

Damn.

Last night, he'd looked sexy as sin in his ball cap and sunglasses. Tonight, though...tonight he was positively panty-dropping.

Standing right at six feet, he was well above her five-feet, five-inch frame. The pale blue of his eyes reminded her of the beach her parents took her to as a little girl. The water was so crystal clear she could see the tiny fish swimming near the shallow bottom.

Gracie continued to study Nate as he slowly made his way toward her. His hair was a little darker than what she would consider light brown, but when the light shone down on it just right, hints of auburn peeked through.

With those mesmerizing eyes and a strong jaw, Nate's face was a perfect combination of chiseled features and boyish charm. And when Nathan Carter smiled, his entire face lit up.

Doesn't matter.

The tiny voice was right. None of that mattered. He was Kole's best friend and, most importantly, a co-worker at her new job.

Of course, Jake had told her during her phone interview that the guys are only at the office a couple times a week, if that. Still, it would probably be in bad form for her to start something up with one of them.

At least she'd have something good to look at on the days he was there. *Just think of it as another perk of the job.*

"Hey," Nate's deep voice rose over the noise of the crowd.

"Hi," Gracie responded loudly. She looked around at the swarm of people. "Is this place always this busy?"

"Not at all. A bus full of tourists pulled up about two minutes after I got here and took all the tables.

Dang. Eating Chinese food while standing would be a bit challenging. Her white shirt would be on the losing end of that, for sure.

Gracie still was trying to think of another alternative when Nate began talking again.

"I hope it's okay, but I went ahead and ordered for us both so ours would get done before theirs." He tipped his head toward the crowd.

She leaned in a little closer so he'd hear her better. "That's fine. I'm not picky."

Nate glanced around the room, then back to her. "It's going to be impossible to get anything done here."

"I agree."

"We should…"

Whatever else Nate said was drowned out by a loud eruption of laughter coming from some of the other customers.

"What?" Gracie practically yelled.

Scooting closer, Nate put his hand on her upper arm and leaned in more closely, talking directly next to her ear.

"I said, we should get our food and take it to my place."

Between the gentle way his fingers were holding her arm and his lips touching her ear as he spoke, she could barely breathe, let alone speak.

The slight hint of whatever cologne he was wearing was simply icing on the delectable Nate cake.

Ignoring the electric jolt she felt from his simple touch, Gracie nodded. "Sounds like a plan."

Mid-answer, she turned her head toward Nate's so he could hear her better. He was still leaning down, and when she made the move, their noses nearly touched.

With their eyes locked, they both froze.

The longer they stood like that, the darker the blue hue in his eyes became. For a second, she was sure he was about to kiss her. She was also certain she would let him.

Instead, Nate blinked then jerked away, bumping into the man standing behind him. Looking over his shoulder, he held a hand up to the guy to show him he meant no harm.

"Sorry." When his eyes found hers again, he forced a smile and said, "I'm going to go check on the food." His back was to her before she could even respond.

"What the hell was that?" Gracie mumbled to herself.

She barely knew the guy, yet she'd almost kissed him in the middle of a crowded restaurant. Worse, she'd just agreed to go back to his apartment with him. Alone.

That was like the first rule in single-woman safety one-oh-one.

Sure, he was Kole's best friend, and it was obvious that Sarah liked him, too. Still...

Walking over to the door where it was a little less crowded, Gracie pulled her phone from her purse and hurried to type out a text to Sarah.

Chu's is super crowded. Going to Nate's apartment instead. Just thought I'd let u know. Love u.

She'd just hit 'send' when Nate's voice hit her ear. "What's the matter, Gracelynn? Don't you trust me?"

Startled, Gracie jumped, nearly dropping her phone in the process. With a nervous laugh, she turned and faced him. "N-no. Of course, I trust you."

Some of the other customers had gotten their food and were beginning to eat, so the noise level had dropped.

Speaking more softly than before, Nate smiled and said, "No, you don't. Not completely. And really"—he shrugged— "you shouldn't."

Okay, now she *was* starting to worry. Her face must have given her away because he chuckled. "Relax, Gracie. I just meant that you're about to go with a guy you don't really know to an apartment you've never been to before. Alone. Texting Sarah to let her know where you'll be? Smart. Giving her the restaurant's name as a last known location? *Really* smart."

Embarrassed, Gracie broke eye contact and focused on putting her phone back into her purse. She was still looking down when Nate gently tilted her chin upward with his forefinger and thumb.

"Sweetheart, look at me." When she followed his soft-spoken order, he said, "We don't have to go to my place. In fact, we can call this whole thing off right now, if it's making you uncomfortable."

Genuine concern filled his eyes as they bore into hers. Suddenly, Gracie felt the exact opposite of uncomfortable. She felt...safe.

"No," she blurted a little too quickly. "I'm good."

"You sure? 'Cause I can give you half of what I ordered, walk you to your car, and you can go back home if that's what you—"

He stopped talking the instant her fingers met his bicep. "I'm sure, Nate. And I'm sorry for getting all weird about it. I guess working for the NSA has made me a bit paranoid. Or I've watched too many Criminal Minds episodes. Take your pick."

With a lopsided grin, which was much too sexy, he assured her, "Nothing to be sorry about, Gracie. Trust me. Experience has taught me you never can be too careful. Now"—Nate held up two bulging sacks that smelled incredibly delicious—"what do ya say we go eat this and plan a kick-ass party?"

Feeling much more relaxed, Gracie held the door open and motioned with her hand. "Lead the way."

Less than an hour later, they had most of the bachelor-bachelorette party planned. They were all going to meet at a restaurant called The Gardens, then go to a bar called Bucky's to have a few drinks and hang out.

According to Nate, The Gardens was owned by Trevor Matthew's wife, Lexi, and was the best restaurant in town.

Gracie had met Trevor last week when Jake was introducing her to the other members of R.I.S.C.'s Alpha Team. Trevor was Jake's right-hand man, and as with everyone she'd met at the company so far, he seemed very nice. And was very nice-looking.

In fact, she'd noticed right off that everyone on both Alpha and Bravo seemed to be attractive in their own way. At one point, Gracie had considered asking Jake if it was some sort of requirement or something.

Smiling at the thought, Gracie wasn't paying close enough attention to the piece of sweet and sour pork she'd just picked up. As she was trying to take her last bite, the piece of meat toppled off the edge of her fork and rolled down the front of her white shirt, leaving a trail of the tasty red sauce all the way down the center.

Nate snickered. "Hope that shirt wasn't special to you."

Rolling her own eyes at herself, Gracie shook her head.

"Nope, not special." She glanced down. "Not white anymore, either."

The two laughed together as Gracie reached for the napkins lying beside one of the sacks. She attempted to wipe the sauce up, but only managed to make things worse.

"Well, it looks like this one's a lost cause."

Still laughing at her, Nate stood from the table. "Come on. I've got a clean shirt you can borrow."

"Thanks, but that's not necessary. My car's just across the ally, and I'm going straight home from here."

"Oh, that'd be great," Nate said sarcastically as he grabbed her hand and pulled her to her feet. "Someone sees you walking down a dark alley with all that red on your shirt, they're probably going to think you've been stabbed or something and freak out. Come on."

Gracie's shoulders shook with silent laughter as he led her down the hallway toward what she assumed was his bedroom.

"I guess you're right. If you really don't mind me using one of yours, I can wash it when I get home."

"Wouldn't have offered if I minded. Give me a sec to get one, and then you can change in the bathroom."

As she waited in the hallway, Gracie found herself drawn to the other room across from where she stood. Her curiosity had her pushing on the half-open door and going inside.

Rather than a bed and a dresser, as one would expect to find in a spare bedroom, the space looked more like a tiny version of one of the US Cyber Command rooms at the NSA.

She'd never personally been inside one. Her job title didn't warrant access to it, but she'd walked by as their doors were being opened or closed and had gotten a good enough peek to get the idea.

Gracie couldn't help but be almost as impressed with the small room she was standing in now.

Along the wall in front of her were two long tables that had been pushed together to make one, large work space. There were five computer monitors, four separate computers, and two keyboards.

Other electronic equipment she didn't recognize sat about the desk area and two expensive, black leather chairs were pushed in at the center of each table.

On the wall to her left hung a white board. It was currently empty, but Gracie could tell it got put to use often by the black streaks left behind by whatever had been wiped away.

To her right was a smart board and attached to the middle of the ceiling was its projector. They were just like the ones in the conference room at work.

"Maybe you're the one who can't be trusted."

Letting out a tiny squeal, Gracie spun around to find Nate standing behind her, a light grey T-shirt in his hand.

She slapped his arm out of reflex. "Stop doing that!"

"Hey!" Pretending to be hurt, he rubbed his arm with his free hand and pouted. "Sarah never mentioned you were prone to violent outbursts."

A little embarrassed by her reaction, Gracie played it off by crossing her arms at her chest and lifted her chin. "Only when provoked by sneaky men trying to scare me."

Laughing, Nate handed her the shirt. "Here. It's my favorite, so please don't eat anything red while wearing it."

Snatching it out of his hand, she playfully narrowed her eyes at him. "Very funny."

Gracie held the shirt out in front of her. It was plain with the exception of the word 'Army' spelled in black across the chest.

"Well, I could probably wear it for a dress, but it's clean, so I won't complain." Glancing back up at him, she offered him a sincere smile. "Thank you."

"You're welcome."

Just like at the restaurant, they stood there, staring at each other. Gracie wanted nothing more than to reach up, take his face between her hands, and press her lips against his.

Instead, she blurted, "So, this room is really impressive."

Nate grinned back at her, his face beaming with pride as if she'd just told him his baby was the most beautiful one she'd ever seen.

"Thank you. It's nice to finally have someone appreciate my equipment."

Gracie bit her tongue to keep from making an inappropriate remark. Though she wanted to take advantage of the golden opportunity he'd just laid at her feet, she remained quiet.

Nate puffed out his chest as he walked past her and into the room. "Yep. This is where the magic happens."

"Interesting." Gracie purposefully made her tone sound as though she were trying to solve some great mystery.

Nate looked over at her. "What?"

Gracie shrugged casually. "Oh, nothing. It's just that most men I know would say that the *bedroom* was wear the magic happened. But for you it's in here." She gave the room an assessing glance.

Okay, so maybe she was flirting a little, but come on. There wasn't a woman out there who could blame her.

"She's got jokes," he smiled. "Good to know."

Giggling at herself, Gracie looked around the room again. "Seriously, though. This is some heavy-duty equipment."

"You do programming?"

"Me? God, no. But I was around a lot of technology at my previous job. I mean, it's the NSA, so of course they're going to have top of the line *everything*."

Nate pulled out one of the chairs for her. "Why'd you really leave?"

Confused, Gracie took the offered seat. "I explained all that last night when we were sitting around the fire."

"I know." Nate sat down in the other one, turning so they were facing each other. "I just got the impression there was more to the story than you let on."

"Oh." Damn. He did have good instincts. Biting her lip, Gracie tucked some hair behind one ear. "Well, you're not entirely wrong."

"You want to share? I'm a good listener, and I promise your secret is safe with me."

Gracie laughed when Nate pretended to zip his lips and then throw away an invisible key.

"It's really nothing big. Honestly, it's a little embarrassing."

"Why'd you leave, Gracelynn?"

Her eyes rose to his. For some reason, hearing her full name falling off his lips made all her girlie parts stand up and take notice. *Easy, girl.*

Clearing her throat, she said, "I felt like the job was becoming toxic."

"How so?"

"Everyone was always whispering behind closed doors. If someone was in the break room when I went in for coffee, they'd stop their conversations and hurry to change the subject. That or they'd leave the room altogether."

The space between Nate's brow scrunched together with concern, so she tried to explain.

"I know it wasn't personal. It's not like they were talking specifically about me or anything. People there had various levels of clearance. With so many employees, it was hard to know who was on your same level and who wasn't. It was safer just to stop talking and move on, rather than risk being fired or prosecuted for accidentally revealing classified information."

"So, when you said you wanted to work someplace more personal…"

"That's what I meant."

"I know you have a pretty high clearance, but you do realize Jake and the teams…we won't be able to share *everything* with you, either, right?"

"I know. But working for R.I.S.C in one office space rather than a building the size of Texas—no offense—is more my style. And the way Sarah talks about Bravo, it seems as if you're more like family than co-workers."

"That, we are."

Gracie smiled. "I could tell that the second I walked outside last night. I know Sarah and Kole think of you all as brothers."

Nate tipped his chin. "And we love them the same way."

"See?" she said wistfully. "*That's* what I want to be a part of. I saw a similar relationship with the people at the VA hospital where I volunteered."

That seemed to pique his interest. "I didn't know you volunteered at the VA."

She nodded. "For the past year. I'd go there a few times a week. Mostly, I'd just sit and visit with some of the patients who'd been there a while. Too many had no one who could or would come to visit them. No family or friends close by. I got pretty attached to a couple of the patients. It was really hard saying goodbye."

"I bet. But, if they knew you as well as you seemed to have gotten to know them, I'm sure they understood why you needed to leave."

Her smile grew. "They did. One of the guys even got together with the nurses and bought me a cake for my last day there. It was nice. Kind of bittersweet."

"Well, you seem like you'll be a perfect fit for R.I.S.C."

"Thanks. I hope you're right."

There was a stretch of silence before Nate stood up. "Speaking of work, you have to be at the office tomorrow morning."

Gracie glanced at her watch. "Oh, my gosh, you're right. I had no idea it was getting so late."

"Come on, I'll walk you to your car."

"Thanks, but you don't have to do that." She followed Nate into his living room where she'd sat her purse and keys.

"It's late, and you're alone." He stepped over to his apartment door. "I'm walking you to your car, Gracie."

Sensing he wasn't budging on this one, Gracie went to the bathroom, changed into his shirt, and grabbed her things before following him out the door.

As they walked, it was hard not to notice how alert Nate was. Even while carrying on a casual conversation, his head was on an almost constant-swivel as they made their way to where she was parked. She also hadn't missed the slight bulge against his lower back.

Knowing he had a gun tucked in his waistband didn't bother her. Despite her moment of unfounded paranoia in the restaurant earlier, nothing about this man scared her. On the contrary, being with Nate made her feel safe. Protected.

"I'm assuming this is you?" Nate nodded to her car. It was the only one in the parking lot.

"Great deduction skills, Mr. Carter. You should really think about getting a job as a security specialist or something." Gracie smirked at her own sarcasm as she unlocked her car and opened her door.

"You know"—Nate leaned his hip against the driver's fender and crossed his arms at his chest—"when I first met you last night, I thought you were this sweet, innocent, young woman."

Gracie did her best to ignore the way his biceps bulged beneath his sleeves. "And now?"

"Now..." He stood straight and moved closer to her. With the open door between them, Nate brought his hand toward her and carefully brushed some hair from her forehead. "Now, I think there's a lot more to you than meets the eye."

The same electric current she'd felt before rushed through her veins. Gracie couldn't remember ever having such an intense reaction to a man.

Nate started to lean in, but just when their lips were about to touch, he stopped himself. Pulling back quickly, he dropped his hand as if it were on fire and looked away.

"Thanks for meeting me tonight. I think Kole and Sarah will like what we have planned for them."

Totally thrown by his sudden change in demeanor, Gracie stumbled over her reply. "Uh...yeah. I-I do, too."

"Drive carefully going home."

"I will." Still thoroughly confused, Grace sat in her driver's seat and started the car's ignition. "Thanks for dinner."

He gave her a tight smile. "Goodnight, Gracie."

Looking up at him one last time, she did her best to smile back. "Goodnight, Nate."

With that, she pulled out of the parking lot and drove off, refusing to look in the mirror to see if he was watching her as she went.

CHAPTER 3

Hours later, Gracie woke to a loud chiming rolling through her apartment. It took her several seconds to realize it was her doorbell.

Groaning, she threw off her covers and sleepily made her way to her door. After checking the peephole, she unlatched the deadbolt, released the lock on the doorknob, and opened the door.

"Why on God's green earth are you ringing my doorbell at…" she turned to look at the clock on her wall. "Oh, shit! Is that really the time?"

"Yep. Looks like someone overslept."

Sounding way too cheerful for this time of day, Sarah stepped into the apartment. Her blonde hair was pulled back in a perfectly executed chignon bun, and her makeup was flawless.

Wearing a grey pencil skirt and matching jacket, Sarah's heels clicked on the wood floor as she walked over toward Gracie's couch. "Better get a move on, or we're both going to be late."

Gracie shut the door and turned back to her sister. "Why are you here before work?"

Sitting on the arm of the couch, Sarah smiled. "I wanted to surprise you by taking you for coffee first. Since you and I both work in the same building now, I thought it would be nice to ride together once in a while." Sarah looked at her watch. "If you hurry, we can still beat the coffee shop rush before we have to be there."

Gracie smiled. "That was sweet of you. I showered before bed last night, so I'll just throw on some clothes and run a brush through my hair. I can do my makeup in the car, since you're driving."

"I'll wait here."

Gracie rushed toward her bedroom but was stopped when her sister grabbed her forearm as she passed.

"Whoa. Stop right there."

The order took Gracie by surprise. "What?"

"Where did you get that shirt?"

Crap. She'd completely forgotten what she was wearing. "It's Nate's. He let me borrow it."

"I know whose it is," Sarah said sharply. "I was there when he got that." She bobbed her chin toward a small, faded stain near the hem. "Gracie, why do you have on Nate's favorite shirt? And why did you *sleep* in it?" Sarah's big, blue eyes widened then. Her head turned toward the end of the hall as she whispered. "Oh, my God...is he still here?"

"Wait. This really is his favorite shirt?"

Her sister looked back at her as if she'd grown two heads. "*That's* what you're focused on right now? Gracie, this is Nate we're talking about. I warned you about him. Yes, he's sweet and funny, not to mention good-looking. He's Kole's best friend, and I love him like a brother, but Nathan Carter is *not* boyfriend material. Not to mention, he's a member of Bravo, and you work for his boss's boss. What were you thinking?"

Frustrated for several reasons, Gracie swiped some unruly hair from her face and straightened her shoulders.

"Okay, that was like a billion questions, so let me see if I can answer them all for you. First off, no. Nate's not here. He never was. Two, remember when I texted you about going to his place and why? While we were there, I dropped a piece of sweet and sour pork on my white shirt. Being the nice guy you know and love, Nate offered to let me wear one of his shirts home so I didn't look like the victim of a psycho-slasher with red sauce all over myself. I came home, took a shower, and threw it back on because I was exhausted and it was within arm's reach."

With a deep breath, Gracie finished with, "Three, I wasn't thinking anything because Nate and I are just friends. But, even if we weren't, I'm twenty-six years old and can decide whom I date, should I so choose. Did I miss anything?"

Sarah took a couple seconds to process what she'd been told. "Nothing really happened between you two?"

Gracie rolled her eyes. It was way too early for drama. "No. Nothing happened. Nate was a complete gentleman the entire night. He even walked me to my car and everything." *And almost kissed me.* "Do you want to see my stained shirt? Will that make you believe me?"

She started toward her bedroom where her dirty clothes hamper was, but her sister's words stopped her.

"Don't get the damn shirt." Sighing loudly, Sarah apologized, "I believe you. And, I'm sorry."

Gracie turned back to her. With her hands on her hips, she didn't even bother to hide her smugness. "Well, thank you."

"Look, I know it's none of my business, sis. It's just that…I want to see you happy, but I also want you to do well with this job. I like the idea of my baby sister only being a short elevator ride away from me, and I don't want to see you get hurt. Either personally or professionally."

Her heart warmed. "I know. And I appreciate that, but I need you to remember I'm not a little kid anymore. I was perfectly capable of taking care of myself out in Maryland without anyone's help or advice." With their little tiff over, she gave her sister a smile. "Now, if you're done interrogating me, I really do need that coffee."

As she rushed to get dressed and do her hair, Gracie felt a twinge of guilt. It wasn't like she'd lied to Sarah. Not really.

Okay, so *maybe* she could have put her own pajamas on as easily as Nate's shirt. And she probably enjoyed the fact that it smelled like him more than she should have.

And, yeah, it was possible the reason she'd overslept was because when Gracie had laid down last night, she couldn't stop thinking about Nate's eyes and that damn sexy smile.

Or how his shirt stretched over his broad, taught chest and arms, and the way his ass fit perfectly in those jeans.

Mostly, Gracie blamed her insomnia on thinking about the way Nate had looked at her just before he'd almost kissed her, and then wondering why he hadn't.

He'd been so close, too. The heat was there, staring right back at her. Then, all of a sudden it was like something had spooked him and he'd pulled back. For the life of her, Gracie didn't know why.

Put it all together and a good night's sleep simply wasn't in the cards. She just hoped things wouldn't be awkward the next time they saw each other.

Dressed and ready to go, Gracie grabbed her cosmetic bag and Nate's shirt from the bathroom counter and headed back to her sister.

"Okay, I'm ready."

Sarah's eyes dropped to the infamous shirt. "What are you planning to do with that?"

"I'm taking it with me so I can give it back to Nate."

"Why don't you let me take it? I can give it to Kole, and he can give to Nate. Might look a bit odd if you bring a member of Bravo Team's shirt back to him at the office, don't you think?"

Sighing at the ridiculousness of it all, Gracie said, "You're probably right. I swear, nothing happened, but I can see how some people might take it the wrong way."

"See? I knew I didn't get all the smart genes."

Gracie rolled her eyes. "Let's go, before I change my mind and decide to walk into work wearing the damn thing."

"We've got a new job."

Nate and the rest of Bravo looked at Gabe.

"McQueen's on his way in now and will explain everything once he gets here."

The men all sat around the long, oval table, shooting the breeze while waiting for Jake McQueen to come in and get started.

They'd been called in for this meeting, though they hadn't been told why. Nate was just glad it wasn't an early one, because he didn't sleep for shit last night.

All night long, he'd dreamt about Gracie. His sleep-induced mind had been filled with those enchanting eyes and that long, flowing hair. He imagined himself running his fingers through it before gathering it in his fist while he tilted her head back and took what he wanted.

He'd have thought jerking off while imagining himself with her would've done the trick. All it managed to do was relax him enough to fall asleep, allowing his subconscious to take over and torture him some more.

Nate woke up in spurts, going back and forth between

kicking his own ass for almost kissing her and beating himself up because he hadn't.

All. Fucking. Night. Long.

When Gabe sent the group text an hour ago alerting Bravo of the meeting, the first thing that ran through his head was that Gracie would be at the office, too.

The level of anticipation he felt surprised him. Nate normally didn't get excited just from the possibility of seeing a woman. Especially one he wasn't even dating.

Not that he didn't have an enormous amount of appreciation for the opposite sex. Nate loved a good roll in the hay as much as the next guy. He wasn't quite the man-whore Turner was, but he had a normal, healthy appetite for sex.

Add to that his good looks and military background, and finding a willing partner was never usually an issue. At least, it didn't used to be.

Lately, the empty, meaningless sex he normally enjoyed was becoming...well...meaningless. More and more, Nate had been feeling as though something was missing. And he fucking hated it.

Just seeing Gracie's smiling face when he'd first walked into R.I.S.C. a few minutes ago gave him more excitement than his last few sexual encounters combined.

He was afraid it would be awkward, given how things ended last night, but she'd greeted him pleasantly and professionally, as if nothing had ever happened.

Which technically, it hadn't.

So, either he was reading too much into things and she didn't feel the same, incredible connection he had—one that, if he were honest, scared the shit out of him—or she was mature enough and professional enough not to let it interfere with work.

Nate ignored the little voice inside his head praying it was the latter.

Jake walked in the room, a welcome interruption to his thoughts. Closing the door behind him, he went to the front. Pushing

thoughts of Gracie aside, Nate sat up a little straighter and got his head into the game.

Dressed in a suit and tie, McQueen bid them all a good morning. Getting right down to business, the highly-respected man used the remote in his hand to power up the interactive board on the wall behind him.

"I asked Dawson to call you in here today because I have a job for Bravo. As you know, Homeland contracts us out, from time to time, when there's something they need done but they are unable to get directly involved."

"I'm guessing this is one of those times," Zade stated casually.

With a nod, McQueen clicked the remote again. Two seconds later, a man's face appeared on the large screen.

"This is Petty Officer Third Class, Craig Wyatt. Up until June of last year, Wyatt served as an active member of SEAL Team Five, stationed in Virginia."

Curious, Matt asked, "What happened in June?"

With another click, the men in the room were shown a picture of two Humvees on a desert road. Or, more accurately, what was left of them.

Both vehicles appeared to have been destroyed by some kind of bomb. Metal was twisted and blown apart, hundreds of pieces scattered on the dry dirt around where they'd been hit.

"Last summer, Wyatt and his team were on their way to a meeting. The mission was to gather intel from a known associate of Achim Akmar in order to locate and capture him. They never made it to that meeting. Team Five lost three men that day. Craig Wyatt was among those who survived, but he lost his leg, effectively ending his Naval career."

Achim Akmar. Nate had heard that name before. He just couldn't remember from where. "Akmar...why does that sound so familiar?"

"Achim Akmar is a cleaner," Gabe answered for Jake. "He's well-known and well-connected."

"Akmar's a monster." Jake looked at Nate. "You want someone gone, he's your man. Need intel extracted, he'll do whatever it takes to get it."

Gabe chimed in again. "He gets off on what he does, which makes him even more dangerous. This guy has no qualms about torturing women, the elderly, anyone who stands between him and his money. Achim Akmar is all about one thing...the bottom dollar. Bastard would kill his own grandmother if you paid him enough."

To Gabe, Nate asked, "Why hasn't he been stopped before now?"

"The guy's a ghost, Carter. Not only is he the best at what he does, he's also a master at disappearing."

"Which is why only the wealthiest of clients can afford him," Jake added.

"Okay," Zade joined in. "This Akmar's a total douche. What does he have to do with Craig Wyatt?"

They all waited as McQueen changed the picture once more. On the left half of the screen was the same picture of Wyatt from before.

Dressed in his military-issued desert camo, the guy was smiling for the camera. In a casual stance, he loosely held his AR-15 with one hand and had his other shoved into his pants pocket.

They each had pictures just like it from their time overseas. Finding something to smile or laugh about in the midst of Hell was definitely worth remembering.

Nate's gaze slid to the right, and his stomach dropped. What he saw there was a thing of nightmares.

Craig Wyatt, or what was left of him, was handcuffed to a chair. It was obvious the man was dead.

From what Nate could see, the former SEAL had been badly beaten, either stabbed or shot in the gut, and his pinky, ring, and middle fingers on his left hand had been severed.

"Jesus," Nate muttered beneath his breath.

"Achim?" Kole asked Jake.

"It certainly fits his M.O."

"What the hell was Wyatt involved in that would bring this sort of shit down on him?" Zade directed the question to Gabe, but it was Jake who answered.

"That's what we've been hired to find out."

"I'm all about taking more of Ryker's money"—Matt piped up—"but Craig Wyatt was Navy. Shouldn't NCIS be investigating this?"

Jason Ryker, the man Matt was referring to, was R.I.S.C.'s Homeland Security handler. As head of a covert intelligence department within Homeland, Ryker often hired R.I.S.C. to perform ops the government couldn't officially be involved in.

"There are complications that come with this particular job," McQueen answered.

He changed the screen again to show United States President, James Russell, and another man.

The picture was taken during a highly-publicized meeting. Both dressed in suits, the two men smiled as they walked together down one of the many White House hallways.

"Isn't that Edric Yavuz?"

Jake nodded. "The current president of Turkey."

"Ah, hell." Matt leaned back in his chair. "I do not have a good feeling about this."

"You shouldn't," Gabe said matter-of-factly.

"According to Homeland's intel, President Yavuz has possible connections to Achim Akmar."

"Connections. What exactly does that mean?" Zade asked their boss.

"It means chatter's been picked up and suspicions have been raised that our guy Akmar is on Yavuz' payroll."

"Hold up," Nate jumped in. "Are we really saying Turkey's president, the same guy who's been all over the news lately professing his love for America, ordered the torture and subsequent murder of an American soldier?"

"That's what Homeland needs to know."

"Again," Matt piped up. "Y'all know I'm not one to turn down money, but why all the secrecy? Why not have the CIA or one of the other alphabet agencies look into this?"

Gabe looked across the table to Matt. "Can you imagine if this shit leaks, and it turns out we're wrong? President Russell is supposed to sign that treaty agreement with Yavuz in a few weeks. If the intel isn't solid and someone's just trying to set Yavuz up, it could end badly for both countries."

"Gabe's right," Jake agreed. "According to Ryker, the Secretary of the Navy doesn't want to touch this one. Frankly, I can't say I blame him."

"But Wyatt was a Navy SEAL, for Christ's sake." Having been in the Navy, himself, Matt was clearly taking this one personally. "I'd think SECNAV would want to find the bastards responsible and bring them to justice."

"He does, Turner," Jake assured Matt. "We all do. Unfortunately, there's a lot riding on this, so it has to be handled with kid gloves. That's where we come in."

"Meaning, the government doesn't want to get its hands dirty and risk upsetting the almighty politicians." Running a frustrated hand through his hair, Matt cursed under his breath.

Making sure they were all on the same page, Nate asked,

"Isn't this agreement the one where Turkey will vow to be an ally of the United States and give up all their mass weaponry, including any nuclear devises they may or may not have in their possession?"

"Yep," Kole answered Nate's question. "Just like the one we signed with Korea a few years back."

"But, if it is a solid lead and Yavuz is dirty, we need to know before the treaty deadline." Jake's expression turned fierce. "No fucking way do we want our country's president signing an agreement with a sadistic fuck who'd do that"—he clicked the remote and, once again, the two pictures of Craig Wyatt filled the screen—"to anyone, much less one of our own."

Nate looked at his boss. "I guess we'd better figure this shit out pretty damn quick. That agreement is slated to be signed in three weeks."

"Which is why we're going wheels up in—"

A knock on the door behind Nate interrupted the discussion. It slowly opened, and Gracie peeked her adorable head inside.

"I'm so sorry to interrupt, but Agent Ryker is on the phone, and he says it's urgent. Something to do with the new assignment he has you working on."

Nate ignored the funny way his heart began to beat just from seeing her again. Jesus, he really needed to get laid.

"Thanks, Gracie. I'll take it in here."

"Oh, and I called the phone company. They're supposed to be sending someone out this afternoon to figure out what's wrong with the intercom system."

"Perfect."

Jake gave her a smile as he sat the remote down and walked over to the small table in the corner of the room. Picking up the phone's receiver, he pressed the button to access Ryker's call.

Before beginning the conversation with the Homeland agent, he turned and said, "Thanks for taking care of that, Gracie."

With a smile and a nod, she started to leave, but froze when her eyes caught a glimpse of the large pictures displayed on the screen.

"Hey, I know him."

"You do?" Kole asked, sounding surprised.

"Yeah. That's Craig Wyatt. He's one of…"

Whatever else Gracie was going to say got cut off when she glanced at the picture on the right.

"Oh, my God!" she gasped, both hands flying to cover her mouth. Blinking back tears, her entire body began to visibly shake as her wide eyes shot to Kole's. "Please tell me that's not Craig."

Cursing, her future brother-in-law scrambled to reach the remote, but Gabe was closer. Snatching it off the table, the large man turned the projector off, but it was too late. The damage had already been done.

"Jason, I'll have to call you back." Not waiting for Ryker's reply, Jake hung up the phone and made his way to Gracie.

Sitting in the chair closest to her, Nate sprung to his feet. "Here. Sit down."

Clearly in shock, Gracie did as Nate said.

With her arms wrapped around her center, she began rocking back and forth. "Oh, God, Nate. Is that really him? Is Craig really dead?"

The grief and sorrow in her voice gutted him. Crouching in front of her, Nate took both her hands in his.

"I'm afraid so."

"W-why?" she cried. "Craig was one of the nicest guys I've ever known." Gracie clutched her stomach. "Oh, God, I think I'm going to be sick."

Within seconds, someone was handing Nate the room's

small, plastic trashcan. Positioning it beneath her, just in case, he brought his gaze back up to hers.

"Easy, sweetheart. Slow your breathing."

A set of beautiful, golden eyes pleaded with him as she drew in several slow, deep breaths.

"Who would do something like *that*"—she glanced up at the blank screen— "to him?"

Nate hated that he didn't have the answers she was looking for. "We don't know yet, but we're going to find out."

Taking several more long, controlled breaths, Gracie nodded. When she blinked again, another tear fell down across her cheek and Nate had to fist his free hand to keep from brushing it from her flawless skin.

Kole came back into the room, carrying a glass of water. Nate had been so focused on Gracie he hadn't even realized his friend had left.

"Here, honey," Kole held the glass out to her. "I called Sarah. She's on her way up."

At that, Gracie lifted her eyes."What? Why?"

"You're obviously upset. I figured you'd probably want to go home. You rode here with Sarah this morning, so I asked if she could drive you back to your place." Kole looked to Jake for his belated approval, which their boss gave with a nod.

"No." Gracie shook her head and set the glass down onto the table. Sitting up straighter, she wiped her face dry and looked at Jake. "I'm fine. I can still work. This was just very... unexpected, that's all."

With the same gentle tone Nate had heard him use with his wife, Jake asked Gracie the one question running through the mind of every man in the room.

"How did you know Craig Wyatt?"

"H-he's..." She drew in a shaky breath and let it out slowly before correcting herself. "Craig *was* a patient where I used to volunteer." Sniffing, she looked at Nate. In an almost-whisper, she added, "He's the one who organized my going-away party."

Gracie's beautiful face crumbled, then more tears began to fall, each one causing the unfamiliar pressure in Nate's chest to increase. Unable to keep from it, he pulled her into his arms and held her close.

He wanted to cry with her when he felt her small hands gripping the back of his shirt. It was as if holding onto him was the only thing keeping her together.

I've got you, baby.

Nate looked over her shoulder to Jake and offered a more detailed explanation to him and the others.

"Gracie volunteered at a VA hospital in Maryland. She'd go there a couple times a week to keep some of the Vets who didn't have family close by company."

Jake nodded. "She shared that with me when we first spoke on the phone."

"That's a really nice thing you did, Gracie," Matt told her kindly. Gabe and Zade muttered their agreements.

She pulled away from Nate and wiped her face dry again before giving Matt and the others a watery smile. "Thanks." She then looked up at Kole and said, "Call Sarah back and tell her I'm fine."

"You just found out a friend of yours was brutally murdered. You're not fine."

Gracie grimaced at Kole's words, making Nate want to kick his friend's ass.

"Kole's right," Jake intervened. "With Alpha Team already indisposed on another op and Bravo going wheels up within the hour, I wasn't planning on staying at the office, anyway."

"But, what if someone calls or comes by?"

"I'll re-route the number to ring into my business cell,

and I'll put a note on the door that says we will be back in the office tomorrow morning."

"But—"

"What did I tell you when I first offered you the job here, Gracelynn? About taking care of my staff?"

Looking a little embarrassed, Gracie whispered, "That everyone at R.I.S.C. is like family."

"That's right. And now *you* are a part of that family."

As an adorable blush began to spread across her cheeks, a certain part of Nate's anatomy began to swell. And it wasn't his heart.

Not now, asshole.

Doing his best to ignore the confusing reaction he was having to this woman, Nate gave Gracie's hands a little squeeze and offered her a smile.

"Jake's right, Gracie. We take care of our own, here."

She looked as though she wanted to say something more, but Sarah walked in before she could.

Rushing to her sister's side, she practically pushed Nate out of the way to give Gracie a hug.

"Oh, my gosh, sweetie. I'm so sorry."

Nate stood to give the two women some space. Moving closer to where Kole was standing, he shoved his hands into his pockets but kept his eyes on Gracie.

"Seriously?" Kole whispered low enough only Nate could hear.

Turning his head toward his friend, Nate's brows turned inward as he mouthed, "What?"

Rather than answer, Kole clenched his jaw and shook his head before looking back at his fiancee and Gracie.

"I'm fine. Really." Gracie tried—and failed—to convince her sister she was okay.

"Come on." Sarah stood straight, pulling Gracie to her feet. "I'll take you home."

Though he could tell she really didn't want to leave, Gracie apparently knew when she'd lost a fight. She quietly thanked Jake before promising to be back to work in the morning.

"Take all the time you need," their boss told her.

With a small nod, Gracie started to follow Sarah out the door.

"I'll walk you two out," Kole offered, not even bothering to ask for their boss's permission. Jake would have given it to him, anyway.

To the rest of Bravo, Gracie turned and said, "Come back safely."

Gabe and Zade both smiled as they nodded their heads.

Matt grinned. "Take care, Gracie." Lifting his chin toward Jake, he added, "Make sure you keep the big boss in line while we're gone."

This made her smile a little wider. "I will."

Nate was taken off guard at how disappointed he was that she hadn't said anything directly to him. Then, as she walked out of the room, Gracie looked at him from over her shoulder.

"Be careful, Nate."

Working hard to school his expression, he gave her a crooked grin and winked. "See you when we get back."

With one final, shared look, Gracie turned and walked away. It was the first time since becoming a part of Bravo that Nate wanted to stay behind while the rest of the team went on without him.

CHAPTER 4

"Hey, Carter. Wait up!"

The sun shone down on the team as they made their way across the tarmac to the private jet Ryker had arranged for them to use. With his go-bag flung across his shoulder, Nate turned and saw Kole jogging to catch up to him.

"What's up?"

"You tell me."

Nate was about to ask his friend what he meant when Kole slapped something against his chest.

Grabbing the bunched-up material before it could fall, Nate held it out in front of him so he could see what had Kole so aggravated. His heart stuttered a little harder when he saw it was the shirt he'd let Gracie borrow.

Knowing Kole had his signals crossed, Nate played it off as if it were nothing. Which it was.

"Thanks, man. I was hoping to get this back."

Still acting casual, Nate unzipped his bag and shoved the shirt inside.

He was zipping it up when Kole growled beside him. "Really? That's all you're gonna say?"

ANNA BLAKELY

From behind his sunglasses, Nate looked back at his friend. "What were you expecting, a hug? Aw, you were. That's why you're so upset." He made the tone of his voice mimic that of someone talking to a toddler. "I'm sorry, Kole. Come here and let Natey-watey give you a big hug."

Moving in closer, Nate held both arms out as though he were actually going to wrap them around the other man.

"Quit fuckin' around, asshole." Kole shoved against Nate's shoulder. "You know exactly why I'm upset. I told you not to start shit with Gracie."

Feeling forced onto the defensive, Nate looked over at his buddy. "And I haven't been."

"Yeah? Then why the hell did she sleep in your favorite shirt last night?"

Nate's heart did more than stutter that time. Schooling his expression, he asked, "How do you know she slept in it?"

"Because, dickhead, she was still wearing it when she opened the door for Sarah this morning."

Okay, so that little tidbit made Nate much happier than it probably should have. Determined not to let it show, he gave a shrug. "We met up last night to plan yours and Sarah's party. Chu's was insanely busy, and there was no place to sit, so we got our food to go and took it to my place. Gracie dropped some meat on her shirt, so I gave her mine to wear home. End of story."

Unfortunately.

Though he was also wearing sunglasses, Nate sensed Kole was narrowing his eyes at him suspiciously.

With a sincere tone, he swore to his friend, "Nothing happened between me and Gracie, Kole."

"That's the same thing she told Sarah."

"Well, there ya go. Mystery solved. Now, can we please get on the plane before Gabe comes out and kicks both our asses for making the rest of the team wait?"

Both men started walking again, but Kole just couldn't seem to let it go.

"If there's nothing going on between you two, then what was all that in the conference room earlier?"

"All what?"

"You sure were quick to give her your seat."

Up to now, Nate had done his best to control his temper, but he'd about had it with Kole's bullshit.

"So what?" he shot back. "You went and got her a glass of water. Hell, man. That must mean you're screwing your fiancée's sister."

In a swift move, Kole stepped in front of Nate and removed his glasses. Glaring, he bit out, "What'd you just say to me?"

Nate knew he was probably out of line. But damn it, he'd done nothing wrong and was sick of Kole making it seem as though he had.

Sliding his own glasses to the top of his head, Nate let out an exasperated sigh. "Calm your shit, Kole. I'm just trying to point out how ridiculous you sound right now. Gracie borrowed my shirt. So fucking what? Yes, I offered her my seat when she got upset. Big deal."

And then, because he was pissed, Nate gave Kole his best teenage drama queen impression when he finished with, "And oh em gee, hold the presses...I put my hand on hers while she sat there, crying her eyes out." Nate shook his head in disbelief. "Christ, Kole. The woman had just discovered a close friend of hers had been brutally murdered. Lighten the fuck up, already."

From the expression on Kole's face, Nate thought his words had finally begun to sink in. But then, albeit using a much calmer voice, Kole said, "I'm not blind, Nate. I saw the way you looked at her in there. Everyone did. It's obvious you two have some sort of connection, or whatever. But, I know Gracelynn, and I'm telling you, she doesn't do the whole casual thing."

"And I'm going to tell you for the last time, Gracie and I are just friends. Now, will you please get out of my way so we can go do the job we've been hired to do?"

Kole stared back at him for a few seconds longer before giving him a single nod and stepping to the side.

"If you two ladies are finished arguing, the rest of us would like to fly our asses out of here."

Both men looked up to see Matt sticking his head out of the plane's open door.

"Keep your panties on, King," Kole yelled back.

Nate expected Matt to flip them off. What he didn't expect was for the guy to push his pants down and start shaking his bare ass at them.

"Jesus, that guy needs to grow the fuck up, already," Kole muttered beside him.

"What, like we have?" Nate asked with an incredulous smirk.

"Touché."

Kole's silent laugh told Nate all was forgiven. Although, deep down, Nate was still a little ticked off.

No, he wasn't looking for a relationship, but if he *did* want to start something with Gracie, it wasn't any of Kole's business.

Nate was a grown-ass man, and Gracie was one fine, intelligent woman. If they wanted to go fuck like bunnies in the back of his truck, they could. And there was nothing anybody could say about it.

Aaaand...just like that, the crotch of his jeans began to tighten.

Nate knew he'd have to keep those and any other thoughts about Gracie at bay for the duration of this op. If

Kole saw him sporting a woody while thinking about his almost-sister-in-law, he'd kick Nate's ass for sure.

Once the team was finally settled and airborne, Gabe walked to the front of the jet to debrief them on the details of their mission. Once their team leader started talking, it wasn't hard to push everything else out of his head.

The bastard they were after was one mean sonofabitch. And if Edric Yavuz was in bed with the monster, the United States could be at risk for a whole lot more than just a broken treaty.

"Alright, gentlemen. Listen up. This man is our initial mark. He's been an informant for Ryker's people for a while now. Our job is to locate him and get him to tell us where we can find our real target, Achim Akmar."

Nate and the others each opened the folders they'd been given. On top was a copy of the same picture Gabe was holding up.

"Who is he?" Zade asked the obvious.

"Name's Baran Karas. Goes by Barry."

"Karas...that's a Greek surname, right?" Nate asked curiously.

"Barry's mom is Turkish. His father was Greek," Gabe explained. "His dad died when he was still a baby, after which, Barry's mom moved them back to Turkey to be closer to family."

"So, how did this guy become an informant for the U.S.?"

Nate couldn't help himself. Curious by nature, he was always that kid who asked a billion questions about a topic no one else in the class gave a shit about.

Probably why he went into the tech field. He loved learning new information. About pretty much everything.

Not bothering to hide his frustration, Gabe answered with, "Don't know, and I honestly don't give a rat's ass, Carter. What's important is, this guy was the informant Seal

Team Five was slated to meet with the day their Humvee's got blown into a million fucking pieces. It's also believed he knows the whereabouts of Akmar. Now, we don't know if Karas was directly involved with what happened to our guys, nor do we even know for sure he has intel about Akmar. Either way, we need to find him."

"Duly noted." Nate motioned for their team leader to continue.

Gabe continued to address the team. "Inside each folder, you'll find the most up-to-date information we have on Karas. When we land in Ankara, we'll check into our rooms, deal with our clothes and shit, and meet back at the café down the block from where we're staying."

Ankara was Turkey's capital and, lucky for them, a relatively safe place for Americans to visit.

"We'll grab a bite to eat then head back to my room to map out our next move."

"Do we even know whether this Barry guy is actually in Ankara?" Zade asked Gabe.

"Homeland's latest intel says he is, though he has been keeping a low profile since last summer. The man is smart. He knows he's a suspect in what happened to our SEALS, so he's been staying out of sight."

"If the Navy and Homeland have both been looking for this guy, what makes Ryker think we can find him?"

Though, Zade was the one who asked the question, Gabe directed his answer to the whole team.

"Ryker believes the way to Akmar is through Karas. Those above Ryker's pay grade only want to focus on the big dogs, which is why he handed this to us."

Matt groaned. "Ankara's a big city, Boss. It would be hard enough to find someone who wanted to be found. Locating a guy who's gone dark is gonna be like finding a goddamn needle in a Turkish haystack."

"Better get your magnifying glasses out, boys. This is the job Ryker's paying us to do."

Four days later, after busting their asses, Bravo Team finally found their needle.

Spread out amongst the crowd, each man was strategically positioned in the seats of the amphitheater located in Segmenler Park, the central point of Ankara.

Tonight's performance was a benefit concert consisting of songs sung by various local artists. Being forced to sit and listen to a bunch of lyrics he couldn't understand was annoying as fuck.

Nate was fluent in several languages including Spanish, Dari, Pashto. But not Turkish.

"Anyone have eyes on our guy?"

Gabe's low voice came through the covert earpiece each team member wore. They served as both receivers and mics, which made concealment that much easier, and their sensitivity was so high, a mere whisper came through clear as a bell.

Even more than the others, Nate appreciated the fact that McQueen spared no expense when it came to buying tools of the trade.

"Nothing yet," he responded under his breath.

The bands were between sets, so several people had gotten out of their seats and were moving around.

"Hold that thought." Zade's voice came through next. Then, just as quickly, he said, "Nope. Never mind. That's a negatory, Boss."

"I've got nothing on my end," Kole spoke up. "I don't get it. If this guy's supposed to be hiding out, why would he come here with all these people around?

"He's hiding in plain sight," Nate explained to his friend a split second before Matt chimed in.

"I've got him. My two o'clock. Second section from the

stage. Fourth row, seven seats from the east."

All coms were silent as they waited for Gabe to give the next directive.

"Stand down for now. Keep him in your sight, Turner. Carter, do you have a visual?"

Nate casually glanced that direction, but his view was obstructed by two young women standing nearby. They whispered and giggled like most women did, but it wasn't until he moved his eyes upward that he realized one was smiling straight back at him.

Both women were attractive, and if he weren't on the job...

Another woman's face flashed through Nate's mind. Suddenly, it wasn't some strange woman smiling back at him. It was Gracie.

She was wearing the same yellow sundress she'd had on at Kole's a few days ago. Like that night, her hair was down and falling across her bare shoulders.

Nate watched as she licked her lips and gave him a look that said she wanted him as much as he wanted her. He was about to stand up and go to her when Gabe's voice hit his ear once more.

"Carter? Do you copy?"

Nate blinked and looked again. Of course, Gracie wasn't there, and now the other woman who *had* been smiling at him wore a wary expression.

She said something to her friend and both women left the area as if they couldn't get away fast enough.

Jesus, man. Get your fucking head in the game.

Rubbing his eyes beneath his glasses, Nate shook off the disturbing illusion and tried to find Karas again. With the women gone, he now had a clear view of the man they needed to talk to.

"Affirmative, Boss. I have Karas in my sights."

"Good. Keep him there. King, I want you to slowly make your way over to that area. Get as close to him as possible without making it obvious. When he leaves, we'll follow him out and box him in."

Two bands later, Karas finally stood and began to make his way to the top of the amphitheater. One by one, the members of Bravo began to follow.

It was a game they'd played often. And they always won.

When they were in the grass and away from the thick crowd, Nate and the others pulled back a bit to avoid detection. Now on a sidewalk near the edge of the park, he watched as Karas veered off toward a small, brown car.

The older, beat up vehicle fit the description they'd been given, and was exactly the kind of car someone would drive if they didn't want to stand out.

"He's about to his car, Boss. I'm only a few yards behind him. Should I approach?"

"If you can. Be careful not to spook him."

"Roger that."

Picking up his step, Nate made it to the car just as Karas was about to start the ignition.

"Excuse me. I'm sorry to bother you, but would you happen to have a light?"

Appearing alarmed, Karas simply stared up at Nate as though he didn't understand him. Pulling a pack of cigarettes from his pocket, Nate showed Karas what he was referring to.

Speaking extra loudly and slowly, as a clueless tourist would, he asked the man again. "A light?" Gesturing with his thumb, Nate mimicked the action one would make while trying to ignite a lighter. "Do you have a light?"

Nate and the others already knew Karas smoked, which was why Gabe had bought each of them a pack to carry around. Depending on the situation, any one of the five men could've been the first to make contact with their mark.

Nate just happened to be the lucky winner.

"Oh," Karas nodded. "Yes. I have light." His accent was thick, and his English broken, but Nate understood what he'd said.

"Thanks, man. I've been jonesin' for a smoke all night."

Nate continued to ramble on while he waited for Karas to dig the lighter out of his pocket, which got caught inside his pants. When Karas looked down as he tried to pull it free, Nate used the opportunity to glance across the top of the car and check on the others' progress.

They were headed his way, but not fast enough. Nate needed to come up with a way to distract Karas before he spotted them and took off.

Karas held the lighter out for him. Thinking on his feet, Nate *accidentally* knocked it out of his hand and onto the floorboard.

"Oh, shit, man. I'm sorry."

Muttering what sounded like a curse, Karas bent over and tried to reach it. Knowing this was his chance, Nate pulled his pistol from beneath his loose button-up and pressed the barrel against the back of the other man's head.

"Very slowly, I want you to move your hands onto the steering wheel and sit up."

"I-I...I no...speak..."

"Cut the bullshit, Barry. I know who you are, and I know you can speak near-perfect English."

"No. You have...wrong...man," he continued the farce. "I not Barry. Name is..."

Nate rolled his eyes and sighed. "Look, Bare. It's been a long fuckin' week, and I'm sweatin' my ass off out here. In fact, my hand is getting pretty slick. I'd sure hate to accidentally shoot you while trying to keep a tight grip on my gun."

Resigned, Barry nodded shakily. "Okay, okay. You win. What is it you want?"

The accent was still there, but the man's words had suddenly become a flowing array of beautiful English.

Nate exhaled loudly. "Thank Christ."

As Barry was sitting up, Nate told him, "I need to know where I can find Achim Akmar."

Hearing the other man's name, Barry shot straight up and started to reach for the ignition. Fortunately, Nate had bought the rest of Bravo enough time to make their presence known.

"Touch that key and you'll be pulling back a bloody stump."

Through the passenger window, Nate smiled at Kole who was currently pointing his own gun at Barry's frozen right hand.

"Hey, man," Nate greeted his teammate. "Nice of you to join us." To Karas, he said, "Dude, if I were you, I'd listen to the guy. I once saw him shoot a man center mass from over a hundred yards away. With a paintball gun."

"How many times do I have to tell you?" Kole looked across at Nate. "It was my sniper rifle, asshole. I just adjusted a few things on her."

"Yeah, but you should have seen this shot, Barry. It truly was a thing of beauty."

More confused than scared, the man looked from Nate to Kole, then back again. "I-I cannot give you Achim. He has eyes everywhere."

"Yet, you came to a crowded concert in the middle of the day. In the open." Nate pretended to think a minute. "Yeah, I'm not buying it, Barry."

"I tell you the truth! I do not work with Achim Akmar. I never have. He is a monster."

"You may not have worked with him," Gabe spoke from behind Kole. "But you can help us find him."

Their team leader gave Nate a nod. He opened the driver's door and pulled Karas from the car.

"Come on, Barry. Let's go have a chat, shall we?"

After walking Karas to the van Ryker had arranged for them to use while in the country, Nate and the others drove him to one of Homeland's secure locations. It was an abandoned apartment building slated for demolition in the next few weeks.

Located on the outskirts of the city's eastern border, there was nothing around but a few crumbling structures. A couple squatters had been using the place as their shelter, but they took one look at Gabe and ran off faster than a kitten in a dog pound.

Having set up shop in one of the spaces on the top floor, Gabe had all but ensured no one would be able to hear Barry's screams, in case it came to that.

From the sounds Nate could hear coming from the other side of the closed door, it definitely had.

His gut tightened. He understood the art of torture, and also knew there was a time and place for it. It was the means to a necessary end, but that didn't mean he had to like it.

"How long is Gabe going to keep at it? If the guy hasn't talked by now, I don't think he's going to."

Kole looked up from where he was cleaning his sniper rifle, just to have something to do. "You know how Gabe works. He does what it takes to get to the truth."

"Isn't that what Akmar does?"

"Seriously?" Turner stood from the box he'd been sitting on. "You're really comparing Gabriel Dawson, a decorated SEAL and our team leader, to that murdering sonofabitch, Akmar?"

"No. Of course not," Nate backtracked. "Come on, Matt.

You know what I mean. When do you decide enough is enough?"

"Not my call. But what I do know is that Akmar tortured one of our own to death. He was a SEAL for fuck's sake. And what about Gracie?"

That had Nate standing from the metal folding chair he'd managed to find. "What about her?"

"I saw the way you were with her at the office the other day. Don't you want to be able to go home and tell her we found the man who murdered her friend? I bet that would make her like you even more than she already does."

"You know what? Fuck you. I'm so goddamn tired of everyone trying to get into my business."

Just then, the bedroom door creaked open and Gabe and Zade stepped out. Gabe was covered in sweat and the knuckles on both his hands were torn and bloody. A strong, unpleasant odor followed the two men through the dense air.

"Ah, God. What is that stench?" Kole asked them.

"Our friend Barry pissed and shit himself." Gabe dug a few liras—the official Turkish currency—from his pocket and tossed them on the makeshift table Nate was standing near. "Go to town and buy him some clean clothes. Take Jameson with you."

Knowing when not to argue, Nate followed Gabe's instructions and grabbed the money. "Got it, Boss. Come on, Kole."

"We're heading out when you two get back."

"Heading out?" Zade asked their somber leader. "Where we going?"

"Home." The big guy glanced back toward the room Barry was in. "If Karas knows where Akmar is, he'd rather die than rat him out."

"You think he knows?" Matt asked their boss.

"No." Gabe's answer was instant and unwavering. "I don't."

"So, what are we going to do about him?" Zade asked. "Akmar, I mean."

"We're going to go back home, regroup, and figure out our next move. We'll find him," Gabe assured the team. "Just not this trip."

Damn. Nate would never admit it, but Matt had been right. He did want to be there to see Gracie's face when they told her they'd caught the bastard who killed Craig. However, what Gabe said was also true.

They would eventually find Achim Akmar. And when they did, Nate prayed he was the one to put a bullet through the bastard's brain.

During the long plane ride home, his thoughts kept turning back to Gracie. As much as he hated to acknowledge it, Nate realized he'd actually missed seeing her these last few days. Which was ridiculous, given they'd only just met.

Regardless, Nate did feel a connection with Gracie. One unlike any he'd never felt before. Shit, just the idea of talking to her again was exciting. A fact that left him wondering once again, what the hell was happening to him?

You know exactly what's happening.

Ignoring the annoying inner voice, Nate put his headphones over his ears. He turned his classic eighties rock playlist up loud enough to drown everything else out. Then, reclining in his comfy, leather seat, he closed his eyes and compelled himself to think about anything other than Gracelynn McDaniels.

By the time he woke up, the pilot was telling them to prepare to land. Feeling the effects of crossing several time zones, Nate wanted nothing more than to go home, shower, and fall back to sleep.

With his bag in hand, he headed down the plane's staircase. It wasn't until he reached the asphalt below that he realized Jake was waiting at the edge of the tarmac for them. Standing next to their boss was Sarah, and she looked anything but happy.

"Kole."

Kole had just cleared the plane's steps when Nate said his name. The other man looked up and followed Nate's gaze.

"The fuck? Why is she here?"

Nate knew Kole wasn't upset at the idea of Sarah greeting them as they got off the plane. He was simply concerned, because this sort of thing had never happened before.

As they got closer to their boss and Kole's fiancée, Nate's chest began to tighten. Sarah's face was red and splotchy, and her eyes were slightly swollen from crying.

"Sarah?" Kole dropped his bag and rushed to her. With his hands on her shoulders, he asked, "Baby, what is it? What's wrong?"

Somehow, Nate knew what she was going to say before she even said it.

"Gracie." Sarah was barely able to say her sister's name.

"What about her?" Nate stepped in closer.

Kole glanced over at him, but Nate didn't give a shit. Right now, all he cared about was finding out what had happened to Gracie.

"She's..."

Please don't say she's dead. Nate didn't think he could take hearing that.

"She's what, Sarah?" Kole prompted, his hand cupping the emotional woman's cheek. "Baby, talk to me."

"Gracie's missing," Jake answered for her.

"Missing?" Nate and Kole both spoke in unison. Nate's stomach fell to his feet.

"What's going on?" Gabe asked as he and the others made their way over to them.

71

"What do you mean, she's missing?" Nate directed his question to Jake.

"Who's missing?" Matt asked, trying to catch up on the conversation.

"I took Gracie home the day your team left." Sarah was speaking to Kole, but everyone around her listened closely. Especially Nate.

"I stayed with her for a while, to make sure she was okay. After a few hours, she convinced me she was fine and just needed some time to process everything. So, I left and..." Sarah's face crumbled, and Kole took her into his arms.

"Shhh. It's okay, baby." He rubbed her back. "We'll find her. Everything's going to be okay."

Hating the look on Jake's face, Nate asked, "What do we know?"

"Like Sarah said, she took Gracie home Monday after she learned about Craig Wyatt's death. Security cameras in the parking lot at Gracie's apartment complex show her leaving again about fifteen minutes after Sarah left. We followed her using traffic cam footage, which led us back to our office."

"She went back to work?"

Sarah lifted her head from Kole's chest to answer Nate's question. "She went back to R.I.S.C., but I didn't see her. I was in my office from the time I got back to the firm until I left at six. If I'd just seen her." Her eyes lifted to Kole's "If I'd known she was there, then maybe—"

"No, Sarah." Kole shook his head. "Don't do that to yourself."

"Office security shows her entering at two thirty-three," Jake continued. "She stayed for almost two hours while the guy from the phone company fixed our intercom system, then drove back home. That's the last time anyone saw her."

"That explains why she went back to work," Gabe mused.

"She must have forgotten to call and cancel the appointment."

"Did you check out the guy the phone company sent?" Nate asked desperately. "Maybe he...did something to her." Christ, he hated to even go there. The idea that Gracie had been hurt in any way gutted him.

"He's clean," Jake broke through Nate's thoughts. "Cameras show him leaving alone. His boss, along with traffic cams and computer records, confirm he went straight from our office to another job on the other side of the city. That company backed up his claim, as well. He's not involved."

Still holding his fiancée close, Kole asked Jake, "When did you first realize she was missing?"

"When she didn't show up for work on Tuesday. I called her, but there was no answer. I went down and talked to Sarah, but she hadn't heard from Gracie since leaving her apartment the day before."

"I went over to her place to check on her," Sarah spoke up.

"And?" Nate prompted, feeling like he was going to implode.

"Her apartment had been broken into." Sarah swiped at a new tear. "The whole place was trashed."

Sonofabitch.

The others cursed under their breaths, but Nate forced himself to remain focused. He needed to find out all he could.

"What did you do then?"

"I called Jake. He told me to get back into my car and wait for him there."

"You did good, baby." Kole kissed the top of Sarah's head. "That was the exact right thing to do."

Nate looked at Jake. "What did you find at her apartment?"

"Nothing. There was no trace of her. Her purse and keys were there. Credit cards were all still in her wallet."

"So, it wasn't a robbery," Zade surmised.

"Doesn't appear to be, no."

If there'd been a way to find Gracie, Jake would have figured it out by now. Still, Nate had to ask. "What about her cell?"

"It was also in her apartment, but it's broken. Looks like whoever was there either threw it against the living room wall or stomped on it."

"Pissed because they didn't find what they were looking for?" Gabe speculated.

"Maybe. I called DPD and they sent over a team to process the scene. The officers took pictures and dusted for prints. The usual. The unfortunate reality is we don't know much of anything at this point. Just that someone trashed her place five days ago, and Gracie hasn't been seen or heard from since."

Five days. Five *fucking* days since she'd gone missing.

Nate's mind swirled with numbers and percentages. He knew the odds of finding someone alive dropped drastically after the first twenty-four hours. Much longer than that, and the search for a missing person becomes a recovery operation.

No. She can't be dead.

Nate pictured Gracie's smiling face. He could still hear her laugh as they'd joked together in his apartment that night. It was the most beautiful sound in the world, and suddenly, Nate forgot all about Achim Akmar and all that other bullshit.

In that very moment, the thing Nate wanted more than anything in the entire world was to hear Gracie laugh again.

CHAPTER 5

Gabe, Matt, and Zade followed Nate to his place to help grab some things. After, the entire team met back up at Kole's.

Less than an hour later, His and Sarah's dining room looked more like control central with Nate's monitors and other equipment spread out across the table.

The three other men stayed a while, offering whatever support they could. Eventually, the guys left with the under-standing that they were all on-call and needed to be ready, in case their assistance was needed.

Nate had spent the rest of the day and most of that night doing everything he could think of to try and find Gracie. With the exception of the occasional trip to the bathroom, he kept his ass parked in his chair.

Today had been more of the same. His fingers were cramping from all the typing and searching, but he couldn't stop. He had to figure out what happened to her.

Unfortunately, they hadn't found out any more than what Jake had already told them. After hacking into Gracie's apartment security, Nate was able to catch a glimpse of whoever broke into her place, but that was it.

The guy wore all black and a hood covered any chance they may have had to see his face.

Unbeknownst to the police, Jake had given Nate Gracie's cell phone. His boss knew if there was something useful on there, he'd find it a hell of a lot faster than anyone on the DPD payroll. Unfortunately, there'd been nothing to find.

After working to recover her texts and emails, Nate had discovered nothing more than some conversations with Sarah and Kole.

He'd gotten excited when he'd found a few old texts their dead SEAL had sent to Gracie just before she moved here a couple weeks ago. Unfortunately, there wasn't anything in any of those to help, either.

By the time he was done searching, Nate was so frustrated he wanted to throw the damn thing against the wall, too.

Needing a break, he got up and walked through the kitchen to the sliding door. Opening it, Nate stepped outside for some fresh air.

He inhaled deeply, filling his lungs with as much oxygen as he could before letting it out slowly. The sky was cloud-covered, and the cool breeze let him know rain was on the way.

Nate looked over to the space they'd all sat the night of the barbeque. A week ago, today.

He pictured Gracie smiling and joining in on the conversation with ease. Though, she'd only just become a part of R.I.S.C., it felt like she'd been there all along. Like she belonged with them, and now, she was gone.

Where are you, sweetheart?

Sarah's soft, exhausted voice broke through his thoughts. "I started more coffee. Figured you might need some."

Running a hand down his face, Nate turned and smiled.

"Thank you." When she yawned, he put a hand on her

shoulder and squeezed. "Come on, honey. You need to get some rest."

Shaking her head, Sarah argued, "I'm fine. I need to stay up in case we find her."

Damn, she was breaking his heart. The poor woman had been doing whatever she could to help, which wasn't much.

Keeping herself busy, she'd played the good hostess, making sure they had enough coffee and food to keep them going. Even when Cam, a friend from Sarah's work, stopped by to check on her, she'd put on a brave face and offered to make him lunch.

Through it all, she'd remained amazingly resilient and positive. But, Nate could tell she was teetering on the edge.

None of the guys had said anything until now, knowing it was her way of coping with everything. But the others were gone, and it was time she got some rest.

"I promise you when we find Gracie, you'll be the first to know." Nate purposely didn't say *if*, because it wasn't a matter of if. He *would* find her. "But you're not going to do your sister, or anyone else, any good if you pass out from exhaustion. At least go lay down for an hour or two and recharge."

"He's right, baby." Kole came up behind Sarah and wrapped his arms around her. Kissing the top of her head, he rested his cheek against it. "You have to take care of yourself."

"I know, but..." Sarah turned in Kole's arms. "I just don't want to miss anything."

Kole cupped her face. "I swear to you if we get even the smallest hint of where she could be, I will wake you up immediately."

Nate watched while Sarah considered this. "Promise? Even if it's..." Her voice broke, so she cleared her throat. "Even if it's bad news? You swear you'll wake me?"

Kole gave her a sad smile. "Cross my heart."

"Okay. But don't let me sleep too long." Turning back around, Sarah stepped out of Kole's embrace to give Nate a hug. "Thank you."

He squeezed her back. "Don't need to thank me, honey. Gracie's one of us, now. And even if she wasn't, she's your sister. I'm going to keep doing everything I can to find her and bring her back home to you." He pulled back to give her a smile. "To all of us."

Resting a hand on Nate's cheek, Sarah smiled and whispered, "I know you will."

Behind Sarah, Kole gave him a nod of thanks then escorted her back to their bedroom. Nate returned to the dining room and began checking on the programs he'd set up to run. He hadn't gotten any hits so far, but he damn sure wasn't giving up.

Several minutes later, Kole returned looking nearly as tired and worn down as Sarah.

"How is she?"

He shrugged, then chuckled silently. "She was actually arguing again about how she should be out here doing something to help as she fell asleep."

Nate grinned. "I'm glad she's finally getting some rest."

"Well, the sleeping pill I crushed into the tea I gave her earlier may have helped a little."

Nate felt his eyes bug out. Keeping his voice down, he half-whispered, "Dude, she is going to be so pissed." Then, he shook his head. "You know what? Doesn't matter. I'm just glad she's finally sleeping. She looked like hell."

"Watch it, asshole." Kole's words were harsh, but his tone held no bite, and one corner of his mouth was curved upward.

"You know what I meant."

"Yeah," Kole sighed. "I do." Stretching his arms above his

head, he yawned before sitting down in the chair next to him. "I still can't believe this is happening."

Nate hesitated a few seconds before asking his next question. "I hate even thinking this, but is it possible Gracie was involved in something illegal? Could she have gotten mixed in with the wrong crowd back in Maryland, maybe?"

He'd known the answer before he'd even asked the question. But, they still had to consider the possibility.

Kole looked at him like he was stupid. "Gracie? Hell, no. That woman's a saint. Fuck, you heard her. She even volunteered at the VA hospital on her free-time. How many women you know, especially ones her age, do something that selfless?"

Nate threw his palms up. "I know, man. I just...I had to ask."

His friend's expression softened some. "I get it. This whole thing just blows donkey balls, you know?"

"Big, hairy ones. Yeah, I know." Nate thought for a minute. "Hey, you bringing up the VA reminds me. So, Craig Wyatt—one of the patients at the hospital where Gracie volunteered—gets murdered, then she goes missing a few days later. They've got to be connected, don't you think?"

Kole perked up. "Sure is one hell of a coincidence if they're not."

"Exactly." Nate rubbed his eyes. "I'm going to do some more digging on Wyatt. See what I can come up with."

"You know, what we told Sarah holds true for us, too."

"What's that?"

"We need to get some rest, man. We've both been going non-stop since we landed. You, more than anyone. Go home. Get some sleep. You've got the spare key, so come back whenever you're ready."

Nate considered this. "Everything's already set up, here. I'll just crash on your couch again."

"You and I both know you don't sleep for shit when you're not in your own bed."

His friend was right. Not that he *couldn't* sleep somewhere else. Hell, during his time in the Navy, he'd actually mastered the art of sleeping while sitting up in his computer chair. But he always felt like shit after.

"Come on, man. Let your programs do their thing. I'm a light sleeper, so if it dings or buzzes...or whatever the fuck it's supposed to do when it finds something, I'll hear it."

Nodding, Nate relented. "Fine, I'll go. I'll set up duplicate programs on the computers I left at my apartment. That way, if one of us misses something, hopefully the other will catch it."

Nate grabbed his keys and sunglasses and both men walked to the door. Sliding the glasses onto the collar of his V-neck, he said the one thing he hated to admit.

"I'll keep checking, but..." Nate glanced back toward the closed bedroom door at the end of the hallway. "Tomorrow will be a week since anyone's seen Gracie. You know our chances of finding her alive are—"

"I know," Kole cut him off. Grimacing, the man swallowed hard and said, "But we can't give up."

"Never going to happen," Nate assured him. "I just want you and Sarah to be prepared in case this whole thing ends badly." God, he prayed that wouldn't happen.

"I understand." Kole nodded. "Unfortunately, so does Sarah."

Nate turned and opened the door, but a hand on his shoulder stopped him.

"Listen. About all that shit I said."

Confused, Nate looked back at his friend. "What shit?"

"About you and Gracie. I know you're a good man, Nathan. I never meant to imply otherwise."

"None of that shit's important, right now, Kole. What matters is finding Gracie. Let's focus on that, yeah?"

Kole bobbed his head in agreement. "Yeah. Thanks."

Nate's heart hurt for the pain he saw in the other man's eyes. "It's what friends do, man. I'll be back first thing in the morning, unless I find something before then."

With a shared look, Nate left and headed home. Once there, he got everything up and running and took a quick shower. Knowing he wouldn't get much sleep anyway, he sat in one of his two office chairs and watched the monitors closely.

For the next hour, he remained diligent. Checking program after program, Nate prayed with everything he had that something would pop up and tell them where Gracie was.

But there was nothing.

Her credit cards were useless, since her purse had been left behind. Her phone was in shambles, and what had been recovered was of no help whatsoever. It was as if she'd simply vanished into thin air.

"Goddamn it!" Nate's arm flew out across his desk, knocking several papers and his empty travel mug onto the floor.

Shoving his chair back, he stood and locked his fingers behind his head, pacing the short length of his office. He couldn't remember the last time he felt this helpless.

Gracie was out there, somewhere, and he couldn't stop the barrage of questions rolling through his mind.

What had happened to her? Was she okay? Had she been hurt? Did whoever broke into her apartment decide to ki—

"Nope." Nate spoke the word aloud, refusing to let his mind go there.

He was a man of facts and data, and nothing they'd found so far indicated Gracie had been harmed in any way. That was what he chose to focus on. Otherwise, the what-ifs were going to drive him fucking batshit.

His stomach growled, reminding him he hadn't eaten since early that morning. Sadly, minus a few beers, his refrigerator was essentially bare.

Glancing at the clock, he decided to run down to the corner to Chu's for some takeout.

Knowing his phone was set up to alert him of any new data found in the programs he had running, Nate grabbed his black leather jacket and keys.

The night air was unusually cool for this time of year, plus, the jacket would hide his gun.

While waiting in the restaurant for his order, Nate couldn't help but think of that night here with Gracie. He smiled as he remembered the way she'd blushed when he'd called her out on texting Sarah about going to his place.

He then thought about the way she'd looked in his shirt. The damn thing nearly fell to her knees, but she somehow still managed to make it look sexy.

The memory of that moment at her car came next, those fleeting seconds when he'd come so close to kissing her. Regret filled him to the core as he wondered if he'd ever get that chance again.

He was still mentally beating himself up for not going for it when someone called out his name.

After paying the man at the register, Nate grabbed the white, plastic sack and headed for the door. It wasn't until then that he realized it had begun to rain. From the looks of things, it wasn't stopping anytime soon.

"Fanfuckingtastic."

Doing his best to pull his jacket collar up to cover his neck, Nate bit the bullet and went outside. Raindrops poured down on him in sheets as he made his way toward the alley.

Some of the cold drops ran down into the neckline of his

shirt, making Nate curse Mother Nature as he picked up his pace.

Half way to his apartment, the hairs on the back of Nate's neck began to stand on end. And it wasn't from the cold, wet weather.

This was something different. A feeling he got when he knew someone was following him.

Nate instantly went on full-alert. Not wanting to spook whoever it was for fear they'd freak out and do God knows what, he continued on as if he were none the wiser.

The sound of footsteps made its way past the pouring rain, their pattern becoming a little louder as the person's pace increased.

Waiting for the perfect moment, Nate let them get closer and closer. Then, he made his move.

In one, fluid motion, Nate dropped the bag containing the food, spun around on the ball of his feet, and reached out for the person wishing him harm.

Growling, he shoved his assailant back into his apartment building's brick wall so hard, he knocked the wind out of the piece of shit.

As he did this, Nate inadvertently bumped into some bulging bags of trash that had been stacked near one of two dumpsters placed there. Keeping a strong grip on the guy's shirt, he ignored the stench of rotting garbage and kicked the bag that had toppled into his path out of the way.

Whoever this guy was, he was of a smaller build. Wearing a pair of baggy jeans and an oversized, grey hoodie, his face was obscured by the hood.

Nate couldn't give a shit what the guy looked like. He just wanted to go home, eat his food—which had probably spilled out of the container and into the bag when he dropped it—and go to bed.

Knowing this was most likely just some punk-ass kid

trying to make a quick buck by robbing him, he decided to try and scare the kid into never pulling a stunt like this again.

Stepping in closer, Nate shouted above the rain. "Listen, asswipe. I've had a long fucking week, and I am *not* in the mood to deal with this shit. So take your skinny ass back home to your mamma. Or, better yet, go find a real fucking job and quit trying to steal from innocent people."

When the kid shook his head beneath the hood, Nate decided he needed to take things a step further.

Pulling his gun from his waistband, he shoved it against the kid's chest. Hard.

"I'm *not* going to tell you again, dipshit. Get the fuck out of here and don't come back. You got it?"

A soft whimpering reached his ears, taking him by complete surprise.

"What the hell?"

Nate yanked the hood roughly off the kid's head. When he saw the face hiding behind it, he felt as though *his* breath had been stolen.

"*Gracie?*"

She tried to smile up at him, but she was shaking too badly.

"H-hi."

A few more seconds passed before his mind caught up with what his eyes were seeing. The woman he'd been searching for, the same one who'd been missing for a week, was standing right in front of him.

Her hair was pulled back and tucked into the hoodie's collar, and her face was void of any makeup. The bruises beneath her eyes made her appear as though she hadn't slept in a week.

Rain continued to fall onto her long, beautiful lashes, and she stared back up at him as though he was the answer to her prayers.

God, she's beautiful.

"I d-didn't know where else to g-go."

Hearing her quivering voice again was like a slap to the face. "Shit," he muttered, remembering he was still holding her at gun point.

Nate pulled the weapon away from her chest and tucked it back into his waistband. Then, without giving it a second thought, he pulled her to him and wrapped his arms around her.

"Jesus, Gracie." He held her tightly. "It's so fucking good to see you."

She said something in return, but her words were muffled against his chest. It didn't matter. She was here, and she was safe.

Realizing she was shivering because she was cold, Nate pulled away just enough to look down at her face. "Come on, sweetheart. Let's get you inside and out of this rain."

Relief that broke his heart filled her worn and weary eyes. "Okay."

Picking up his food, Nate used his other hand to grab one of hers. He didn't think about the why, he only knew he couldn't stop touching her right then if his life depended on it.

Back inside and out of the rain, Nate sat the bag with the surprisingly still-closed container onto his dining room table and shrugged out of his dripping jacket. Hanging it on the back of one of his chairs, he pulled his phone from his pocket.

"Wait!" Gracie practically shouted. "Who are you calling?"

"Who do you think? I'm calling Kole. He and Sarah have been worried sick about you." Nate licked his lips and swallowed hard. "We all have."

"You can't call them, Nate. They might be listening or something."

This gave Nate pause. "They? They, who? Gracie, who's after you?"

"I-I don't know." She shook her head.

When she did, a few wet strands of hair stuck to her cheeks, and Nate resisted the urge to pull them away.

"All I do know is some guy broke into my apartment the night you left, and he knew my name. Said he'd be back."

"You talked to him? Who was he? Did he hurt you?" Without giving her a chance to answer any of his questions, Nate started running his hands down her arms, looking her over for possible injuries.

"No." She pushed his hands away. "H-he didn't see me. I overheard him talking on the phone to someone."

Nate started to ask what the guy said but stopped himself. "Okay, let's back up a few steps. I need to let Kole and Sarah know you're okay."

Gracie's face filled with alarm. She started to argue again, but Nate held up a hand to cut her off.

"Just listen a minute. I can call him on our secure phones. The ones we take with us when we go on an op."

She still looked unconvinced, so he asked, "You trust me. You must, otherwise you wouldn't have come to me, yeah?"

Gracie nodded slowly in agreement.

"Good. Then, I need you to trust me on this, too, okay? These phones are highly encrypted. No one's going to be listening to them. You have my word."

"Okay," she whispered softly.

She may have agreed, but Nate could still hear the trepidation in her voice. Could see the fear reflected in those beautiful, golden eyes.

Putting the phone on speaker, Nate dialed Kole's number. Sounding groggy, as if he'd been sleeping, Kole answered on the third ring.

"Nate? Why the hell are you calling on this line?"

"I found her."

"What?" Kole instantly sounded alert and fully awake. "You found Gracie? Where is she?"

"Well, actually…" Nate gave Gracie a tiny smile. "She found me. She's here, at my place." With a tilt of his chin, he motioned for Gracie to say something.

"H-hey, Kole. I'm here. I'm okay."

"Gracie? Oh, thank God."

"Where have you been?" Sarah's voice came through next. "We've been looking all over for you!"

It sounded like she was crying, but at least this time, they were tears of joy.

"I'll explain everything when I can. For now, please just know I'm okay. And I'm sorry I worried you." Her eyes found Nate's as she added, "I just didn't know what else to do."

When Kole began to bombard Gracie with his rapid questioning again, Nate could tell she was feeling overwhelmed and wasn't sure what to say. Taking the phone off speaker, he gave her a wink before putting it to his ear.

"Hey, Kole, it's me. Listen, I think Gracie needs a minute to regroup."

"Regroup? She vanished for six fucking days. She doesn't need to *regroup*. She needs to tell us what the hell happened."

"And she will. Look. Let me talk to her first. I'll get the whole story, and then I'll call you back with the details."

"I'm coming over."

Gracie must have heard Kole's voice through the phone, because she began to adamantly shake her head.

Understanding her concern, Nate told Kole, "No. Don't come here."

"The fuck you mean? Of course I'm coming there."

"Kole, listen to me a minute, okay? Whoever broke into Gracie's apartment knows her. She overheard him mentioning her name to someone on the phone and saying he'd be back. I'm assuming that's why she didn't go to Sarah in the first place. She didn't want to risk the guy following her there."

Gracie bobbed her head, letting him know his assumption was spot on.

"Now, I know you both love Gracie, and you're worried about her," Nate continued. "I also know you don't want anything to happen to Sarah. Especially not after what went down with Prescott."

Ian Prescott used to be a lawyer at the firm where Sarah worked. The guy became obsessed with Sarah and began stalking her. He even went so far as to break into her and Kole's apartment and assault her.

Luckily, Nate and Kole showed up before the maniac could cause her any serious harm.

"You're right," Kole begrudgingly agreed. "I don't. But, damn it, I don't want anything to happen to Gracie, either."

"And it won't. How about this? She stays here with me tonight, and then we'll all meet up at the office tomorrow. I'll text Gabe and tell him to get ahold of the others. You can text Jake and let him know what's going on. We'll plan on meeting at the office at oh eight-hundred. We can figure everything else out, then."

There was a long pause, and Nate waited. He could hear Kole relaying the plan to Sarah. From what he could make out, she didn't like it, but in the end, she agreed.

"Fine. We'll see you at the office at oh eight-hundred. I'd tell you to give her a big hug and a kiss from me, but that would probably come back to bite me in the ass. So, just tell her goodnight, we're glad she's safe, and we love her."

Nate chuckled. "Will do. 'Night."

"Goodnight. And Nate?"

"Yeah?"

"Thanks for taking care of her."

"Never have to thank me for that, brother."

Not waiting for Kole's response, Nate ended the call and shoved the phone back into his pocket. He drew in a deep breath and let it out slowly then locked his eyes with Gracie's.

"First things first. Let's get you a hot shower and some clean clothes. I'll order some more food to be delivered, and then, you're going to tell me what the hell it is you've gotten yourself into."

CHAPTER 6

With her head tilted forward, Gracie stood beneath Nate's large shower-head, letting the hot water run down her shoulders and back. It was the first time in nearly a week she'd felt safe enough to give herself more than a handful of minutes to wash, rinse, and get out.

The hotels she'd stayed at the past few nights were less than stellar, but they were off the beaten path and within her meager cash budget. She was very careful to make sure she wasn't followed, but still. Her paranoia was in full form lately, and she'd been too afraid to let her guard down, even for a second.

"Gracie?" Nate's voice carried through the closed bathroom door and over the noise of the shower.

Opening the frosted shower door, Gracie stuck her head out. "Yeah?"

"Just checking to make sure you are okay."

A warm sensation spread across her chest, and it had nothing to do with the temperature of the water.

"I'm good. I'll be out in just a minute."

"Take your time. The food's here, but we can warm it up if we need to."

"Okay."

She waited a few more seconds to make sure he wasn't going to say more before closing the door and finishing her shower. After, she got out and dried off, then squeezed as much water from her long hair as she could into the towel she'd used.

Gracie looked down at the pile of clothes she'd been wearing and cringed. They were still damp from the rain, so there was no way she was putting those back on.

That's when it hit her.

Her extra set of clothes was still at the last place she'd stayed. *Damn.*

She couldn't explain why she left there in such a hurry. There'd been no sign of the man she'd seen at her apartment. Still, something had told Gracie she needed to get out of there tonight.

Knowing the general details of their current op, she'd assumed—and prayed—Bravo had made it back home. Banking on that, she'd grabbed what cash she had left and called for a cab.

Because she'd been so worried about possibly being followed, Gracie had told the cab driver to drop her off a few blocks from Nate's. From there, she walked down a block, went into a nearby alley, backtracked, and crossed the street before heading down the next block.

She continued the erratic behavior, hoping to throw whoever it was off…just in case they were back there somewhere, following her.

Gracie reached Nate's block just as he was walking into Chu's. The relief she'd felt from just seeing him again was almost indescribable.

As the rain poured down, she'd stood across the street,

watching him while he waited for his food. As soon as he left the restaurant, she'd high-tailed it across the street and into the alley behind him.

She was trying to catch up to him when he'd taken her by complete surprise, spinning around and pushing her against that wall. She'd tried to tell him who she was, but he'd knocked the wind out of her, making it impossible to speak.

By the time she could talk again, he was pushing his gun against her chest. Right above her heart.

Fear had left her frozen. To be fair, Gracie had never even had a gun pointed in her direction, much less had one pressed against her body like that.

She looked down at the small, round bruise beginning to form on her skin. She wasn't mad at him for it. How could she be?

Her thoughts returned to that moment in the alley. Not the fear and uncertainty she'd felt, but the powerful way Nate had moved.

He didn't appear to even have to think about what he was doing. He just attacked with strength and purpose. In a weird, twisted way, it was almost beautiful to see.

Shaking those thoughts away, Gracie went back to the task at hand. Wrapping the large, black towel she'd used around her body, she secured it between her breasts before opening the door and walking out into Nate's bedroom.

She started to look around for something to throw on when she spotted his favorite shirt laid out on top of his bed. Next to it were some running shorts and a pair of socks.

Smiling for the first time in days, she started to undo the towel when the door opened, and Nate stepped inside the room.

Letting out a little squeal, Gracie quickly covered herself and held the towel in place. Their eyes met and Gracie froze. She wasn't the only one.

They both stood like that for a solid ten seconds before talking all over each other.

"I was just changing into—"

"I'm so sorry. I was just checking to see—"

They both laughed nervously.

"You go first," Gracie offered.

"No, please." Nate held out a hand. "Ladies first."

"I-I saw these and assumed you'd left them for me."

"I did. You weren't carrying anything with you in the alley, so I figured you'd need something for tonight."

Nate's thoughts must have returned back to that moment because his eyes lowered toward her chest. Not in a sexual way, but more of a clinical, assessing manner.

"Shit."

He mumbled the low curse before closing the distance between them. Slowly, as though he were afraid to hurt her, Nate raised his hand to the small bruise.

His fingertips traced the tiny, reddish-blue circle, sparking a flame of desire as they moved across her delicate skin.

Gracie felt her pulse quicken and tried with all her might to control her breathing. It was so hard to do when the man who'd invaded her most recent dreams was this close. Touching her in such a gentle, caring way...while she was practically naked.

"I'm so sorry, sweetheart. I didn't mean to—"

"I know." Gracie covered his hand with hers. "You didn't know who I was," she spoke softly. "How could you? You reacted the way you've been trained, that's all."

Nate's stunning eyes rose to meet hers. Gracie stared into those deep seas of blue and then lowered her gaze to his mouth.

She wanted to kiss him. Had thought of little else ever since the last time she'd been here.

Gracie didn't know if it was her adrenaline running on full steam or the roller coaster of emotions she'd experienced as of late. But something inside her said to go for it. So, she did.

Rising on her tiptoes, Gracie glanced back up at him one last time before closing her eyes and pressing her mouth to his.

At first, Nate didn't reciprocate, and Gracie feared she'd made a terrible mistake. Just as she started to pull away, he cupped the back of her head with one hand and pressed his other at the small of her back.

Taking over, Nate began to kiss her back forcefully, his lips pressing against hers with a hunger matching her own.

Exhilarated by the fact that he wanted her just as badly, Gracie took things a step further. Using the tip of her tongue, she traced the seam of his mouth, enticing him into letting her in.

Nate grunted as they tasted each other for the first time, the sound making her even more aroused than before. As their tongues danced and twirled together, Gracie became bolder with her movements.

Closing the remaining few inches left between them, she pressed her hips against his. Wearing nothing but a towel, it was easy to feel his jean-clad erection against her lower belly. Slick heat began to pool between her legs as she imagined herself setting it free.

Sliding her hand in that direction, Gracie's fingers had almost made it to Nate's belt buckle when he stopped her. Placing the hand that was once against her back over hers, he pulled his lips free, abruptly ending the kiss.

Their panted breaths mixed together as Gracie tried to figure out what had just happened. It didn't take long to get her answer.

"I'm sorry, Gracie. I shouldn't have done that."

"What? Kiss me back?" Gracie teased.

She waited for him to make some sort of joke, but the look of regret on his face said he was one hundred percent serious. Her heart sank inside her deflated chest.

"Oh, um..." She licked her lips, hating that she still tasted him there. "I think I'm the one who should apologize. I thought you wanted—"

"I did," he answered quickly. "I do." Nate took a couple steps backward, raking a hand through his hair.

Even when it was messy, he looked sinfully delicious.

"You're a very attractive woman, Gracie," he remarked.

Just not attractive enough.

Mortified, Gracie became focused on her bare feet so she wouldn't have to look him in the eye while he let her down easy.

"Hey, look at me." Nate used his thumb and forefinger to lift her chin, forcing her to make eye contact despite her efforts to the contrary. "You are the most beautiful woman I've ever seen. Don't doubt that for a second, sweetheart."

Oh, God. Had she actually said that out loud?

She closed her eyes and regained her composure. Doing her best to salvage what was left of her dignity, Gracie moved out of his reach.

"It's fine, Nate. I'm probably all hyped up on adrenaline or something. Really, it's fine."

"Gracie..."

Trying to pretend like nothing happened, she purposefully made her voice overly cheerful.

"You said the food's ready, right? Because I am *starving*."

Yeah, she knew it was lame, but it was the best she could come up with. What she really wanted to do was crawl into a hole and never come out.

Thankfully, Nate didn't push the subject. "Uh, yeah. I'll go warm it up while you get dressed."

"Perfect." She gave him her best, *everything is fine* smile. "I'll be out in a minute."

After giving her a final, assessing look, Nate left the room, quietly closing the door behind him.

Growling at herself, Gracie turned and plopped face down onto the bed. She lay there, wallowing in self-pity for a few more seconds before sitting back up and pulling herself together.

Once she was dressed, she went into the bathroom and used a brush she'd found in one of the vanity drawers to tame her still-damp locks. There was nothing more she could do to try and look any more presentable—not like it would matter, anyway—so, she took a deep, calming breath and went to find Nate and the food.

She wasn't lying when she'd claimed to be hungry. With only a bit of cash she'd had stashed away in her apartment, she'd been very stingy on what she spent money on these past few days.

The delicious aroma of sweet and sour pork hit her half way down the hall, the scent reminding her of the night she was here with Nate. Gracie looked down at the letters sprawled across her chest and found herself wishing she were wearing it for a whole other reason.

Pushing those useless thoughts away, she decided to focus on the fact that she was safe, and be thankful Nate was kind enough to let her stay here.

"Food's on the counter, and I set a plate and fork out for you to use. Help yourself."

"Thanks," Gracie muttered as she walked past him. Hating the uneasy look in his eyes, she added, "And thanks, again for letting me stay here. I didn't know where else to go."

"Of course."

That was all she got, making her feel even worse for

forcing herself on him like she had. Although, he did kiss her back, and *damn.*

For someone who wasn't interested, he sure as hell kissed like he was.

They both filled their plates in silence before taking a seat at Nate's table. It didn't seem possible that a week had gone by since she was last here, laughing and joking around.

It's crazy what a difference a few days can make.

Hating the awkwardness between them now, she tried to apologize. "Nate, I'm sorry. I never should've—"

"Tell me what happened at your apartment," he interrupted. "Exactly. Don't leave anything out."

His abrupt tone took her off guard. "Um, okay. Sure. Let's see, I left the office with Sarah. We went back to my place and hung out for a while."

"What did you talk about?"

Her heart rate increased. "Is that relevant to what happened?"

Nate shrugged. "I don't know. Probably not, but the more details you can give me, the better chance I have of catching this guy."

Gracie really didn't want to divulge her entire conversation with Sarah, given that Nate had been the main topic for the last portion of it. *I'll leave that part out, for now.*

"We talked about Craig. I told her some funny stories from my time with him at the hospital. I showed her the pictures..." Gracie cut herself off. "Oh, no. The pictures."

"What pictures?"

"On my phone." Knowing she needed to explain a bit further, she added, "I left it in Craig's hospital room one day when I went to go check on something with one of the nurses. It wasn't until later that night I realized he'd taken a bunch of silly selfies before putting my phone back exactly how I'd left it. As a joke, you know?"

Grinning, Nate nodded. Gracie couldn't help but think it was totally something *he* would do.

Nate surprised her when he said, "I have your phone. I should be able to recover all your pictures."

"Really? That would be great!" Then, she scrunched her brow. "Wait. Why do you have my phone?"

"When we got back from Ankara…" Nate hesitated, clearly unsure of what he could share about the op.

"It's okay, Nate. I know where your team was sent. I helped Agent Ryker with some of the arrangements."

With a nod, he started again. "When we got back from Ankara late Saturday afternoon, Jake and Sarah were waiting for us at the gate. They told us you'd gone missing, and Jake gave me your phone. I restored all your texts and emails to see if there was something in them that could help us find you. I didn't specifically go in and download the pics, though."

"There aren't many, but the ones I do have, I'd like to keep. If that's possible."

"I'll do my best to get them back for you."

Nate grinned at her from across the table, and Gracie's heart did that whole skipping-a-beat thing. *Focus, Gracelynn. Focus*

"Thanks. I forgot to grab it and my purse when I went back to the office that night. I guess I was still so shocked about what happened to Craig, I just grabbed my keys and drove. When I got back home and saw what had happened, I was afraid whoever that guy was would be able to trace my location, so I left it all on purpose."

There was a stretch of silence before Nate pushed on. "Let's back up. So, you and Sarah talked about Craig. Then what?"

"She left to go back to work. I started to run a bath, thinking it would help me relax. But, then I remembered someone from the phone company was supposed to be at the office at three, so I went back there to wait for them."

"Why? You could've called Jake. Had him take care of it."

Gracie shook her head. "He left, remember? He told me he was going to finish up with you guys, then close the office for the day and work from home."

"You're right. I stand corrected. Anyway, it's probably a good thing you weren't home when that guy got there."

"No kidding."

"Okay, so you went to the office. What happened next?"

"I went to R.I.S.C., the guy came and fixed the intercom system, then I went back to my apartment. Only, when I got there, my door was cracked open. I was sure I'd locked it when I left, but started to second guess myself. I pushed the door open a little more, and that's when I saw the mess."

"And the man? Where was he?"

"In my bedroom. I could see his reflection in the mirror hanging above my nightstand."

"Jesus, Gracie." Nate sat back in his chair and ran a hand over his five o'clock shadow. "If you could see him, he just as easily could've seen you."

"I know. That's why I didn't keep the door open like that. Once I saw him, I pulled it so it looked like it did when I got there. Then, I just stood and listened at the door."

She could tell Nate wanted to reprimand her for sticking around rather than going for help. Instead, he asked, "What did he say?"

Hating that she could still feel the pure, unadulterated fear from that day, Gracie licked her lips nervously and took a breath before telling Nate everything she could remember.

"He told whoever he was talking to that he couldn't find it. And before you ask, no. I have no idea what *it* is. Then, he said not to worry. That he'd keep looking for the"—she made air quotes—"'McDaniels bitch' until he found her. Me. Whatever. Anyway, the bastard swore he'd do whatever was necessary to get me to tell him where to find whatever it was he was looking for." Gracie looked down at her hands, which were clenched into fists atop the table. "That's when I got really scared."

"And you could hear what he was saying from all the way outside?"

Gracie gave him a half smile. "He talked really loudly for a burglar. Almost like he didn't care if anyone heard him. His voice really carried, too, so that made it easier."

"Do you think you'd recognize it if you heard it again?"

"Absolutely. Between his vocal tones and his accent…I'll never forget it."

"Accent?" Nate perked up at that. "What kind of accent?"

"It sounded middle-eastern. I've never been great at accents, though, so don't quote me on that."

"You said you got a good look at him?"

"I did."

"That's good. I'll have you sit down with Zade tomorrow and give him the description so he can put together a sketch for us."

"Zade can draw? Wow. Who knew?"

Nate chuckled. "He's a man of many talents."

Gracie grinned but then hid a yawn behind her hand. "Sorry. I haven't slept well since…well, this whole week, really."

"I can imagine. Where did you go after you left your place? And where have you been staying this whole time?"

"I hid in the bushes behind my apartment building and waited until the guy left. When I felt it was safe enough, I ran inside, grabbed a change of clothes and a few hundred dollars I keep stashed away for emergency money, and flagged down the nearest cab. From there, I changed hotels every couple days, just in case. Then, I came here. To you."

Gracie's mind whirled from memories of that night. She didn't even notice Nate getting up and coming over to her until he spoke again.

Much like he'd done in the office after she'd first learned about Craig, Nate squatted down in front of her and put a hand over hers.

"We're going to figure this out, Gracie."

"I know you will."

He gave her a sweet smile. "Listen, why don't we call it a night? Jake will probably want to go over all this again with you tomorrow, anyway."

"Great. Can't wait."

Chuckling as he stood, Nate pulled her to her feet. "Come on. You can take my bed. I'll sleep out here on the couch."

"Oh, Nate, no. I've caused you enough trouble as it is. I don't want to take your bed, too." *Unless you're going to be in it. With me. Naked.*

"Don't worry about me. I can sleep anywhere."

Clearing her throat—and her X-rated thoughts—Gracie decided it best not to argue. "Only if you're sure."

"I'm sure. Now, go. Those sheets haven't been slept on since I got back, so they're still clean. You know where the bathroom is, and if you need anything else, just ask."

Trying to talk past the big knot that had suddenly taken up residency in her throat, Gracie blinked quickly and whispered, "Thank you, Nate. I didn't...I didn't know who else to turn to. I would have gone to the police, but I got the feeling the person the man was talking with was important. I don't know why, but my gut said to stay low and not say anything to anyone until you got back." She looked at his handsome face and smiled. "Something told me you'd know what to do." Glancing away, she laughed nervously. "Silly, right? I probably should have gone straight to the cops."

Like before, Nate lifted her chin. "Don't waste time

second-guessing yourself, sweetheart. You did good. You stayed calm, waited until it was safe to get your emergency money, and remained hidden until you had someone you could trust to go to. I wish you'd have found a way to contact Sarah to let her know you were okay, but only because we were all worried sick, thinking of what could have happened to you."

"I know. I'm sorr—"

Nate stopped her with a finger to her lips. "No more apologies. You're safe now, and that's all that matters. Got it?"

Gracie nodded and tried to say "Got it", but it came out all jumbled, since his finger was still in the way.

The man's eyes danced as he laughed, making him look even younger than his thirty-three years. She made a mental note to try and make him laugh as much as possible.

"Go on, now. Get some rest. If you're lucky, I'll make you some breakfast in the morning. I think I have a box of Pop-Tarts in there, somewhere."

"You do drive a hard bargain, Mr. Carter. But, if Pop-Tarts are on the line, I'm all in. Unless they're strawberry." She scrunched her nose. "I don't really like those."

"Which kind are your favorites?"

"The brown sugar and cinnamon, of course."

"Well, how 'bout that. They're my favorite, too." Nate gave her a wink and a smirk. God, the man was too freaking sexy for his own good.

Knowing she needed to leave the room before she did something ridiculous like kiss him again, Gracie smiled and said, "Goodnight, Nate."

"Goodnight, sweetheart. Sleep tight."

Turning around, she walked back to Nate's room. He said the sheets were clean, and they were, but she could still smell hints of him on the pillowcase.

Just like the shirt she was wearing, it was a mixture of

laundry detergent and whatever cologne Nate used. It was light, not like the strong, make-you-gag type some men wore. And it was quickly becoming her most favorite scent in the world.

Given all that had transpired, she expected this to be just like the previous nights. Every night for the past week, she'd lay awake, tossing and turning, while listening for any signs of someone trying to break into her room.

Every little sound would make her jump, and she was constantly checking the flimsy locks on the hotel door. It would take hours for her to actually fall asleep, then she'd wake up in a panic, fearing she'd been in the same place for too long.

Tonight, for the first time in a week, Gracie closed her eyes and fell asleep almost immediately. And she stayed that way, knowing the man in the other room would gladly stand between her and any danger that may come her way.

CHAPTER 7

Edric Yavuz calmly removed the crystal stopper from his decanter and poured himself two fingers of his favorite bourbon. Typically, he'd take a moment to appreciate the bottle's intricate etchings, but today he had more pressing issues occupying his thoughts.

"You said you'd find her." Edric replaced the stopper. With both it and his glass in hand, he turned to face his most trusted associate. "I pay you well to keep your word."

"And I will."

"When?"

"I will find her, Edric. You just have to give me more time."

Edric slammed the expensive tumbler down onto the serving table. "It's been over a week, Achim. People like Gracelynn McDaniels do not just disappear. She is nothing. A nobody. She should not have the means to simply vanish like this."

"You're right. She will turn up. And when she does, I will be there."

"Well, you'd better hope it happens soon. That treaty is to

be signed in less than a month. If that file is found before then..."

"I will find the woman and the file, Edric. She couldn't have gone far. Her purse and phone were still at the apartment when I was there."

"And you're certain Wyatt didn't send the file to her in an email or text?"

"I already told you he didn't. There were no emails and I went through each and every text he sent to her. It was all foolish pictures and worthless conversations."

"Well, check it again."

"That's not possible."

"Why not?"

"I already went back for it. Either the police or the people she works for must have taken it. It doesn't matter. I crushed it before I left, just in case."

Swallowing the warm liquid remaining in his glass, Edric poured himself another. "Tell me more about this company she works for."

"It's called R.I.S.C. They do private security. Bodyguards, shit like that. It's owned by a man named Jake McQueen. He's former Delta, and from what I've heard, his operatives are the best. All former military. The McDaniels woman recently took a job as McQueen's office manager and public relations contact. Her soon-to-be brother-in-law is a security specialist for one of the two teams McQueen put together."

At least the man found out something useful. "Is this going to be a problem?"

"On the contrary."

Intrigued, Edric motioned for Achim to continue.

"With no ID and limited funds, the bitch will have to reach out for help soon. Given what they do for a living, I'm thinking she'll go to someone with R.I.S.C., and I plan to be there when she does."

"And the sister?"

"There's been no sign of Gracelynn anywhere near her sister's apartment. She's smart. Much smarter than we gave her credit for. My guess is she knows someone's after her and doesn't want to put her sister in danger."

"Maybe that's where you should start. Get to her through her sister."

"That's one route we could take."

Edric thought for a moment. "Is your friend who discovered the McDaniels woman close by? I don't want to waste time having to wait for him to show."

"I can have him here by morning," Achim said with certainty.

"Make the call."

"Yes, sir." He turned and started to leave the room, but Edric stopped him.

"Achim?"

With his hand on the expensive doorknob, the killer-for-hire turned to face him.

"As always, do—"

"Whatever it takes," Achim finished for him. "Don't worry, Edric. I'll take care of everything."

"You always do, my friend."

Long after Achim had left, Edric was still in his office. Sitting behind his large, mahogany desk, he studied the framed photo of him with President Russell.

They were smiling and shaking hands, having come to an agreement on the terms of the treaty. Edric laughed to himself, knowing once Gracelynn McDaniels was in his possession, he'd have everything he needed to destroy Russell and the precious United States of America.

* * *

Nate stole another glance at Gracie. She was sitting between her sister and Kole in the conference room while they waited with the rest of the team.

They'd all arrived twenty minutes ago, but Jake had gotten caught up with something at home and was running a few minutes late.

After a tearful reunion in the office's reception area, Nate and Kole had escorted Gracie and Sarah back here to go over everything and figure out what their next move was.

He and Gracie hadn't spoken a whole lot this morning, outside their awkward greeting in the kitchen and small talk over Pop-Tarts and coffee.

Knowing she was more than ready to see her sister again, Nate hadn't wasted any time getting her here.

Sarah had brought her a change of clothes so she wouldn't have to wear what she slept in. Although, if it were up to Nate, she'd wear nothing but his favorite shirt. Forever.

Not that the T-shirt and denim capris she had on now weren't every bit as sexy. Hell, the woman could be wearing a moo-moo and she'd still look good enough to eat.

Nate shifted in his seat as his cock began to swell. He really needed to get a grip on his hormones. But, fuck.

All he'd thought about since last night was that goddamn kiss. That, and how—had he not been a complete dumbass— it would have turned into a whole hell of a lot more.

He was just so taken off guard when she'd kissed him like that. He knew he should've stopped her sooner, but a bigger part...okay *two* bigger parts...wanted nothing more than to feel those full, supple lips on his.

So, like a complete loser, he'd waited for her to make the first move.

Then, when she did kiss him, what did he do? He stood there. Frozen. Just like the geeky, high school dork he used to be.

Thankfully, he finally got his ass in gear and kissed her back, and ho-ly-*fuck* could she kiss! Their tongues met, and his dick went from half-mast to ready-to-explode in less than a second.

It was a damn good thing he stopped her when he did, because had her fingers made it down any further, he would have completely and unequivocally embarrassed himself.

Guilt settled in his gut again. He hated knowing Gracie had been embarrassed afterward. Nate could tell she thought it was because he didn't want her, which was the farthest fucking thing from the truth.

He'd tried to tell her that, too, but she'd changed the subject to food, and he was such a chicken shit, he'd let her.

Because of that, he'd then been forced to lay there all night, knowing she was alone in his bed…wearing that damn shirt.

For the first two hours, he did nothing but shift this way and that, trying to get comfortable enough to fall asleep. Of course, that was an impossible task when his dick was as hard as a fucking two-by-four between his legs.

For a minute, he'd considered going in and taking a shower in the second bathroom so he could relieve the pressure and maybe get some rest. In the end, he decided against it.

For some reason, jerking off to thoughts of Gracie while she was in the very next room made him feel like a creep. Instead, he'd tried to think of anything and everything that wasn't sexual, eventually falling asleep.

The door to the conference room opened, and Nate blinked rapidly as he brought his thoughts back to the present. Kole looked over at him with a strange expression, mouthing *you okay?*

With a single tilt of his head, Nate silently assured his

friend he was fine as Gracie stood to greet Jake when he entered the room.

"Gracie." Jake drew her in for a hug. "I'm so glad you're okay."

Clearly surprised at their boss's show of affection, Gracie stumbled over her own words as she belatedly hugged him back. "I-I...um...thank you."

Pulling back, Jake kept his hands on her upper arms. He spoke with sincerity when he looked at her and said, "We were all incredibly worried about you. I understand your reasons for staying away, and while I admire your selflessness, I wish you'd come to me when this all started."

"I'm sorry, Jake. I panicked. I was afraid whoever that guy was would be watching the building here, and I..." Gracie sighed loudly and shook her head. "I'm sorry. You'll have my letter of resignation before I leave here, today."

Resignation? Now, Nate was the one panicking.

Gracie hadn't mentioned anything to him about quitting. If she quit, she might move back to Maryland. If she moved, he may never see her again, and if that happened...

Calm your shit, dude. That little voice was right. No way Jake will let her quit over something like this. Would he?

Nate waited with bated breath for his boss's response.

"Resignation?" Jake dropped his hands. "You just started. Why the hell would you resign?"

Hiding a smile, Nate shifted his attention to Gracie. Looking even more nervous than before, she said, "I...uh...I just assumed since I didn't show up or call for an entire week, you'd already be looking for my replacement."

"If you think I'd fire you for putting your safety above being here to answer the phone, you don't know me very well. But, that's okay." Jake grinned and patted her arm. "You'll get there. Our priority right now is finding out who was in your apartment and why. As far as the job goes, we'll figure all that out later."

Walking past Gracie, Jake turned his attention to the entire room. "Sorry, I'm late. Olivia wasn't feeling well this morning, and I didn't want to leave her alone until I was sure she was going to be okay."

"What's going on with Liv?" Gabe asked.

"She caught some sort of stomach bug. She seemed to be doing better when I left." He took a seat at the head of the table and looked to Gracie. "Let's start from the beginning. Gracie, why don't you tell us all what happened. The more details you can give, the better."

Gracie looked over at Nate, who gave her a wink and a nod. He could tell she was remembering him saying almost those exact words to her last night.

Everyone listened as Gracie retraced what happened from the time she got back to her apartment the previous Monday to arriving at Nate's last night.

Nate was grateful she left out the part about him nearly shooting her ass in that alley. She also—thank you, Jesus—skipped over the felt-it-in-his-boots kiss they'd shared.

He was especially thankful for that particular omission, knowing Kole probably would've leapt over the fucking table and beat his ass if he knew.

"Nate said you got a look at the guy. If now is a good time"—Zade looked to Jake—"I could take her to your office and do a quick sketch. See what we come up with."

"That's a good idea. Come back in here when you're done."

Zade stood and walked around the table. "Come on, Gracie." He grinned. "Let me show you how the magic's done."

Returning his smile, Gracie stood and started to follow.

"Can I come with her?" Sarah asked.

Zade shrugged. "Don't see why not."

Both women followed him out of the room. Jake waited until they were gone to begin speaking to him again.

"Nate, is there anything else you can think of? Anything she shared with you last night but forgot to mention?"

Only that I put a gun to her chest and later stuck my tongue down her throat.

"She told you everything she told me, Boss."

"What are your thoughts?"

"I think it's a big fucking coincidence that a former SEAL she was friends with is found tortured to death a few days before her apartment is broken into, and she's scared into hiding. And I know what we all think about coincidences."

"No such thing," all five men said in unison.

"Okay." Jake leaned his elbows on the table. "We need to look into Craig Wyatt more closely. Carter, I want you to dig deep. His financials, love life. All of it."

"Boss, I've looked. There's nothing there."

"Look again. Wyatt's death and the target on Gracie's back have to be related somehow. We figure out that connection, we find the person behind it."

"Roger that. I'm on it."

They continued to discuss the situation involving Gracie before Jake shifted the conversation to an update on Alpha Team's latest op. Jake stopped talking a few minutes later when the conference door opened.

Zade came in with a piece of paper in his hand and a worried expression on his face. Shutting the door behind him, he looked to Jake and said, "We have a problem."

"Talk to me."

"I got finished with the sketch of the man Gracie saw in her apartment. I gotta say, I'm impressed. Most people don't remember that many details about someone they just caught a glimpse of. Especially in a situation like the one she—"

"Zade." Jake said the other man's name sternly to stop his rambling. "What did you find out?"

"I—" He glanced nervously to Kole before locking his eyes with Nate's. "It's not good."

Zade handed the drawing to Jake, who immediately let out with a low curse.

"What?" Nate asked, tired of waiting for the bomb to drop. Zade looked back in his direction, but still didn't answer. "Who was in her fucking apartment, King?"

Jake turned the sketch around for them all to see.

"Ah, hell." Kole sat back in his chair and ran a hand down his face.

"Correct me if I'm wrong"—Matt looked at the picture more closely—"but that sure looks a lot like—"

"Achim Akmar," Nate finished the thought, his gut churning. *Sonofabitch.*

"Think we should tell her?" Matt looked to Kole, but it was Gabe who answered.

"Don't think we have a choice."

"I agree," Jake nodded. "Gracie's already proven herself to be tough and resourceful. She can handle it, and frankly, she needs to know what she's up against."

"Fuck me," Kole bit the words out.

"Just so we're all on the same page here," Zade began to reiterate their theory. "The man who went after Gracie is the same guy who managed to capture and brutally murder a former Navy SEAL. Is that really what we're saying?"

"Yeah, King," Nate shot back. "That's what we're fucking saying."

Unable to hold back the sudden need to see her again, Nate got up and headed for the conference room door.

"Where are you going?" Kole asked as Nate passed by him.

"To get the girls. The sooner Gracie knows what's going

on, the sooner we can put together a fucking game plan to keep her safe."

Knowing he needed to calm his ass down before Gracie saw him, Nate stepped inside the restroom located across the hall. He splashed some cool water on his face and then used a paper towel to wipe away the evidence.

With his hands clenching the sides of the sink, Nate stared at his reflection and wondered when this woman had become so important to him. They weren't dating. Hell, they'd barely even kissed.

So, why did the thought of an evil bastard like Achim Fuckstick Akmar coming anywhere near Gracie fill him with such terror?

He couldn't explain it, but the second he saw that picture in Jake's hand, all Nate wanted to do was drag Gracie away to someplace safe. Somewhere he could make sure nothing bad ever happened to her again.

You're scared because you care about her.

"No shit, asshole."

Great. Now he was talking to himself. What the fuck was happening to him?

Rather than wait for another response from his inner self, Nate did his best to shake off his concerns and headed to Jake's office. He knocked and opened the door, but the room was empty.

Assuming Kole or one of the other guys got the two sisters while he was in the restroom, Nate walked back to the conference room. But when he got in there, Gracie and Sarah were nowhere to be seen.

"Where's Gracie?"

Matt gave him a confused look. "I thought you went to get her."

"I did." Feeling the need to clarify, he turned to Jake. "I went to the restroom, then your office. They're not in there."

113

Kole stood and headed for the door. "Well, they couldn't have gone far. I mean, this place is only so big. They're probably in the ladies' room. I'll go get them."

He'd just stepped into the hallway when his phone buzzed with a new text notification. Pulling it from his pocket, Kole glanced at his screen. "You've gotta be shittin' me."

"What?" Nate went to his friend's side.

"They went across the street to get some coffee." Kole held up the phone to show Nate Sarah's text.

"Gracie seemed like she was getting pretty tired in there," Zade spoke up. "Sarah mentioned going for coffee when we were done with the sketch. Said something about wanting to stretch their legs before coming back in here."

Nate took a menacing step toward him. "So, you let them go alone? Knowing who's after Gracie, you just let them walk out of here, unprotected?"

"Hell, no," Zade stood his ground. "I told them to wait in Jake's office for one of us to come back and get them. Jesus, Carter. I'm not a fucking idiot."

"It's right across the street, and mid-morning." Matt tried to diffuse the rapidly growing tension in the air. "That place is always packed this time of day, so they probably figured there'd be plenty of people around."

"Yeah, 'cause no one's ever been taken against their will in public before. Jesus," Nate growled as he spun on his heels and headed toward the office reception area. "I'm going to go keep an eye on them."

"Right behind you." Kole walked swiftly in order to catch up.

Both men left the office and made their way to the elevator at the end of the floor's main hall. Nate ground his teeth together to keep from howling out in anger. Apparently, Kole still noticed.

"I know you're worried about Gracie, Nate, but you really

need to take it down a notch. Realistically, the chances of something happening to her this time of day, right across from where we work are..." Kole thought for a moment. "Fuck, I don't know. You're the genius; you do the math. My point is I'm sure they're probably fine."

Nate knew he was over-reacting, but couldn't seem to control the overwhelming fear he felt for Gracie. The primal need to protect her was a living, breathing thing.

They'd lost her once, already. He sure as hell didn't want to lose her again.

"Maybe you're willing to risk her life on a probably, but I'm not."

Several seconds of intense silence filled the air as the elevator continued its decent.

"You know," Kole finally spoke up again. "At this point, Gracie's pretty much already my sister. Yet, you're the one acting all caveman right now. Makes me wonder if there's more to her staying at your place last night than either of you are letting on."

Shit. *Game face, game face, game face.*

Keeping his eyes on the door in front of him, Nate acted as casual as possible. "Meaning?"

"Oh, come on, man. You know damn well what I mean. Did something happen between you and Gracie last night, or not?"

Turning to face Kole, Nate did his best not to lie to his friend for the second time. "You told me to stay hands-off, so that's what I'm doing. Now, will you please stop looking for shit that isn't there?"

Surprisingly, Kole gave him a half-grin before turning away again. "I believe you."

"Thank you."

"But, for the record, if it did happen, I wouldn't be *completely* against it."

Whoa. "What?"

Still looking straight ahead, Kole shrugged a shoulder. "I'm just saying. I did a lot of thinking this week. When we couldn't find Gracie, I realized the only thing that really mattered was knowing she was safe. And happy. So, as long as Gracie chooses to be with someone who can ensure both those things, I guess I can't really complain too much about who it is."

Nate didn't know quite how to respond to that, so he remained silent. Kole, however, had more to say.

"You're the one she trusted enough to go to. You're the person she felt safe with when all this shit went down." Kole glanced over at him. "I don't know, man. That just says a lot to me, I guess."

Huh. Well, ain't that a kick in the crotch?

One of the main reasons Nate had pulled back last night was because he kept hearing Kole's voice in his head, making him promise to keep things platonic with her. He didn't know if that meant he was ready for a relationship or anything, but Nate was damn sure certain about one thing.

If Gracelynn McDaniels ever tried to undo his belt again, he sure as fuck wasn't going to stop her.

* * *

"I can pay for the coffees, Sarah. It's the least I can do after all the worrying I caused you."

"Put your money away, sis. This is my treat."

Gracie put the twenty back into her wallet and closed the flap on her purse. She was lucky Jake was able to get it back from his detective friend. Apparently his brother was a member of Alpha Team, so she guessed that made things a little easier.

The barista at the other end of the counter called Sarah's name, and the two women went over to pick up their drinks.

"I'd love to sit here and enjoy these, but we'd better get back to the office."

Gracie agreed with her sister. "Yeah. I'm sure Nate probably had a conniption when he realized we came over here unsupervised." She took a sip through her straw and swallowed some of her delicious caramel Frappuccino before asking, "Is Kole like that, too?"

"Like what?"

"All...what's the word?"

"Overprotective?"

"That's it!"

Sarah laughed. "You think?"

Holding up her phone so Gracie could see it, Sarah showed her the text Kole had just sent ordering them to keep their asses there and not move until he and Nate got there.

"I am curious, though." Sarah stopped talking for a minute to give them time to squeeze through the crowd of people. "I mean, I get why Kole is that way with me. We're engaged to be married."

Gracie threw in, "Not to mention the whole stalker incident."

"Ugh, don't remind me." Sarah shook her head. "But, back to my original thought. Why is Nate so overprotective of you?"

Gracie's heart thumped a little harder. "What do you mean?" she asked way too innocently.

"You said you two are just friends, right?"

"Yeah." Friends who shared a hot and heavy, incredibly amazing kiss in his bedroom. "So?"

"So..." Sarah drug the word out. "I saw the way he kept looking over at you in the conference room earlier."

He did? "H-how was he looking at me?"

Her sister raised a brow. "Like he was thinking about being a whole lot more than just friends."

Gracie had thought that, too, when he was kissing her last night. But then he'd apologized for it and had been acting pretty distant ever since.

Remembering the regret in his voice when he'd started the whole, you're-so-beautiful-but speech, Gracie said, "Well, I don't know what you *thought* you saw, but I can assure you, it wasn't that."

They finally made their way out of the coffee shop and back onto the sidewalk. Gracie was about to push the button on the light pole so they could cross the street safely when Sarah's hand grabbed her forearm.

"Gracie, wait."

Doing her best not to spill her drink, she turned toward her sister. "What?"

Sarah looked torn, like she wasn't sure if she should say whatever it was she was thinking.

"Sarah?"

With a look of sincerity and love, her sister said, "I just want you to be happy. You get that, right?"

Gracie smiled. "Of course. I feel the same about you."

"I know you do. And I thought you should know, Kole and I both agreed that, if you and Nate want to date or whatever, we won't stand in your way."

Laughing, Gracie hugged her sister. "Well, thanks for that, but trust me. Nate isn't interested in being anything more than friends." *Unfortunately.*

Sarah rolled her eyes. "If you say so."

Still grinning wide, Gracie shook her head at her sister. "I say so. Now, come on. We'd better get back before he and your fiancé decide to run over here and rescue us from ourselves." She pushed the button.

"Uh, oh."

"What's the matter?"

"We're too late."

Gracie followed Sarah's line of sight across the street to their building's entrance. Sure, enough, Nate and Kole had just come through the doors and they did *not* look happy.

Gracie couldn't help but focus solely on Nate. He'd rolled the sleeves of his white button-up to the middle of his sinewy forearms and was standing with his hands on his hips, glaring at her.

She stared back, wondering how the hell the man could look pissed off and sexelicious, all at the same time.

"Just friends, my ass."

Blinking, Gracie looked over at her sister. "What?"

"You can't hide shit from me any better now than you could when we were younger. You're totally into him."

"Am not." The bold-faced lie fell right off her tongue.

"And he's just as into you."

"No, he's not."

"Are you kidding me? Look at how mad he is right now. The man practically has lasers shooting out from his eyeballs."

Gracie looked back over to where Nate was still waiting. "He's upset, so that means he's into me? That makes absolutely no sense, Sarah."

"Sure, it does."

"In what universe does that make sense?"

Her sister rolled her eyes again and sighed. "If he didn't care, he wouldn't be so worried. And because he's worried, he's pissed. Kole does the same thing with me." A wicked grin formed on her face. "It's a major turn-on when he gets like that."

"You get turned on when your fiancé is mad at you, and you're trying to give me advice about my dating life?" Gracie teased.

"I know." Sarah laughed. "It's totally twisted, but what can I say? It works for us."

Both women started laughing, and Gracie looked back at Nate. She thought about what Sarah had just said, and yeah. She could see it, now.

Still giving her the same you're-gonna-get-it look, she could almost feel his nervous energy from all the way over here.

"It says to walk." Sarah grabbed her elbow. "Come, on."

The closer they came to the men, the more turned on Gracie felt. Too bad her apartment was still marked as a crime scene. She and her vibrator could really use some serious quality time about now.

All she'd have to do is replay the memory of that kiss over and over, and she'd be able to release the tension that had been building up ever since last night.

"What's going on?"

Sarah's voice snapped her back into focus. "Huh?"

"What are they looking at?"

Gracie and Sarah both turned their heads to their right, the same direction Nate and Kole were facing. A black panel van was gaining speed at a rapid pace.

And it was coming straight for them.

Her eyes shot to Nate, who looked as scared as she felt. Though, she could barely hear him, Gracie knew exactly what he was saying. Nate was screaming at them to run.

"Sarah, move!" Kole yelled so loudly his voice cracked. Both men were waving their arms, telling them to get out of the way as they pushed their way through the growing crowd of people.

Feeling as though everything was happening in slow motion, Gracie grabbed hold of Sarah's sleeve and propelled her forward as they started to run. But the van was already right up on them.

She could hear Nate and Kole hollering for them and shouting orders. People screamed from the sidewalk, but Gracie's sole focus was on trying to get herself and her sister as far away from the van as possible.

They were almost to the curb when it stopped directly behind them. Gracie turned her head to see what was going on and screamed.

A man in a black baseball cap and all-black clothing slid open the side door and jumped out. In a hail-Mary move, Gracie pushed Sarah as hard as she could, hoping to at least get her sister to safety.

People who'd gathered to see what the commotion was all about scattered now, trying to get out of the way. Gracie saw Kole grab hold of Sarah and felt a moment's relief from knowing her sister was safe.

At the same time, Nate drew his weapon and pointed it directly at her. No, not at her. At the man now pulling her back toward the van.

"Gracie!" Nate screamed at the top of his lungs . "Let her go!"

More Criminal Minds episodes ran through her head. She'd seen enough to know if she got into that van, she was as good as dead.

"Don't worry about the lawyer," the driver yelled at his accomplice. "This is the one we wanted, anyway. Just get her into the van and let's get the hell out of here!"

Oh, God. That voice. It was the man from her apartment. Gracie was sure of it.

With renewed motivation, she began to fight with everything she had. Gracie kicked and twisted her body, trying with all her might to break free from the man's tight grasp.

Her arms flailed about as she attempted to slap her assailant as hard as she could. Any place she could.

The only thing she managed to do was knock the guy's

hat off his head. For some reason, though, that small act seemed to enrage him.

"You bitch!"

In a surprising move, he spun her around so she was facing him. Trying to commit every detail of his angry face to memory, Gracie didn't see his fist as it swung toward her head.

The last thing she heard before a blinding pain exploded across her temple was Nate's voice as he screamed her name.

CHAPTER 8

"Gracie!"

Gun drawn, Nate watched in horror as the bastard trying to kidnap Gracie reared his fist back and punched her hard in the side of the head. Protective instincts unlike any he'd ever felt before reared up and took over.

With his pulse racing and heart pounding, Nate pushed his way through the crowd of gawking people. He'd never wanted to pull his trigger more, but there were too many innocent bystanders to risk taking a shot.

"Get out of the fucking way!"

He continued to shove people aside who were just standing there, watching like it was some sort of goddamn reality show. By the time he got to the curb, the man had already slid the door shut, and the van was speeding off.

Nate's eyes shot down to where Kole was hovering over Gracie. His heart damn near stopped when he realized she wasn't moving.

"Sarah's inside. I've got Gracie," Kole yelled. "Go!"

Running as fast as his feet would take him, Nate followed the van down the street. Horns honked, and the sound of sirens grew louder and louder, but he didn't stop. Not until he realized his efforts were futile.

The van was too fast and had covered too much ground. Not caring that he was still in the middle of the busy street, Nate stood there a minute, catching his breath as the van peeled around a corner two blocks down and vanished.

His gut churned, and his chest ached, knowing the men who'd just tried to take Gracie from him had gotten away. At least the fucker didn't get her in the van before they took off.

Gracie.

Tucking his gun into his waistband, Nate sprinted the rest of the distance back to where she was. Once again, he found himself pushing against several strangers' shoulders to make his way to the woman who had, in a week's time, managed to become one of the most important people in his world.

Finally clearing the group of people, Nate looked down at one of the most beautiful sights he'd ever seen. With Kole by her side, Gracie was sitting up and talking.

"Gracie?" he choked out her name.

A set of gorgeous, terrified eyes rose up to his. She opened her mouth to speak, but nothing came out. His chest tightened as he realized she was struggling to keep it together.

Crouching down next to her, he did his best to keep his own voice calm and steady. It was nearly impossible, given the fear and rage still threatening to consume him.

Very slowly, Nate brought his hand to where she'd been hit. To her credit, Gracie only flinched a little. Thankfully, she didn't completely pull away from his touch.

Brushing some hair back so he could get a better look, Nate literally had to bite his tongue against the stream of curse words threatening to fly out of his mouth when he saw the nasty bruise already forming on her cheekbone.

"Are you okay?"

"Y-yeah. I think so."

Her voice was small and shaky, but just hearing it again sent a wave of relief coursing through his system.

"Ah, thank Christ."

Nate blew out a loud breath as he wrapped his arms around her and pulled her close. He couldn't deny the bit of satisfaction he got from feeling her hands on his back, gathering his shirt in her fists.

Not caring in the least that they were surrounded by a bunch of people, they sat like that for several seconds, each holding on to the other as tightly as they could.

Jake's booming voice spread over the crowd. "Let us through, please."

"Come on, guys," Matt offered Jake support. "Give us some room."

Gabe wasn't quite as polite with his request.

"You heard 'em. Back the hell up."

"Gracie?" Sarah came bolting through an open space. "Oh, thank God!"

She pulled Gracie from Nate's arms and into her own. "I was so afraid I'd lost you again."

"I'm okay, sis. I-I'm okay."

"What the hell are you doing out here?" Kole scolded his fiancée. "I told you to stay inside until it was safe."

Sarah glared at Kole. "I saw the van drive off and I wanted to make sure my sister was okay."

"I'm fine." Gracie wiggled herself out of Sarah's tight embrace. Both women stood, and the men followed suit. "He just hit me and then jumped b-back into the van and t-took off."

Nate's eyebrows shot up at the flippant way she'd just described what happened to her.

"He *just* hit you?"

Gracie turned to him, wide-eyed. He started to reprimand her, but Jake's sharp tone stopped him.

"Carter." Nate's boss gave him a look that said he needed to back off.

Pressing his lips into a hard line, Nate inhaled a deep breath through his nostrils to keep from shouting at the damn-fool woman.

He was about to suggest they go inside and away from the crowd when another loud, authoritative voice rose over the others.

"Officer Warren, I want you and Reynolds to clear all these people out. Get them behind the tape. Now."

"Yes, sir."

Nate recognized the detective giving orders as he approached them with purpose, the man's frustrated gaze zeroing in on him and Jake.

Ah, hell.

"The second I heard a report of two gun-wielding cowboys trying to stop an attempted kidnapping at this address, I knew Jake McQueen had to be involved."

"West," Jake greeted the detective with a handshake. "Gotta admit, man. I'm glad you're the one they sent."

The detective let out a snort. "Nobody *sent* me. Like a dumbass, I volunteered. You're welcome, by the way."

"Detective," Nate offered his hand.

Eric West was a detective with the Dallas Police Department. He also happened to be the twin brother to Derek West, Alpha Team's technical analyst. D was a total jokester, but a literal genius. Especially when it came to computers.

"Carter." The man shook his hand, then offered it to Kole. "Jameson. We really need to quit meeting like this."

Eric had been the detective assigned to Sarah's case when she was attacked.

"You know, Nate, my brother said you're almost as smart

as he is. But, given your choice of employer, I'm inclined to think you're both idiots." West turned and gave Jake a smartass grin.

"This one's big, Eric." Jake looked back at the man grimly. "This was an attack on one of my people. Tried to take her right here, in front of our building, in the middle of the fucking day."

To the detective's credit, he lost all traces of humor and got down to business. "Tell me."

More than ready to get Gracie away from all the stares, Nate asked, "Can we continue this inside? I don't want her out in the open any longer than necessary."

Eric's gaze shifted to Gracie. When he realized who the victim was, the man softened his expression. "Miss McDaniels. Like I said, I'm Detective West. It appears trouble has found you, again. Are you hurt? Do you need medical attention?"

"N-no." Gracie shook her head then winced. "No ambulance. I just…" She glanced up at Nate. "I just w-want to go h-home. Or…crap. I g-guess I don't really have a h-home right now, do I? That's okay. I c-can go s-somewhere else. Somewhere other than h-here."

She was rambling, and her words were beginning to stutter. Recognizing the signs of shock mixed with an impending adrenaline dump, Nate didn't wait for the detective's permission.

Wrapping an arm around her trembling shoulders, he started to guide Gracie toward the building's entrance.

"Come on, sweetheart. Let's get you inside."

Boasting no argument, Detective West and the others followed them into the building and back into R.I.S.C.'s office. Once inside, Nate took Gracie into Jake's office for some privacy.

To the detective, he said, "Give us a minute?"

Compassion filled the other man's eyes. "Sure." To Gracie, West said, "Take your time. I'll get the others' statements, then come back and talk to you. That sound okay?"

"Sure," Gracie nodded and tried to smile.

With Sarah by her side, Nate looked to Gracie. "Wait here. I'll be right back."

Not waiting for a response, he headed for the break room to get some ice from the freezer. Grabbing a clean dish towel, Nate wrapped the cubes up and twisted the cloth at the top to hold them in.

When he returned to Jake's office, Gracie was in near melt-down mode.

"I-I don't understand this. I d-don't understand any of it. I haven't d-done anything w-wrong. I don't know those m-men. I have n-no idea what they w-want." Wild eyes found his as she silently begged him for answers he didn't have. "W-why is this h-happening?"

Nate slowly walked over to where she was sitting and pulled up a chair next to hers. Facing each other, he carefully pressed the makeshift ice pack against her swollen cheek.

"I don't know why those men are after you, Gracie. But I can promise you, we are going to find out. In the meantime, I need you to trust that I will do everything in my power to keep you safe."

"I-I believe you."

"Good girl." Looking up, he started to say something to Sarah, but Gracie interrupted him.

"I-I don't know w-why I'm sh-shaking so b-badly."

"It's just adrenaline, sweetheart. It'll stop soon. You just have to ride it out, okay?"

"Ok-kay."

God, his heart hurt for her.

To Sarah, he asked, "Can you take over for me?"

Nodding, Gracie's sister slid over and took the ice pack from his hand. "Sure."

"Y-you're leaving?"

Goddamnit. He fucking hated the fear still consuming those beautiful eyes.

"I'm just going in the other room. I need to let Detective West know what happened out there. I'll come right back once I've given him my statement. Okay?"

"Okay."

"Do not leave this room," he ordered both women fiercely.

He couldn't give a shit less that he was stepping up and taking charge. His woman had nearly been taken from him, right before his very eyes.

The thought had Nate's steps faltering.

No, no, no. Gracie wasn't his. She was a friend. A friend he cared about in a friendly way.

Ignoring the tiny voice calling bullshit, Nate walked swiftly to where Detective West was waiting.

Fifteen minutes later, he'd gone over everything he could remember about what had happened. Kole also gave his official statement, and then West asked Nate to go get Sarah, so she could tell him her side of things.

Full of nervous energy, Nate left the room. With his own adrenaline still pulsating through his veins, he was tempted to make another stop at the men's room.

Since that didn't work out so well for him last time, he bypassed it and went straight to Jake's office.

Gracie watched her sister as she walked out of the room, leaving her alone with Nate. He shut the door, presumably to give them some privacy.

The guy's face was a sea of emotions. As she looked up at him, she recognized anger, concern, and...fear?

"Are you okay?" Her question came out much softer than she'd meant for it to.

Nate gave her a humorless smirk as he shoved his hands into his jeans pockets. "Shouldn't I be asking you that?"

"I'm better."

And she was. The pounding in her head had quieted to a dull ache, and the intense trembling had subsided.

When he continued to stare without saying another word, Gracie realized he was probably waiting for an apology. One that was well-deserved.

Standing, she laid the ice pack down onto the cushioned seat and began to say what needed to be said.

"I'm really sorry, Nate. We never should have left the building without one of you. Or, at the very least, we should've checked with you beforehand."

She waited, but he remained silent. *Okay.* Apparently, more groveling was going to be required.

Stepping toward him, Gracie continued nervously. "I-I know it wasn't very smart of us, and you and Kole have every right to be upset. It's just that, I was exhausted from going over everything with Jake and the others and then doing the sketch with Zade. Sarah mentioned coffee and I..."

She let her voice trail off, hoping he'd say *something.* Instead, he began walking slowly toward her, the muscles in his strong, sexy jaw bulging as he moved.

Stopping mere inches from where Gracie stood, Nate stared into her eyes, but remained silent. The look he was giving her was so intense, she half-expected steam to start shooting out of his ears.

"Okay, look," she said defensively. "I get that you're upset, but we just wanted to go grab a quick coffee. That was all. I mean, you saw us, right? We were coming straight back. Yes, it was probably stupid, but you can't seriously stay mad about this forev—"

The rest of the word was cut off when Nate grabbed the back of her neck and slammed his mouth down onto hers.

A tiny squeak escaped the back of her throat just before he used his tongue to pry her lips apart. Assuming she was forgiven, Gracie opened her mouth and let him in.

Standing in the middle of their boss's office, she wrapped her arms around his neck and held on tightly as Nate began to devour her. He took, and she gave.

It was the most sensual, raw-emotions moment of her entire life.

When he was done feasting, Nate pulled away slowly and rested his forehead against hers. They remained locked in each other's arms, their chests heaving in sync as they attempted to catch their breath.

Regaining some control, Nate lifted his head. His eyes locked onto hers when he said, "I thought I'd lost you."

He sounded different. His voice was low, and there was this darkness to it she'd never heard before.

"Nate?"

"You scared the shit out of me, baby." He swallowed hard and shook his head back and forth slowly. "Don't ever do that, again."

Baby? Completely thrown by his behavior, Gracie was still trying to figure out what the hell was going on when there was a knock at the door

They both turned, and when Kole walked in, she expected Nate to pull away from her touch. Her insides did a little cheer when he didn't.

Gracie knew they should be focused on what had just happened outside, rather than making out in Jake's office like a couple of teenagers. But, hey. Life was short, right?

Her scattered thoughts took her back to before. Instead of

Nate's hands on her back, it was that man's, and he was trying to take her away from everyone and everything she cared about.

Her breathing picked up, and her body shivered from the terrifying memory. Of course, Nate noticed.

Misunderstanding, he dropped his arms and took a step back. Gracie wanted to explain, but not with Kole there.

She could tell her sister's fiancé was surprised at the intimate embrace she and Nate had been sharing, but rather than comment on that, he said, "Uh, sorry to interrupt. West needs Gracie's statement. When she's done with that, Jake wants us all to meet back in the conference room." His eyes slid to Gracie's. "You, included, honey."

"Okay," she agreed nervously.

"Be right there," Nate told his friend.

After another assessing glance at Gracie, Kole left the room. Nate turned to her, his expression softer than before.

"Gracie, I—"

Not this time, buster. She threw her hand up. "If you're going to apologize for kissing me again, just save it. Please."

His brows rose and he shook his head. "No." He closed the distance he'd put between them and rested his hands on her hips. "I'm not apologizing, Gracie. Not for kissing you, anyway."

Still skeptical, she waited for him to explain.

"I like you." One corner of his mouth rose, forming his lips into a hot-as-hell half-smile. "Of course after that kiss, I'm pretty sure you got that."

"It's still nice to hear you say it," she whispered back.

With a silent laugh, Nate admitted. "Yeah, I guess I have been throwing out some pretty big mixed signals lately."

That was a serious understatement. She was beginning to feel like a batter at home plate, trying to figure out what the hell her coach wanted her to do.

"Alright." He looked her right in the eye. "Then let me be clear. I like you, Gracie. A lot. And after this is all over, I'd really like to take you out." He licked his lips. "See what this could turn into."

Gracie realized Nate was nervous, too. The man had just pulled his gun and chased after a van carrying the two men who'd tried to kidnap her. He'd done so without even blinking an eye, yet, *this* made him nervous.

It was absolutely adorable.

"I-I'd like that, too." Her voice shook.

Okay, so maybe he isn't the only nervous one.

Giving her that sexy half-smile she was beginning to love, he whispered. "Good." Then, clearing his throat, he got a little more serious. "The thing is, right now, I need to stay focused on keeping you safe. Which means I can't be distracted with"—he paused a moment—"whatever's going on between us."

"I understand," she told him truthfully.

He still felt the need to reassure her. "It's not that I don't want you, Gracie. Trust me, I do. I just can't run the risk of you getting hurt because my head's somewhere else. So, this"—he motioned back and forth between them—"is going to have to wait until we catch the bastards who are after you. I hope you can understand that."

"I do," Gracie whispered back. "Really."

With a gentle hand, he brushed some hair away from her face. A low, growling sound came from his throat as he studied the swollen area.

"I'm going to kill them."

"What?" Gracie felt her eyes widened. "Nate, no."

A fierce hatred crossed his face. "They almost took you from me. From Sarah and Kole. Not trying to scare you, sweetheart, I'm just giving you fair warning. Anyone tries to hurt you again, they're dead."

"O-okay." Because, really. How else does one respond to such a statement?

With a smirk, Nate said, "I'd better go get West before he sends Kole back in here to nag us again."

Minutes later, Nate stayed by Gracie's side while she gave Detective West her statement. After saying their goodbyes, she took a deep breath and got ready for her meeting with Jake and the others.

With her hand in his, Gracie followed Nate out of Jake's office. If anyone thought it odd to see the two of them holding hands as they entered the other room, they didn't say anything.

Nate waited until she sat down in the open chair next to Sarah before taking his own seat to Gracie's left.

She looked at her sister, whose knowing eyes moved from her, to Nate, and back again. With an almost indiscernible shake of her head, Gracie silently told her now wasn't the time to talk.

"Gracie," Jake addressed her directly.

Nervous for a whole other reason, she looked at her boss. "Yes?"

"Are you sure you're okay? Matt's Bravo Team's medic. He can check you out."

"I'm fine, Jake." She glanced around the table at the others. "Really. I have a small headache, and I'm sore. Other than that, I'm good."

"If you start to feel worse or have any dizziness or nausea, let one of us know right away," Jake ordered kindly.

"Yes, sir. I will."

Moving on, Jake took a deep breath and dove in. "I know this has already been a long and eventful day for everyone, but given the turn of events, we need to have a game plan in place before we leave."

With the remote in his hand, Jake turned on the interactive board and looked at Nate and Kole.

"While you two were giving your statement to Detective West, Gabe and I went through the video feed from the building's external security cameras. Because the driver remained inside the van and was wearing a hat and sunglasses, we couldn't get a clear picture of his face for identification."

"It's the man from my apartment."

All eyes went to Gracie.

"I-I recognized his voice when I heard him shouting at the other guy," she explained.

"What did he say?" Nate asked from beside her.

"He told the man who had ahold of me not to worry about the lawyer and just get me into the van."

Sarah gasped, and Gracie reached for her sister's hand. Kole nearly lost it.

"They were after Sarah, too? What the fuck?"

"Gracie, how sure are you that the man behind the wheel was the same one you saw in your apartment?"

Lifting her chin, Gracie straightened her shoulders. "I'd stake my life on it."

At this point, she pretty much was.

"Okay." Jake took her word for it. "So, we know the driver was Achim Akmar."

Though, fearful of the answer, Gracie asked, "W-who is he?"

"I'll fill you in later," Nate offered.

Jake continued. "Thanks to Gracie's admirable attempt at fighting off the second assailant, our facial rec software was able to find a match."

The man who'd hit her appeared on the screen, causing a shiver to race down her spine once more. Noticing this, Nate reached over and gave her forearm a light squeeze. Thankful he was there, she gave him a small smile and covered his hand with hers.

"Fucking hell," Matt growled from across the table.

Looking to his teammate, Nate asked, "Who is he?"

"Adrian Walker."

"Thought you might recognize him, Turner." Jake commented.

Matt began to rub the back of his neck. "Unfortunately."

"Since you're familiar with Walker, why don't you go ahead and share what you know."

Sitting up a little straighter, Matt told the group about the man on the screen.

"Adrian Walker was a member of a FAST platoon I tagged along with on an op a few years back. I served as their medic for the duration of the mission."

Nate leaned over closer to Gracie and quietly explained, "FAST stands for Fleet Anti-Terrorism Security Team. It's part of the Marine Corps Security Forces Regiment."

Confused, she addressed Matt. "So, this guy was on an anti-terrorism team and then, what? He left the Marines to become a terrorist, himself?"

"Yep."

It was obvious Matt was still very much affected by what happened.

"Why would he do that?"

Matt shrugged. "Same reason people do all sorts of crazy, stupid things, Gracie. Money."

Jake clicked another button, and the picture on the screen switched again. Looking back at them now was a group of soldiers.

Gracie immediately recognized Matt, appearing almost invincible in his camo combat gear. Standing to his right, looking every bit as patriotic as the others, was Adrian Walker.

"Six years ago—" Matt began. "Their team and I were stationed near a small village a few miles south of Kuwait. We were guarding a high profile naval installation. One involving nukes. Everything was going as planned. Then, one day, Walker just up and vanished."

"He went AWOL." Zade surmised.

Matt nodded. "At first, we thought he'd been captured by the enemy. Spent weeks busting our asses looking for him. Every day we'd wake up, thinking that was going to be the day we either got a ransom demand or worse, a video of Walker's execution. But, nothing ever came. A few months after the op ended, I learned he'd switched sides."

"Walker began selling US military intel," Jake jumped in. "Names of men and women currently serving. Locations where they'd been stationed and what their objectives were. If he knew it, he found someone willing to buy it."

"So, he fucked us." Gabe sounded almost as pissed off as Matt.

Matt pointed at the picture. "Thanks to that bastard, the entire military intelligence community was chasing its own ass for months. They had to re-route and re-plan all kinds of shit just to keep our people safe. More recently, he's turned gun for hire. The problem is he's always a step ahead and stays just outside our reach."

"Until today. Our girl, here, nearly took him down." Zade looked at Gracie and winked.

Gracie felt herself blushing but did her best not to react. She never did like being the center of attention.

"That's right," Jake agreed. "Walker's back, and apparently, whoever he's working for now has hired him and Akmar to take Gracie."

"And possibly Sarah, too, from the sounds of it." Kole looked to his fiancée, his loving eyes filled with worry.

"But, why?"

Gracie knew she sounded desperate, but she didn't care. Someone had just tried to freaking kidnap her, for crying out loud. She should at least know the reason why.

Gabe addressed her directly. "Are you sure you can't think of any reason these guys would be after you?"

"No!" She sighed. "Don't you think, especially after what just happened, I would tell you if I knew something?"

Gabe put his hands up defensively. "Had to ask. I'm sorry."

Nate gently rubbed his hand up and down her back. When she turned to him, Gracie saw something different in his eyes. It was the exact same look each of the other men had.

"*You* know something, though. Don't you?" She glanced around the room, her gaze landing on Jake's. "If you know what's going on, then tell me." When the room remained silent, she raised her voice. "This is my *life* we're talking about. My family's life! If you know—"

"We don't know anything for certain," Jake cut her off. "But we do have reason to believe that what's been happening to you is somehow related to Craig Wyatt's death."

Gracie felt her eyes grow big as saucers. "Craig? I-I didn't even know he'd been killed until the day I came in here and saw that horrible picture."

"Gracie, did Wyatt ever give you anything?" Gabe continued his questioning. "Any sort of gift or maybe something he asked you to hold onto for safekeeping while he was in the hospital?"

"No. He never gave me anything. The patients weren't allowed to give volunteers gifts. It was against hospital policy." When Gabe didn't respond, she said, "You still haven't told me why you think Craig's murder and what happened today are related."

Rather than respond, Gabe looked to Jake. Thankfully, he shared their theory with her.

"We have reason to believe Achim Akmar—the man who broke into your place and you say was driving the van today —is the same man who tortured and killed Craig."

"Oh, my God." She didn't even try to hide the shock she felt from that revelation.

"Which means, boys and girls," Jake addressed the entire room. "This is now official R.I.S.C. business."

Nate's gaze moved from hers, then to Kole's before his focus landed on Jake.

"You know, the only way we're going to be able to stop either of these men is to find out who hired them and why."

"I agree." Jake set his gaze on Gracie. "Which is why we're going to need you to disappear again."

CHAPTER 9

"Hold up. You want Gracie to stay with *Nate*?"

Nate looked over at his best friend's fiancée. "Gee, Sarah. Your confidence in my abilities is overwhelming. I'm touched, really."

Her expression changed from shocked to sympathetic in less than a second. "I'm sorry, sweetie. That came out wrong. I have no doubt you can do your job. I just assumed Gracie would stay with me. I mean, she's my sister. Kole can protect us both."

"Gracie needs to be someplace else *because* she's your sister."

Sarah looked even more confused by Gabe's statement. "I don't understand."

With his elbows on the table, Gabe leaned forward and explained. "Akmar mentioned leaving the lawyer. That's you. They were after you, too, Sarah."

"That makes no sense. You said this Achim guy wanted Gracie. She's the one they nearly..." Sarah's voice cracked, and Kole grabbed ahold of her hand while Gabe continued with his thoughts.

"My guess? They weren't expecting your sister to be there. Prior to today, she'd gone dark. Most likely, they thought they could use you to get to her."

To that, Nate added, "The fastest way to get a person to come out of hiding is to use someone they love."

"That was the whole reason I didn't come to you in the first place," Gracie told Sarah. "I was afraid that man would follow me and end up hurting you. I wasn't going to risk something happening to you, sis."

"Yet, you had absolutely no problem going to Carter and risking his ass." All eyes shot to Zade, who gave her a wide grin before looking at Nate. "I think I like her even more, now."

Flipping his teammate the bird, Nate ignored the snickers from a couple of the guys.

Looking horrified, Gracie started shaking her head. "No. That wasn't it. I thought maybe you could help, that's all."

Nate squeezed her shoulder and smirked. "He's just teasing you, sweetheart."

"Oh." Relief filled her beautiful eyes. "Good. Because I was really careful to make sure no one followed me to your apartment."

"I know."

"Carter," Jake stole his attention. "You got a secure place you two can go to lay low for a while?"

"Yeah, I know a place."

"Good. Kole, what about you? I think it's a good idea for Sarah to be out of sight, as well, until this whole thing blows over."

Kole gave Sarah a half smile. "I was going to surprise you with a pre-wedding getaway." He shrugged. "Guess now's as good a time as any."

Sarah gave her fiancée a loving smile. "That was really sweet of you."

"You know me. I'm all about the sweetness."

Sarah laughed, which Nate knew had been Kole's goal.

"Kole, be sure to give Gabe the address where you'll be staying. Take your work phone and leave your personal cells here. One of us will let you know when it's safe to return home. Nate, same goes for you."

"Got it."

"The rest of you..." Jake looked at the other members of Bravo. "I want you back here at oh seven hundred. Go home and get a good night's rest. It may be your last for a while."

The team stood, along with Sarah and Gracie. Matt, Gabe, and Zade all wished Nate and Kole well, vowing to do what it took to make it safe for them to return.

Nate followed Kole, Sarah, and Gracie to the doorway, but Jake's voice had him pausing.

"Hey, Nate. Hang back a minute. I wanted to go over a couple things with you before you leave."

To Kole, Nate said, "Wait for me up front."

After those three left the room, Nate turned to Jake. "What's up?"

"Shut the door and have a seat."

With an uneasy feeling in his gut, Nate did as his boss instructed.

"This place you're taking Gracie to. How secure is it?"

"It's solid. I'm going to rent a cabin at Lake Livingston. My parents used to take us there every summer."

Concern passed through Jake's eyes. "These people are good, Nate. If you went there as a kid, there's a chance they could figure that out."

Nate shook his head. "We always met up with another family. A guy my dad grew up with. They lived near there, and Dad's friend would always make the reservations in his name. He'd get there early, pay for everything, and then Dad would pay him cash for our half. There's no way they can trace it to me. Plus, the business has changed hands several times over the years."

Jake considered this a moment. "I'd still use an alias, just in case."

"Roger that." Several seconds of awkward silence passed before Nate asked, "Was that all you needed?"

His boss looked at him with an assessing eye. "You got this one?"

What the hell? "Are you asking if I can handle this assignment, Boss?"

"I know you can do your job. I just want to make sure you have your head on straight where Gracie is concerned."

Forgetting who he was talking to for a moment, Nate shot back with, "And what the hell is that supposed to mean?"

Jake rested his palms on the table in front of him and locked his arms. "It means I have fucking eyes, Carter. Jesus, man. You can practically cut the sexual tension between you two with a goddamn knife. So, before I put her under your protection, where you'll be sharing a tiny as fuck cabin, I want to hear you say the words. Are you good to watch her? If the answer's no, I'll put her with Gabe. And if you tell me that's what needs to happen, I will respect that decision."

Christ, this was not something Nate wanted to discuss with his boss. Or anyone else, for that matter.

"Gracie and I aren't"—he thought about how to word it —"We haven't," Nate paused again, clearly not helping his case any. "I'm good, Jake. I've got this."

"Good to know."

McQueen stood straight, finally putting Nate out of his misery. Almost.

"Look, Nate. I get it. When someone you care about is in danger, you want to be their first line of defense. But, I also know when emotions get involved things can get messy.

People tend to make mistakes. And in our line of work, those mistakes can get people killed."

More than ready to put an end to the uncomfortable-as-fuck conversation, Nate stood and pushed his chair in.

"I'm good, Jake. Really. Now, if that's all, I'd like to get on the road. I want to get there and get settled before dark so I can do a good perimeter search and set up surveillance outside our cabin."

With one final look, Jake tipped his chin. "That's all. Keep your phone close. We'll do everything we can on our end. In the meantime, I want you to keep looking for a connection between Akmar and Craig Wyatt."

Nate held out his hand. "I'll let you know if I find something."

With a strong grip, Jake returned the handshake. "Good luck, Nate. Stay safe."

* * *

Full of anxious energy, Gracie waited in Nate's living room as he rushed to gather his things.

He'd been fairly quiet since his private meeting with Jake.

She wanted to ask what it was about, but he'd been bouncing back and forth between his computer room and bedroom for the past twenty minutes. She got the feeling now wasn't the time for questions.

A picture on the mantle above Nate's electric fireplace caught her attention. She walked over to it and began tracing the edge of the wooden frame with her fingertip.

With nothing else to do but wait, Gracie studied the two boys smiling back at her.

One was clearly older. She guessed him to be around seventeen. The other boy looked as though he were eight, maybe nine. Gracie smiled when she realized the youngest boy was Nate as a child.

The two were standing side-by-side and each was holding a fishing pole and a small, plastic tackle box. Behind them was a cabin near a large lake, the setting sun reflecting beautifully off the water's smooth surface.

It looked like such a happy time. Definitely a much simpler time.

"You ready?"

Gracie turned to face him.

"Yeah." Eyeing the three bags and backpack he was attempting to lug around, she went to him and pulled the small one from his hand. "Here. Let me carry this one."

"Thanks," he mumbled as he handed it to her. "Okay, so just like when we came up here. You stay behind me at all times, and if I tell you to do something, you do it. No questions. Got it?"

"Got it."

Gracie wasn't stupid nor did she have a death wish. This was Nate's area of expertise, so she had absolutely no problem doing as he asked.

As soon as they made it outside, they turned in the opposite direction from where his truck was parked. She started to ask, but Nate beat her to it.

"We have to assume those men know about the team. If that's the case, then they most likely know where each of us lives, what we drive, all of it. So, instead of taking my truck, we're going to take this."

Gracie glanced at the white, four-door sedan Nate was already loading his bags into. "Whose car is this?"

"Jake's." He took the bag from her hand and put it into the trunk next to the others. "Well, technically it belongs to R.I.S.C." He slammed the trunk shut. "We have a few like it."

She studied it again. "Meaning, cars that don't stand out or draw any unwanted attention?"

Smiling, Nate winked. "Smart girl." Opening the passenger door for her, he said, "Come on. If we hurry, we'll have time to stop and get some food for the cabin before we check in."

"Cabin?" Gracie asked as she got into the car. She thought back to the picture.

Rather than answer her right away, Nate shut the door and walked around the car's rear bumper. He kept his eyes peeled on their surroundings the entire way.

Once he'd sat down and shut his door, he turned to her. "You trust me, right?"

"Yes." There was no hesitation in her answer.

"Good. Then, you should know I'm going to do everything in my power to keep those men from finding you again. Starting with getting us out of the city and to a place I know you'll be safe."

"Okay."

With one final nod, Nate turned the key and started the car's ignition. They'd no more hit the highway and she was out like a light.

Gracie thought she'd be too wired to sleep, but the events from the past week, plus her earlier adrenaline surge and subsequent drop, had apparently taken their toll.

The next thing she knew, he was waking her with a gentle nudge and a soft whisper.

"Gracie."

She could hear the sweet sound of his voice but couldn't seem to open her eyes. Nate nudged her harder.

"Gracelynn."

Hearing her full name, she cracked open a heavy eyelid. "Hmm?"

"We're here."

Gracie blinked a few times and sat up straight. Once the cobwebs finally cleared from her brain, she remembered what had happened.

Licking her dry lips, she ran her fingers through her hair. "Where exactly is here?"

"A small resort along Lake Livingston." When she looked at him expectantly, he added, "We're about three hours southwest of Dallas."

"I slept three hours? Why didn't you wake me?"

He shrugged. "Figured you needed the rest."

Gracie rubbed the sleep from her eyes. "I guess I must have."

Looking through the windshield, she saw the log building they'd parked next to. It was small with a sign that read *Livingston Cabins* near the door. Shining brightly from one of its two windows was a neon sign letting customers know they were still open.

Gracie started to open the door, but Nate's hand on her arm stopped her.

"Wait."

She turned to him. "What?" Then, it dawned on her. "Oh, right. I should probably let you get out first to be sure it's safe."

"There is that," he said with a tiny smirk. "But, there's something else I wanted to talk to you about first."

Scooting down in his seat a bit, Gracie watched as he reached into his jeans pocket. He pulled his hand out and opened his palm to her, its contents leaving her both confused and a little breathless.

"Are those what I think they are?"

"Depends. If you think they're wedding rings, then yeah. They are."

Her gaze landed back on his. She half-expected him to be wearing that smartass grin she was beginning to enjoy seeing. There wasn't even a hint of a smile in his expression.

Heart beating rapidly, she asked, "Nate, why do you have wedding rings?"

Using his free hand, he held up the smaller of the two bands. "Akmar and Walker won't be looking for a married couple."

"Oh. Right. That makes sense."

She took the thin gold band and slid it onto the finger that was supposed to symbolize everlasting love.

Since she was a little girl, Gracie had always imagined what it would be like to see a ring such as this on her hand. In her wildest dreams, she never would have guessed she'd be wearing one in order to hide from a professional killer.

Another thought hit.

"Before we left, you said it was likely they knew who you were. What if they start calling around to hotels and places like this looking for us?"

Nate reached into the back seat for the smaller duffle he'd brought along. With it on his lap, he unzipped a small side pocket and pulled out what appeared to be two drivers' licenses.

"One, businesses like these aren't supposed to give out that type of information." He handed her one of the plastic cards. "And two, I've got us covered in case they do."

Gracie stared down at the I.D. in her hand. It was the same picture as the one on her actual license, but everything else was different. Unfamiliar.

"Who is Lynn Winters?"

"She's you. Until we get back home, that is." He paused a moment. "The key to being undercover is to stick as close to the truth as possible without giving yourself away. There aren't many variations of Gracie or Gracelynn, so I used the last half of your name."

"What about you? Who will you be?"

Nate held up his license for her to see.

"James Winters." She tried it out to see how it felt on her tongue. It felt…off.

"James is my middle name. Winters was my grandmother's maiden name. It's an alias I've used before, but it has no ties to anything Walker or Akmar would know about."

"When did you even have time to make these?"

"I already had mine from before. I threw yours together while we were at my apartment."

He just threw a fake I.D. together in a matter of minutes. Gracie didn't even know what to think about that.

Rather than respond, she glanced back down at her picture. Absentmindedly, she began to run her thumb across the fake name and address and wondered how her life had come to this.

Placing his hand on her knee, Nate softened his voice. "It's just a precaution, Gracie. You'll be safe here, I promise."

She glanced down. Heat radiated from his hand to her leg. Even now, in the middle of the freak show her life had become, his touch sent her pulse racing.

Gracie knew she shouldn't be going there. But, when it came to this man, her body seemed to have a mind of its own.

Nate pulled his hand away before muttering, "Stay there. I'll come around and open your door."

"Wait." This time it was Gracie who threw her hand out.

He looked over his shoulder. "Yeah?"

With her fingers clutching his impressively solid bicep, she licked her lips nervously before pulling herself up to him and pressing her mouth to his.

It wasn't a passionate kiss like the one in Jake's office. It was a bit awkward and clumsy, which was the whole point.

Pulling back, she nearly laughed at the shock reflected in Nate's widened eyes.

"What was that for?"

Gracie shrugged. "I know you said nothing more can happen between us, but we're supposed to be married, right? Depending on how long we're here, we're bound to be around other people. I know we've already kissed, but that was before." When Nate remained silent, she tried to better her explanation. "I thought, in case we have to actually *act* married or something, we should probably get the awkward, unexpected kiss out of the way now. You know, so we don't blow our cover or whatever."

His Adam's apple bobbed up and down as he swallowed hard. After staring at her a few seconds longer, Nate gave her a tiny smile. "That was smart. Thanks."

Feeling better about the impromptu kiss, Gracie watched as he walked around the front of the car. Opening the door for her, he waited until she got out to give her the run-down for the rest of the night.

"We'll go check in and get some snacks for tonight. In the morning, we'll drive into town, grab a bite to eat, and then go find you some clothes and a few necessities to get us through the next few days."

Right. Because they couldn't go to her apartment for her own clothes prior to leaving Dallas.

"Do you think that's all it'll take to find Akmar and Walker? A few days?"

"I hope so."

Nate glanced out at the area behind her as he spoke. *Always protecting me.* Too bad that meant they had to be hands-off.

Shaking those thoughts away, Gracie stood a little taller. Whining and complaining wouldn't help the situation, so she decided to try and make the best of it. After all, they were going to be sharing a cabin on a lake. *It won't be so bad, right?*

A long stretch of rolling thunder passed over them and a big, fat raindrop landed on her cheek. She nearly laughed at its ominous timing.

It would be just her luck to be stuck inside a cracker-box cabin with the one man she wanted but couldn't have.

Naturally, for the next three days, that was exactly what happened.

It had rained and stormed nearly non-stop since their first night there. The good news was that Nate was able to spend a lot of quality time with his computer, working to figure out why someone wanted to take her. The bad news? There was no T.V.

While Nate was busy working his magic—as he called it— she'd already finished reading the last of the only two romance novels the little log shop had for sale.

And why she'd decided to read romance at a time like this was beyond her. The last thing she needed rolling through her head right now were stories of endless love and hot, steamy sex.

With a loud sigh, she put the book down onto the end table next to her chair and went to the sliding glass door. The view would be beautiful, if it weren't for the constant cloud coverage and pouring rain.

Wrapping her arms around herself, Gracie stared out at the dismal-looking lake. For what felt like the millionth time lately, she wondered how she'd gone from being excited to start a new chapter in her life to hiding out from someone who tried to kidnap her with a man who'd barely spoken to her since they'd gotten here.

It didn't help that every time he walked into one of the cabin's three rooms, her heart did this funny fluttering thing, and her insides began to tingle. The man had kissed her like a sexual god after she'd nearly been taken. Too bad he'd barely given her a second glance these past few days.

Logically, Gracie understood why Nate hadn't made any sort of advances toward her since that day in Jake's office. He'd been upfront with her from the start about how things had to be.

Their boss had declared this an official R.I.S.C. case, and Nate was in charge of keeping her safe. He'd told her he needed to stay focused on that, which meant nothing more could happen between them until this whole thing blew over.

He was definitely a man of his word.

Though, she'd argued with him that first night, Nate had insisted on taking the couch and giving her the bed. The bottom half of his legs hung out over the arm, and it was so narrow he'd had to remove the back cushions just to keep from rolling off.

Gracie was deciding whether or not she should try to get him to take the bed tonight when a pair of strong hands began rubbing her shoulders from behind. Startled, she jumped, but didn't turn around. Instead, their eyes met in the reflection of the glass.

"Sorry. I didn't mean to scare you."

Afraid to move for fear he'd stop touching her, Gracie shook her head and smiled. "You didn't." She could see one of his dark brows lift at her claim. "Okay, so maybe you startled me a little."

She loved the way his reflection smiled back at her. "You seemed very deep in thought. Anything you want to share?"

Uh, definitely not. Gracie did her best to act completely normal.

"Just tired of all the rain. I know we aren't exactly here for fun, but I was hoping since we *are* here, maybe we could...I don't know. Go swimming or hiking or something."

Immediately wanting to smack her complaining self, she

turned to face Nate. As expected, his hands dropped back down to his sides.

Ignoring the intensity with which she missed his touch, she apologized.

"Sorry. That sounded completely ungrateful. I didn't mean it to be."

"I know what you meant." He smiled down at her. "I'm sick of being cooped up, too."

Tilting her head toward the computer set-up on the coffee table, Gracie asked, "Have you been able to find anything useful?"

"Not yet, but I'm not giving up. Neither is anyone else. Gabe texted earlier to say he and the others were checking up on a possible lead Ryker found, so I'm waiting to hear back about that."

Gracie nodded, but didn't verbally respond.

"Hey." He tilted her chin up then waited for her eyes to meet his before continuing on. "I know this is hard. The waiting's the worst. Not to mention being stuck in here with me."

Nate smirked, and she knew he was trying to make her smile. Good thing he didn't realize *why* it was so hard being trapped in the cabin alone with him.

The man was seriously lethal, and not just in a professional way.

Giving him the smile she knew he was waiting for, Gracie said, "Well, I'm sure there are a million other things you'd rather be doing than babysitting me. Especially, when I know for a fact you haven't been able to sleep worth a damn since we got here."

"I'm good. The couch is actually more comfortable than it looks."

Gracie waited until she was certain he was going to stick with the lie before responding. "I sure hope your undercover skills are better than that, *Mr. Winters*. Otherwise, we're screwed."

Feigning hurt feelings, Nate put a hand to his chest. "I'll have you know, I'm the first person the team comes to when they need someone to go under. What do you have to say about that, *Mrs. Winters?*"

Crossing her arms, Gracie studied him a moment. "Better. I almost believed you that time. Maybe there's hope for us, yet."

"You think I'm lying?"

"About the undercover part? I'm not sure. But you were lying through your teeth when you said the couch was comfortable."

"Yeah?" he challenged with a smart-ass grin. "What makes you so sure?"

"I've been sleeping less than twenty feet away. I can literally hear you tossing and turning throughout the night, which is ridiculous seeing as how there's a perfectly comfortable bed with plenty of room for the both of us."

At the mention of sharing a bed, Nate blinked, and his demeanor completely changed. Gracie could see the wall going back up and actually felt him pulling away again.

Damn her and her big mouth, anyway.

"So, I looked at the weather." He turned around and started for the kitchen. "The rain's supposed to continue throughout the night, but be cleared out by morning. I thought, if you wanted, we could rent one of those canoes we saw when we checked in and take it for a spin around the lake."

"Really?"

The idea probably excited her more than it should have, but the walls in this place were seriously starting to close in on her.

"Sure. If it stays nice, we could even go down to the beach

area and swim a bit. Then, I thought maybe we could go into town for some pizza or something after. If you want."

Gracie felt like jumping up and down. "God, yes," she moaned.

Nate's gaze shot to hers for a split second before refocusing on the glass he was filling with water. He swallowed a big gulp before clearing his throat.

"We'll plan on that, then."

Not sure what that was all about, she smiled and said, "Great. I can't wait."

With a renewed spirit, she went over to the kitchen table and began to arrange the deck of cards Nate had bought for them.

Just the thought of being able to go and do all those things tomorrow made playing another game of solitaire bearable.

Sneaking a sideways glance, she saw the grimace crossing over Nate's face as he sat back down onto the not-so-comfortable couch and went back to work on his computer. Gracie decided right then she'd give him one more night of misery on the damn thing, and then she was going to convince him to share a bed with her.

And she wasn't going to take no for an answer.

CHAPTER 10

"Tell me you found something."

"Not yet, but we're still looking."

With the phone to his ear, Achim walked across Nathan Carter's apartment. While he continued searching for what he was almost certain wasn't there, he braced himself for the tongue lashing that was about to come.

"I do not pay you to simply *look*, Achim. I pay you to do what needs to be done. So far, you haven't given me shit on this." There was a moment of silence, and then, "If you cannot give me what I want, perhaps I should consider finding someone else to do this job. Someone more *capable*."

Achim rolled his eyes. Edric Yavuz wouldn't be where he was today if not for him, and he knew it.

"There is no need to go looking elsewhere, Edric. I told you I would find the woman, and I will."

"When?" Edric's demand mimicked that of a small child. "I am running out of time, Achim. Maybe you've forgotten, but my future hangs in the balance until we find that fucking file."

"Well, maybe you should have thought about your future

a little more before making deals with a nuclear weapons dealer at the same time you were supposed to be making a public appearance."

"I told you before," Edric snapped back. "The press had already left the area, and Shamir was close to the village I was in. It only made sense that we meet then to get the deal finalized."

"In a fucking alley like some two-bit criminal? There were still American soldiers present, Edric. And not just any soldiers, but SEALS. I've known you to make some mistakes in the past, but allowing yourself to be photographed while making an arms deal not two weeks after meeting with the President of the United States about signing a treaty with them is by far your worst."

"How was I supposed to know one of them would be outside snapping pictures for some goddamn government report?"

"It is your job to plan for such things," Achim bluntly pointed out. "Instead of waiting to be certain you were secure, you let your greediness and impatience overshadow your common sense. Now, as usual, I'm left to clean up your mess."

"You get paid a hefty sum to clean up my messes, so quit your incessant whining and find Gracelynn McDaniels."

Achim looked around Nathan Carter's living room. Like the rest of the man's apartment, he'd turned it upside down, but found nothing.

"She and Carter are in the wind. So is the sister."

"Surely there is something there that would tell us where Carter would take her to hide."

Achim rolled his eyes again. "The man is former Naval Intelligence, Edric. He's not going to leave us a map with a big, shiny arrow pointing to his hideout."

He'd no more said the words when his attention was

drawn to a picture on the fireplace mantle. Kicking a throw pillow out of his path, Achim made his way across the disheveled room.

He studied the picture of the two boys in the woods. The lake in the background looked oddly familiar, as did the cabin. A few moments passed before he realized why.

The night before last, Achim had been sitting in his hotel room flipping through the multitude of useless television channels when a local advertisement for cabin and canoe rentals came on. He remembered thinking maybe, when this job was done, he'd take a few weeks off and go there.

Then, he'd laughed at the thought of someone like him hiding out amongst a bunch of normal, unsuspecting families.

Achim looked at the photo again. The commercial for the lake had mentioned it was only a short drive from the city. Knowing it must be a special place for Carter to have a framed picture of it on display, he realized he may have just found that shiny arrow, after all.

"I think I found something. I'll be in touch."

"What is it? What did you—"

Edric was still talking when Achim ended the call. Yavuz may be the Turkey's president, but Achim knew he was really the one with all the power.

* * *

What the fuck were you thinking?

The silent question burned through Nate's mind again as he stared at the mouthwatering site before him.

Sitting on the seat opposite him, Gracie's head was tilted back and her eyes were closed as she soaked up the sun's rays. He clearly hadn't thought this plan through.

Not. At. All.

When he'd first mentioned spending the day on the lake, Nate's entire focus had been on giving her a relaxing, normal day outside the cabin. What he hadn't taken into consideration was the fact that the most beautiful woman he'd ever known would be wearing a bathing suit the entire time.

This wasn't just any bathing suit, either. It was yellow, which complimented her golden skin tone perfectly, and was made from the tiniest scraps he'd ever seen.

The woman was gorgeous in a pair of running shorts and his old t-shirt. Gracie in a bikini? Holy fuck, he was so completely screwed.

His dick jumped behind his shorts, reminding him he hadn't actually been screwed by *anyone* in quite a while.

The combination of the canoe's shallow bottom and his long legs had Nate's knees drawn up closer to his chest than when he normally sat. Between that and his baggy swim trunks, the raging hard-on he was sporting was incognito. He hoped.

Desperate to think of anything other than how badly he wanted to reach across and dip his fingers beneath the yellow material covering the space between Gracie's thighs, Nate forced his mind to take a different direction.

"Tell me about Craig."

Clearly taken off guard, Gracie opened her eyes and sat up. "W-what do you want to know?"

For the past three days, Nate had learned more about Craig Wyatt than his own mother probably knew. As wonderful as technology was, however, some things couldn't be found on the web or in a file.

Nate shrugged, rowing them slowly across the water's calm surface. "What was he like?"

"Oh, um, he was nice." She smiled sadly. "Funny."

"Did he ever say or do anything that made you, I don't know, suspicious of anything?"

"Never. I mean, he was just like everybody else there. He had his good days and bad days. But, overall, he was a very positive, upbeat kind of guy. I can't imagine anyone wanting to hurt him."

"Any visitors come by while you were there? Any family members or former teammates come to see him?"

"No. Never." She shook her head. "Remember? At your apartment that night, I explained to you that's why I would go and sit with him. Why I sat with several of the patients there."

"No, I remember. I just needed to be sure." Nate paused for a moment, hating the next question he had to ask. "Did you and Craig ever—" God, he didn't want to say it. "Were you two just friends?"

Gracie's brows turned inward, and from the tone of her voice when she answered, she didn't care for the question any more than he did.

"Of course we were just friends. I would never have hooked up with one of the patients there. Not only would that have violated the volunteer policy, it would be wrong of me to use my time with them and their vulnerability to try to score a date."

Thank God.

"I'm sorry." Nate held up as much of his hands as he could without completely letting go of the oars. "I had to ask."

Gracie bit her bottom lip and nodded, but said, "Look, Nate. I appreciate how hard you've been working to try to figure this whole mess out. I really do. But, do you think maybe, just for an hour or two, we could talk about something other than Craig or the fact that someone tried to kidnap me?"

From behind his sunglasses, his eyes found the bruise that was beginning to fade. His pulse instantly spiked, and his hands fisted around the oars' wooden handles.

He'd never had such an animalistic reaction just from seeing someone get hurt. Not even when that asshat lawyer threatened to kill Sarah a while back.

It was different with Gracie. Like so many things were.

Nate couldn't explain it. Frankly, he was afraid to even try. But somehow, some way Gracelynn McDaniels had wormed her way into a place inside him he never knew existed.

Realizing he hadn't answered her yet, he forced a smile and said, "Sure. What do you want to talk about?"

Using both hands, Gracie gathered her hair and pulled it to one side so it all fell over her left shoulder.

"You."

"Me?" He couldn't hide his surprise. "What about me?"

"I don't know. Stuff like, where did you grow up? Do you have any brothers or sisters? Did you play sports in high school? Ever been married? You know, the normal stuff people talk about when they're first getting to know one another."

"Normal stuff, huh? I can do that." Knowing the oarlocks would keep the oars from falling into the water, Nate released their handles and rested a minute. "Let's see. I grew up in Studley, Virginia."

Gracie busted up laughing. "I'm sorry. Did you say *Studley?*"

Nate chuckled at her reaction. "Yes. Studley."

Her face filled with skepticism. "That's an actual place?"

"Yes, Miss Doubty McDoubtster. It's a tiny, unincorporated town northeast of Richmond. It has a gas station and everything."

Though, she was trying hard not to, Gracie snickered from behind her pursed lips.

"You don't believe me?" Nate acted hurt. "Fine. When we

get back to the cabin, I'll pull it up on the map and prove it to you."

"Oh, I believe you." She smiled. "I just find it fitting that you would be from a town with the name 'Studley'."

"That's right." Nate held his right fist up and flexed his bicep. "Pretty sure they changed the name to Studley after I was born."

Gracie laughed, but her eyes seemed mesmerized by his bulging muscles. Normally, Nate would make some inappropriate comment right about now. Probably something referring to his 'size'.

Rather than fall down that masochistic rabbit hole, he lowered his arm and said, "So, that's where I'm from. What else did you ask? Oh, yeah. Siblings. I had an older brother."

Those adorable eyebrows scrunched together again. "Had?"

"Scott was nine years older than me. I was what my parents affectionately call their 'Oops' baby. Anyway, Scott was a Lieutenant in the Navy and during his second tour in Afghanistan, the chopper he and five other members from his unit were in got shot down. There were no survivors."

"Oh, God, Nate. I'm so sorry."

The sincerity in her tone was touching. "Thanks. It sucks, and I still miss the big jerk like crazy. But, it was a long time ago. It helps to know he died doing what he loved." Nate smiled sadly. "From the time I can remember, Scott always wanted to be in the Navy."

"What about you? Did you always know you wanted to go into the military?"

Nate snorted. "Not at all. I'd planned to go to college, major in computer science, and then make a shit ton of money working for some big fortune five-hundred corporation."

"What made you change your mind?"

"My brother died serving his country."

"I'm sorry," she apologized again. "I didn't mean to drag up bad memories."

"Nothing to be sorry for. Honestly, it's been a while since I've talked about Scott, so thank you. Talking about him keeps his memory alive. Oh, and to answer your last two questions, I played second-string quarterback all four years in high school, and no, I've never been married."

She gave him a smirk. "See? This is nice. We're getting to know each other more."

"Well, then. In keeping with that spirit, what about you? Any secret husbands I need to know about who might be jealous of your fake one?"

When Gracie laughed, it was as if her entire soul lit up from within. Jesus, he didn't think he'd ever get tired of hearing that sound.

"Definitely not. I've only had a couple relationships you could even consider labeling as serious, and even then, it would be a stretch. My dad and Becky, Sarah's mom, got divorced when Sarah was two, and Dad took a job in Maryland. Six months later, he met my mom, and three months after that, they were married. Nine months later, I came along."

"Wow. Sounds like they had quite the whirlwind romance."

"It was." Gracie smiled wistfully. "When I got older, Dad explained that he and Becky had loved each other in the beginning, but they married really young, and as they grew up, they grew apart."

"What about your mom? Is he still with her?"

"Oh, yeah. Those two can't keep their hands off each other. I swear, most days it's like they're still in their twenties."

"I noticed you and Sarah have different last names."

"Yeah, that's a bit of a touchy subject with my dad. Becky remarried not long after their divorce, as well. Since Gordon, Sarah's stepdad, was the one physically helping to raise her, Sarah's mom asked my dad if Gordon could legally adopt Sarah when she was younger. It was a hard decision, but Dad said he thought it would be easier on Sarah if she had the same last name as Becky and Gordon. So, he signed off on it."

"I can see that."

"But," Gracie was quick to add, "My dad loves Sarah very much. They talk on the phone and send cards all the time. He always made sure she and I got together whenever we could, growing up. Plus, Dad gets along really well with both Becky and Gordon, so it all worked out."

"Sounds like he made the right choice for both himself and Sarah's mom."

"Yep. We're all just one, big happy family." As if she realized she'd said something wrong, Gracie began to apologize. "I'm sorry."

Nate looked at her questioningly. "For what?"

"You just shared that story about your brother, and here I am, going on and on about my sister."

He smiled. "You didn't go on and on, Gracie. And I asked, so there's nothing to be sorry for." Nate glanced up over her shoulder, only then realizing exactly where they were on the lake. His smile grew. "Speaking of Scott. There's something I want to show you."

Nate grabbed the oars again and began to paddle them toward a small sandbank not far from where they were. After rowing them onto shore as far as he could, he stepped into the water and helped Gracie out of the canoe.

"Oh! The water is colder than I thought it would be," she said as they walked carefully onto the bank.

"I'm just glad we went ahead and decided to buy the

water shoes. Definitely don't want to go barefoot where we're going."

That same skepticism flashed behind her beautiful eyes. "Where exactly is that?"

Purposely ignoring the question, Nate grabbed her hand and grinned. "I'll show you. Come on. It's this way."

Five minutes and a couple of stubbed toes later, Nate guided Gracie through the clearing and up to the top of the cliff he'd spotted from the lake.

"Watch your step."

Gracie cautiously leaned over a bit and looked down. "Um, Nate? You wanna tell me what we're doing up here?"

Keeping hold of her hand for more his peace of mind than hers, he said, "My brother and I used to come up here."

Her head swung around, and her eyes widened a bit just before they filled with recognition. "The picture."

"What picture?"

"On your fireplace. The one with the two boys. That was you and Scott, wasn't it?"

"Oh, yeah. I'd almost forgotten about that being there."

"And it was taken here? At this lake?"

"Yeah," Nate smiled, remembering that summer fondly. "I was eight, and he was eighteen. My parents used to bring us here every summer. We always rented one of the really big cabins that slept like twenty people. It was us and Clint's family." For clarification, he added, "Clint and my dad grew up together."

"Sounds nice."

"It was. Most of the time, anyway."

"Only most?"

"I was the youngest, so Clint's kids had a tendency to pick on me."

"I bet Scott didn't let that go on for long."

Nate smiled. "No. In fact, the last time I ever remember it

happening was in this very spot. It was the same year the picture was taken."

"Really? What happened?"

"We all came up here. Clint's boys dared Scott and I to jump. It's only a twenty-five foot drop, so Scott was all for it."

"But, you were scared."

Nate laughed at his younger self. "I wasn't just scared. I was terrified. My knees were shaking, and I remember the roof of my mouth tingling. My palms became sweaty, and I was on the verge of tears just thinking about jumping."

"I can't imagine you being scared of anything."

He glanced up at her, his heart swelling a bit when he realized she was being serious. "Well," he played it off. "Keep in mind, I was only eight. My fearless bravery didn't come until a few years later."

Gracie laughed. "So, did you jump?"

"I did. I wasn't going to, though. I'd actually started to walk back down to our canoe by myself."

"What stopped you?"

"Scott."

"He made you jump?"

Nate grinned. "The exact opposite, actually. He told me it was perfectly fine if I didn't want to do it, and what those boys were saying didn't mean jack shit."

"I'm confused. If you didn't want to jump, and Scott made you feel okay about not jumping, then why do it?"

"I don't know." Nate looked out onto the shimmering water below. "Maybe it was because I knew Scott was leaving for boot camp the week after we got back home, or the fact that I didn't want those boys to keep teasing me the rest of the time we were here. All I do know is the minute Scott held out his hand and offered to either jump with me or walk me back to our cabin, it was like a switch was flipped. Suddenly, there was nothing that would have kept me from jumping with him."

"What happened after?"

Nate's smile grew wider. "We spent the rest of the day jumping into the lake."

Gracie smiled. "That's a really great memory, Nate."

"It is," he nodded. "So, what do you say?"

Not understanding, she asked, "What do I say about what?"

He tilted his chin toward the edge of the cliff. "You want to try it?"

"Me?" Her jaw dropped, and she put her hands palms-up. "Oh, I-I don't know."

"You can swim, right? You told me you could when we rented the canoe."

"Yeah." She nodded her head. "I'm an okay swimmer, I guess." She looked back over the edge and swallowed hard. "But, that's a really long way down."

"I know it seems like it, but it's actually not. You'll only be in the air a few seconds before we're in the water, and I promise I'll be with you the whole time."

If she didn't want to jump, Nate wasn't going to pressure her. Gracie seemed to be considering it, though.

Biting her lip, she studied the distance to the water closely. Through the mesh of her water shoes, he could see her big toe bouncing up and down and felt guilty for making her feel so nervous.

"You know what? Never mind. Forget I said anything. We'll just go back down to the bank and swim around for a while."

Nate took her hand in his and started back toward the trees. They'd made it three whole steps before he felt a strong tug on his arm.

"No."

He turned to face her. "No?"

Gracie straightened her shoulders. "I want to do it. I want to jump."

"You sure? It's seriously fine if we don't."

"I'm sure."

He could tell she was still nervous, but a new look of determination had begun to take over.

"Okay, then. Let's do it." Once they got to the edge of the cliff, Nate gave her a few tips. "You want to land feet first. Try to make yourself as straight and tall as possible before you hit the water. Think pencil."

"Just not the bendy kind, right?"

Nate chuckled. "Right. You ready?"

Gracie looked down one last time. She drew in a deep breath then let it out slowly and nodded. "Ready."

Like Scott did with him all those years ago, Nate grabbed her hand and said, "Together on three." With their eyes locked, he counted aloud, "One. Two. Three!" Then, they jumped.

Gracie screamed as they fell. Though, he tried to keep ahold of her hand, they became separated as their bodies hit the water.

Nate torpedoed deeper and deeper, his momentum finally slowing when his toes met a much cooler area beneath the surface.

He then began to move his legs and arms as he'd been trained, and within seconds, his head was above water again.

"So." He used one hand to rub his eyes before running it roughly across the top of his head a couple times. "What did you think?"

Blinking against the few droplets still remaining on his lashes, Nate looked to where he thought Gracie had landed. Assuming he'd gotten turned around, he spun himself in the opposite direction. He saw only rippling water.

"Gracie?"

Nate looked to the spot where they'd secured their canoe thinking maybe she'd already began swimming to the shore, but it sat empty. Bobbing up and down easily from the miniscule waves he and Gracie had caused.

Heart in his throat, Nate's head whipped back around, but there was still no sign of her.

"Gracie!" he yelled loudly, waiting another second before diving under to search for her there.

The sound of Nate's panicked heartbeat filled his ears as he tried to see through the cloudy, green water. His arms swiped this way and that in hopes he'd bump into her, but he felt nothing.

When he resurfaced again, she was nowhere to be seen.

"Gracelynn!"

Terrified she'd landed wrong and was under the water and unconscious, Nate prepared to go back down and continue searching. Filling his lungs with as much air as they could hold, his face had almost hit the water when he felt something touch his back.

"Yes?"

He twisted his body around. A strange, guttural sound of relief escaped his throat when he saw her.

Treading water with ease, Gracie smiled back at him as though she didn't have a care in the world.

"What the…where the hell were you?"

She looked confused. "What do you mean? I've been here." Gracie glanced around them and smiled again. "The water felt so nice and refreshing, I decided to stay under and swim around in it for a while."

"You decided to…" Unable to believe what he was hearing, Nate clamped his teeth together and began breathing through his nose. Still attempting to slow his racing pulse, he opened his mouth then closed it. Then, he opened it again. "You're kidding."

"What? And you were right, by the way. That was a total rush. We should do it again."

"You want to do it again?" He bit out. "You want to do it *again?* I thought you'd fucking drowned, Gracelynn. I came up, and you were just...gone. What the fuck were you thinking?"

"You're mad."

"Damn right, I'm mad. I thought—" Nate cut himself off when he noticed the way she was looking at him.

Gracie was trying to hold her serious expression, but she'd rolled her lips inward and laughter lit up her mischievous eyes.

It had taken him a few minutes, but Nate finally realized what had just happened.

"You did that on purpose, didn't you?"

Now biting her lip, Gracie remained quiet. The damn fool woman was clearly struggling to keep from laughing.

"Damn it, woman. You about gave me a goddamn heart attack!"

"S-sorry," she barely sputtered out the insincere apology before losing it. With a near-hysterical laugh, she managed to say, "You should...have seen...your face."

"Oh, you think that was funny?"

She laughed even harder. "A little bit, yeah."

Anger gone—Because, how the hell could he stay mad when she seemed so happy?—Nate stared to swim toward her. "I'll show you funny."

Knowing what was coming, Gracie's eyes widened, and she screamed. Turning with lightening-like speed, she laughed as she fought hard to swim away.

Nate was on her before she ever had the chance to escape. She squealed and laughed even harder when his fingers found her ribs. Tickling her mercilessly, he continued the torture until Gracie begged for him to stop.

"Please," she pleaded breathlessly. "Oh, God. Please stop!"

Talking loudly enough she could hear him over her own laughter, Nate asked, "You gonna scare me like that again?"

"No!" She shook her head emphatically.

"Promise?"

"I promise! I promise!"

Nate stilled his hands. "Okay, then."

"Oh, my God," Gracie's words escaped with an exhale of relief. With her hands on his shoulders, she steadied herself. "I can barely breathe right now."

"Speaking of breathing..." Nate kept hold of her, his legs kicking to the sides to help keep them both afloat. "Where'd you learn to hold your breath like that?"

"Impressed?"

Nate parroted her words from before. "A little bit, yeah."

With a smug grin, she told him, "I was on my high school swim team. Then, in college, I made extra money working as a lifeguard at the campus rec center."

"So, that whole scene up there." Nate lifted his chin toward the cliff. "Acting all scared and nervous. That was just an act?"

Gracie gave him an unapologetic smirk. "A girl can't reveal all her secrets at one time, now, can she?"

Narrowing his eyes, Nate squeezed her ribs a bit tighter and playfully growled. This caused her to laugh again, making his already half-hard dick rise to full mast.

Something Gracie felt the instant she moved in to give him a hug.

CHAPTER 11

"Oh," Gracie pushed herself away from Nate. "Sorry." She was both surprised and embarrassed by his body's reaction to her.

"Sorry," he said at the exact same time. Then, he gave her that damn-sexy, lopsided grin. "That tends to happen a lot around you. Just ignore it."

Not likely. With butterflies dancing around in her lower belly, she continued to tread water and brought her eyes to his.

With a slightly pinker tint to his cheeks, Nate swallowed hard. Though, a part of her—a throbbing, aching part—enjoyed the hell out of the fact he'd basically just admitted to having had multiple erections because of her, she also didn't want to make things harder on him than they already were.

Pun intended.

"After this craziness is over, right?" Gracie tried her best to sound perfectly fine with waiting for anything more.

Heat instantly filled his eyes. "Right."

Her heart thumped powerfully inside her chest as she

imagined the hard shaft she'd just felt against her belly sliding into her aching core.

She licked her lips and whispered, "Good."

Nate had just opened his mouth to say something else when a loud string of thunder rolled above them.

Gracie looked up at a large, gray cloud making its way toward them. "That doesn't look good."

He followed her gaze. "Damn. We should probably head back."

With their mutual flirting session over, Gracie hid her disappointment by turning and swimming back toward the canoe. She could hear Nate making his way through the water behind her, but it was obvious he was keeping a safe distance between them.

It's for the best. That little voice in her head was right. At least she fought to convince herself it was.

An hour later, they were back inside the cabin. After taking turns showering, Nate fixed them some ham and cheese sandwiches.

It was still thundering but hadn't started to rain, so they decided to sit out on the small porch to eat.

Rocking in one of the two wooden rocking chairs, Gracie sat her empty plate down and sighed. "That was really good. Thank you."

"You get enough to eat? I can make you another one, if you'd like."

"No, thank you. I'm actually in the mood for something sweet."

"We could make S'mores."

Gracie felt her face light up. "I forgot we bought the stuff for those."

Smiling back at her, Nate stood. "I'll go start the fire."

More than okay with that plan, she rushed to gather their plates before going inside. After washing the two saucers and sitting them in the small, plastic drying rack, Gracie went to the cabinet where Nate had stored all the dry goods.

Once the ingredients had been collected, she grabbed the two roasting forks by the door and headed back outside. She grinned, not surprised in the least that Nate had already managed to get the fire going.

The stone fire pit was positioned between their cabin and the one next door. Before today, that cabin had remained empty, but when they'd gotten back from their little outing, she'd noticed a small, gold car sitting in its parking space.

"Wonder who our neighbors are," she mused as she made her way to one of the two benches provided for the guests. Positioned on opposite sides of the pit, she chose the one closest to their cabin.

"Larry and Connie Hays. Larry's a retired sheriff from a few counties over, and Connie is a retired school teacher. Neither have any priors and they both appear to be good, upstanding citizens."

When Gracie's jaw dropped, Nate innocently asked, "What? I ran their plates as soon as we got back."

Of course he had.

Before showering, she'd seen him checking the feed from the almost-invisible security cameras he'd installed the first night they'd gotten here. She hadn't realized he'd ran complete background checks on their poor, unsuspecting neighbors, too.

"For a minute there, I sort of forgot why we were here."

"For a minute there"—his gaze bore into hers—"so did I."

Knowing he was thinking of the earlier moment in the lake, Gracie tried to come up with something else to talk about. Before she could, a sing-song voice travelled over to them.

"Hello!"

A tiny bit of a woman was walking toward them next to a

man who towered over her. Her short hair was a pretty blonde and she looked to be around sixty or so. The man appeared a bit older, and the cowboy hat and boots he was wearing were definitely not just for show.

The woman walked straight up to Gracie and held out her hand.

"Hi. I'm Connie. This is my husband, Larry. We're staying in the cabin next door."

"Hello. I'm…"

Panic struck. This was the first time they'd really talked to anyone since checking in and Gracie realized she couldn't remember the name she was supposed to be using. Thankfully, Nate picked up on it and jumped right in.

"James Winters." He practically shoved his hand into the other woman's. "And this shy beauty right here is my wife, Lynn. Nice to meet you."

After exchanging smiles and handshakes with the seemingly sweet couple, Gracie gave Nate a sideways glance. He responded with a wink and a smile, making her feel slightly better about her near flub-up.

"So, where are y'all from?" Connie asked.

"Dallas," Nate answered for them both. "Well, I'm originally from out east, but I transplanted here a few years ago."

"You mind if we join you for a few?"

"Sure." Nate held out his hand toward the other bench. "We were just about to cook us up some S'mores. You're welcome to have some."

"Oh, I do love chocolate."

As the four of them sat down, Larry chuckled. In his deep, smoker's voice, he joked, "She'd probably find a way to marry it, if she wasn't already attached to me."

Nate laughed, and Gracie awkwardly joined in. She opened one of the candy bars and broke off two pieces. One for her, and one for Connie.

Chewing slowly, she knew she needed to figure out a way past the guilt of their deception, or she'd end up completely blowing their cover.

I can do this.

Drawing in a steady breath, she swallowed the sweet treat and spoke up. "What about you? Where are you from?"

"Beaumont. It's about an hour and a half south of here."

"Beaumont," Nate repeated the city's name. "That's just north of Port Arthur, isn't it?"

"That's right." Larry gave him a nod. "Home of the world's largest oil refinery."

"I remember. My parents drove my brother and I through there once when I was younger."

"Larry, here, used to be the sheriff of Jefferson County."

"That was a long time ago, Con."

"I know." Connie nudged her husband with her shoulder. "I still like to brag about you, though."

Gracie smiled. These two were absolutely adorable.

"So." Larry looked to Nate. "What brings you two out here?"

"Actually"—Nate put his arm around Gracie's shoulders and pulled her closer—"We're celebrating our two-year anniversary."

"Two years? Oh, my. Larry, do you even remember when it had only been two years?"

The other man gave his wife an ornery smile. "Hell, yeah, I remember." Then, he lowered his voice and winked at Nate. "Those days were a lot of fun."

"Larry!" Connie playfully smacked his arm, but Gracie didn't miss the look the two shared after.

"Yeah, I sure can't complain," Nate grinned.

"Well, take it from an old fogy like me. You treat each other right, and you'll have a whole lot of great years together."

"Oh, I plan to, Larry. Don't worry." Nate glanced down at Gracie. She could have sworn he was being serious when he said, "I can't imagine my life without her."

"So, tell me. How did you two meet?" Connie asked sounding genuinely interested.

Still blushing, Gracie decided to take the lead. "We met outside the building where we both work." When Nate gave her an approving smile, she asked, "Would you like to tell the story?"

"Go ahead. It's always better when you tell it."

Biting her bottom lip, Gracie thought a moment, and then remembered what he'd told her before.

Stick as close to the truth as possible without giving yourself away.

"I'd gone to this little coffee shop across the street from our building."

"What do you do?" Larry directed the question to Nate.

"I work for a security company."

"Like, home security systems, that sort of thing?"

"Stuff like that, yeah," Nate answered without batting an eye.

Okay, so that was partially true.

"And what about you?" Larry looked across at her.

"I'm just a secretary for one of the offices in the building."

"Oh, honey. Don't ever call yourself *just* a secretary. I was a teacher for thirty years and trust me. We all knew our secretaries were the ones holding that place together."

Gracie smiled. "Thanks, Connie."

"Sorry. Didn't mean to interrupt. Please"—Larry held out a hand—"Continue with your story."

As requested, Gracie went on with the fictional tale filled with half-truths.

"So, I was in the crosswalk headed back to work when this strikingly handsome man exited my building. Suddenly, it was as if everything else around me disappeared until we were the only two people left in the world. He was standing there, looking so strong and formidable. Like he was ready to take on the world. I couldn't take my eyes off him." She turned to Nate, surprised to find him staring down at her.

"Go on," Connie prompted.

"Yeah, honey." Nate's voice had turned low. Sexy. "Go on."

Even though Gracie knew it was all part of their twisted game, she couldn't help but love the way he sounded just then.

"Well, I should have been looking where I was going, because the next thing I knew, this car was headed straight for me. It was clear it wasn't going to stop for the red light."

"Oh, my gosh. So, what happened next?"

"Let her tell the story, Con, and you'll find out."

Gracie laughed softly and then looked at Nate again. With their eyes locked, she said, "The handsome man from across the street saved me." She smiled. "He pulled me into his arms and back onto the sidewalk just in time for the car to miss me. Then, he held me there for what seemed like forever, making sure I was okay."

"And I knew right then," Nate chimed in. "I needed this woman in my life."

"Oh, how romantic!" Connie exclaimed wistfully.

"Romantic? This poor young lady was almost killed. Was the dumbass driving the car texting? I bet he was. Everyone's always texting and driving these days. I swear nearly every driver I pass is looking at his or her phone instead of the road."

"But what a story they have to tell."

"Yeah, the story of how she damn near became road kill."

"Larry!"

"I'm just saying."

As the other couple continued their bantering, Gracie's

entire focus remained on Nate. His gaze bore down into hers so deeply it felt as though he was touching her soul.

She was still trying to decipher whether or not the emotion behind his eyes was real or part of his act when the skies opened up, breaking whatever spell she'd been under.

Rain began to pour down on them in sheets. Connie and Larry said their goodbyes and began walking as fast as they could back to their place.

Gracie stood and reached for the food, but Nate grabbed her hand and started to pull her toward their cabin.

"But, the food," she glanced at the bench now behind her.

"Leave it," Nate ordered gruffly.

Blinking against the rain, Gracie struggled to understand the expression on his face. He almost looked upset, but for the life of her, she couldn't figure out why.

She had to walk double-time to keep up with his long strides, and as they covered the remaining distance to their cabin's porch, she desperately tried to figure out what she'd said that had him so upset.

Nate threw open the door and pulled her roughly inside. Slamming the door shut, he locked it then turned back to her.

The cabin was dark, but light from the porch lamp shone through the window behind him, allowing Gracie to make out his tall silhouette.

Standing there, sopping wet and dripping all over the wood floor, she had to know what she'd done wrong.

"What did I do?" she whispered softly.

Nate shook his head slowly. "I can't do this."

Her heart dropped. "I tried sticking to as much of the truth as possible, just like you said. I'm sorry." She started to turn away. "I thought my story was—"

He reached for her forearm and pulled her flush against his chest. "Perfect. Your story was perfect. You..." he swiped some wet strands from her face. "Jesus, Gracie. *You* are fucking perfect."

Her pulse spiked and her knees shook. "But, you just said you can't do this."

He spun them around and pushed her up against the door. "I meant, I can't keep looking at you and not touch you. I can't hear that beautiful fucking laugh of yours and not want to swallow it up with my own breath." He cupped her damp face with both hands. "I can't be around you another second and not do *this*."

Nate slammed his lips against hers with such force her head would have banged against it had he not slid one of his hands around to protect her.

Always protecting me.

For all of two seconds, she considered asking him about his hands-off rule. Then, he slid his tongue into her mouth.

Kissing him back with the same level of passion and desire, Gracie gave as good as she got. She allowed her hands to begin their own exploration, reaching for the bottom hem of his T.

Her insides did a major happy dance when Nate broke away just long enough to pull the shirt up and over his head. He leaned in, his mouth continuing its delicious assault, as she began to slide her fingers against his hard, bare chest.

Gracie felt his sharp inhale when the pads of her fingers gently rubbed across his taught nipples. Loving how reactive he was to her touch, she ran her fingertips over the tiny nubs again.

He must have decided all was fair in passion and sex, because Nate pulled away suddenly and tore her t-shirt from her body. He then expertly released the clasp on her new bra and slid the straps off her shoulders and down her arms until it fell onto the floor beside them.

"Holy God," he exhaled loudly as he stared. "You truly are beautiful."

Wearing nothing but her panties and a pair of yoga pants, Gracie reached for his chest again.

"So, are you," she whispered honestly.

Nate's eyes moved from her bare breasts to her shadowed gaze as he gently filled both his hands with her firm globes. He kissed her again as he kneaded the sensitive flesh, and when he leaned down and sucked one of her solid nipples into his mouth, she moaned.

"Oh, Nate."

Rather than verbally respond, he flicked her nipple with the tip of his tongue. Gracie cried out from the torturous pleasure, so naturally, he did it again.

An electric line of pleasure ran from her nipple straight down to her clit, causing her hips to push toward him on reflex.

"Patience, sweetheart." Nate smiled as he moved to the other breast. The hot, wet heat from his lips and tongue were nearly enough to set her off.

"No patience," she panted. "I need you."

Sliding her right hand between their bodies, Gracie found the object of her desire and gave it a squeeze.

Nate sucked in a breath, followed by a guttural moan. In a surprisingly fast move, he positioned both wrists above her head.

Pushing them gently against the door, he shook his head. "Touch me like that again, and this is over before it even gets started."

"Please, Nate," she begged shamelessly.

With the most intense look she'd ever seen from him, he stared down into her eyes and vowed, "Don't worry, baby. I'll always take care of you."

Before she could overthink the promise he'd just made,

Nate transferred both wrists into one of his large fists and began sliding his free hand down the front of her body.

Purposely taking his time, he teasingly traced the space between her breasts. Then, moving his hand down further, Nate followed an invisible line down over her flat stomach to her elastic waistband.

Gracie's heart felt as though it would fly out of her chest as the anticipation built deep within her core. Thankfully, Nate didn't wait any longer before dipping his finger beneath the lace edging of her panties.

She cried out when he touched her most treasured flesh for the very first time. They'd only just started, yet she was already about to explode.

Tracing her slit from top to bottom, Nate began moving his fingers as though he'd already mastered the art of pleasuring her body. His mouth moved over her jaw and down to her neck as he slowly inserted his index finger into her core.

Moaning again, Gracie didn't think about whether or not she was being too loud. In fact, Nate seemed to like it, because he grunted against the pulse point on her neck before pushing a second finger inside her tight sheath.

Gracie spread her legs farther. "Oh, God. That feels so good."

He remained silent, but began moving his fingers in and out at a faster, harder pace. His teeth scraped carefully against the skin on her neck, and Gracie cried out again when he gave her a little love bite.

"More," she begged. "Please. Give me more."

Nate pulled his mouth away and yanked his fingers free.

"No." She started to shake her head in protest, but stopped herself when she realized he'd only separated their bodies in order to remove her pants.

In one, smooth motion, Nate hooked his thumbs in the sides and shoved both them and her panties down her legs.

With him squatted down in front of her, Gracie lifted her feet, one at a time, to allow the garments to be removed altogether.

Falling to his knees, Nate's face was directly in line with the apex of her thighs. Gracie thought she should probably be embarrassed. She wasn't.

Knowing the pleasure this man was about to give her superseded any inklings of shyness or embarrassment she may have normally felt.

Nate sensually ran a hand up the side of her left calf, lifting her leg when he got to her knee. He placed the leg over his right shoulder and then used his fingers to open her up to him completely.

"Ah, baby. You're so wet for me, aren't you?"

Unsure whether or not it was a rhetorical question, Gracie silently nodded her head.

"I can't wait any longer." He looked up at her from between her thighs and smiled.

Mother of all that's holy. It was the most erotic scene she'd ever witnessed.

Then, he said, "I have to taste you."

Her insides clenched with anticipation as he leaned his head in and ran his tongue along her opening. Unable to control her body's reaction Gracie bucked against his face.

"Oh, shit. I'm not going to last long, Nate."

She felt him smile against her most sensitive flesh. "Just means there's time for more after this one."

Did he mean multiple orgasms? She'd never had that happen to her before. Honestly didn't think they actually existed.

"I can't. I mean, I've never…"

"Relax, Gracie." His hot breath hit her slick folds, making them contract again. "Told you before. I'll take care of you."

Pressing his mouth against her, Nate used his tongue to

lick and fuck her pussy with perfection. Occasionally, he'd work his way up to her clit and slowly roll his tongue around the swollen bundle of nerves.

He'd bring her *just* to the edge of explosion and then pull away, repeating the torturous cycle until she thought she'd die if she didn't get release.

"I can't take it anymore. Please."

He shoved two fingers into her channel again. Moving them in and out slowly, she could hear how wet she was as he said, "Tell me what you need, Gracie. I want to hear you say it."

"I need to come. Oh, God…please make me come."

He moved his fingers faster, then. Pumping them into her body with more force than before. She was almost there. She just needed…

Nate leaned forward and sucked her clit between his lips. As he did, he flicked it with his tongue over and over again. The sensation, coupled with the thrusting of his fingers, proved lethal.

Gracie exploded. She cried out his name as her head flew back against the door, and she could actually feel the rush of her arousal coating the fingers still moving inside her.

Tiny, white dots flashed behind her closed eyes, and she felt as if she were flying.

By the time she came down from her erotic high, Nate was sliding his hand free from her body. Carefully, he moved her leg from his shoulder and placed it back down so she was standing on both feet again.

He stood before her. Through heavily-lidded, satiated eyes, Gracie was rendered speechless when he held up the fingers that had just been inside her and sucked them into his mouth.

Savoring the last of her arousal from his hand, Nate licked his lips and moaned. "Delicious."

"That was," Gracie tried to talk. "I've never felt so…" Her heavy breathing and muddled mind prevented her from completing her thoughts.

"That was the most beautiful thing I've ever seen," Nate stated sincerely.

Gracie smiled. "Now, it's your turn."

Nate moved in closely and cupped her face with his hand.

"You need to be sure, Gracie. There's no turning back from this."

Leaning forward, she licked then nibbled his chin. "I've never been more certain of anything in my entire life."

Without giving it another thought, Nate bent down and swung her into his arms.

Letting out a little squeal, Gracie started to laugh. "What are you doing?"

Walking toward the room she'd been sleeping in alone, Nate's voice rumbled low.

"Taking you to bed."

CHAPTER 12

We should stop. Hell, they never should have started.

The thought ran through Nate's head on loop as he carried Gracie to the bedroom at the end of the hallway.

He'd been sitting there, listening as she told the story of how they'd supposedly met and fell in love, and all he could think about was how badly he wanted the story to be true.

Nate didn't bother trying to worry about what that meant. Yeah, he should be focused solely on protecting her, but come on. A guy could only take so much, and he wasn't a fucking saint.

The way Gracie had looked at him while sitting by the fire was all the proof he needed. She wanted him, too.

After seeing her come apart in his arms the way she had just now, Nate didn't know how he'd ever get enough of her. Or ever let her go.

Laying her gently down onto the bed, he went to the duffle bag sitting in the corner by the window. Nate opened the new box of condoms he'd brought with him and pulled out one of the square, foil packets.

Setting it on the bedside table, he looked down at the

angelic beauty staring back at him. Gracie's delectable, naked body was splayed out like an offering, and he had no idea what he'd done to deserve her.

With a tiny smile, she looked to the packet then back to him. "Planning ahead?"

Nate began working his belt buckle. "Condoms have a multitude of uses in the field."

"Oh, I see. So, you didn't buy those with this in mind?"

"Didn't say that," he grinned.

Pulling his belt free, Nate released the button on his damp jeans and slowly lowered his zipper. Gracie's eyes slid down to his hands.

Her lids were still heavy from the release he'd just given her, their golden brown darkening with excitement as they continued to follow his movements.

Her chest rose and fell a little faster and Nate about lost it in his pants when her tongue began to run along her bottom lip.

Damn. If just watching her watch him like that nearly set him off, he'd have to proceed with extreme caution. Otherwise, he'd end up embarrassing himself.

Pushing his jeans and boxer briefs down together, Nate kicked them aside, uncaring of where they landed. Gracie's sudden intake of air went straight to his aching groin, and he grabbed hold of his cock, giving it a squeeze to help stave off his impending release.

Nate's hips jerked back a little when his fingers pinched the swollen head. The sensitive skin there becoming slick with moisture.

"This first time's gonna be quick," he warned her. The mattress dipped as he knelt onto the bed. Hovering above her, he used his elbows to keep his weight from crushing her. "We're talking a few minutes. Maybe even seconds."

Gracie giggled. "Well, I've already gotten mine, so the rest is all about you."

"Wrong," Nate shook his head. He used a finger to brush some hair from her forehead. "I plan to make you come again," he leaned in for a short kiss. "And again," his lips left a trail across her jaw. "And again," he whispered into her ear just before pulling the perfect lobe between his teeth.

She moaned and he smiled. Nate had always thought her laugh was the most beautiful thing he'd ever heard. However, the sounds of pleasure coming from her now, a result of his making love to her, damn near caused him to erupt.

Her hands pressed against his chest, and he went with what he knew she wanted. Rolling flat onto his back, Gracie leaned over him and kissed him.

The taste of sweet chocolate was still present on her tongue as it began swirling and dancing in perfect rhythm with his.

Nate had never been big on just lying around and kissing, but with this woman? He'd be perfectly content doing nothing but this for the rest of the night.

There were no complaints from him, however, when she began to move her lips down the length of his body.

With an evil grin, she looked up at him and said, "My turn to taste."

Leaving small, loving kisses as she went, Nate watched as Gracie slowly made her way over his rippled abs...and lower.

Ah, hell.

He wasn't sure if he'd survive, but prayed for at least a few seconds before releasing the massive explosion currently building in his groin.

His hips shot off the mattress as a sudden, wet heat hit his throbbing dick. Moaning loudly, Nate used one fist to clutch the bedding beside him and the other to gather some of Gracie's hair as she ran her tongue over the tip before taking more of him in.

Due to his generous size, most women he'd been with had trouble getting past the first few inches without gagging. Gracie, however, lowered her head until he felt himself hit the back of her throat.

"Jesus," Nate exhaled loudly then moaned again. He felt her smile around his solid shaft.

His sounds of approval must have spurred her into action, because Gracie began sucking and licking with a little more force, then.

She fisted the base as much as her small fingers would allow, and when she began pumping even faster, that familiar tingling in his spine warned him the end was near.

"Nope."

In one fluid motion, Nate pulled her off and spun them around so he was on top, once again.

"What?" Gracie looked up at him with confusion. "I-I thought you liked what I was doing."

"Trust me, I liked it." He kissed her, using those few seconds to regroup. "Too much."

"Oh." She smiled wide then, clearly proud of her ability to please him.

He hopped up from the bed and grabbed the foil square from the nightstand. Using his teeth, he opened the wrapper.

A small, almost indiscernible noise came from the back of her throat when he slid the protection over his pulsing cock.

I know the feeling, baby.

Crawling back onto the bed, he repositioned his body over hers. Supporting his weight with one elbow, he used his other hand to tuck a tuft of hair behind her ear.

Concern flittered behind her eyes as she quietly admitted,

"It's been a while, Nate." She licked her lips nervously. "Like, over a year."

His chest swelled. It was a Neanderthal way to think, but he loved that no one else had been given the pleasure of experiencing her body in so long.

Needing to make sure she felt safe with him, he gave her his own admission. "I haven't been with anyone in a long while, either. Several months, actually."

"Really?"

Nate chuckled. "Really. I'm not quite the hound dog Kole makes me out to be."

This clearly made her happy, because Gracie lifted her hips toward his even more. Her body's way of telling him it was ready to join with his.

Repositioning himself above her, Nate reached between them and aligned his cock to her core. Christ, just the of feeling her hot, drenched opening pressing against him was almost all the pleasure he needed. Almost.

Because he felt like it, Nate leaned down and kissed her slowly. When he pulled back, he whispered, "Ready?"

Gracie nodded. "More than."

With his eyes locked on hers, he linked their hands together on either side of her head then slowly began pushing himself forward. She was tight and he was big, so it took a few seconds just to get the tip all the way in.

Determination flashed across her face and they both moved together to work him inch by inch into her molten core.

Holy. Fuck.

Gracie's body was like a vise, gripping him with such strength, he wasn't sure she'd ever let go. Not that Nate wanted her to.

For the first time in his life, he felt truly connected to a woman. And not just physically.

"God, you feel good," he moaned as he pumped his cock in and out slowly. "Never felt anything so fucking good."

It wasn't just a line. Being with Gracie was like finding the piece to a puzzle. One he never realized was missing.

Picking up the pace, Nate continued thrusting into her. His movements became a little more intense and it didn't take long for her body to start quivering again.

"Holy crap! I'm close again," she announced, sounding surprised.

Even in the midst of such intense pleasure, she managed to make him smile. Knowing he wasn't going to last much longer, himself, Nate was determined to make her climax one more time before he did.

Sliding his hand between them, he gathered some of her essence from where their bodies were joined and began rubbing it over her clit.

"Oh, yeah. Oh, God, Nate. I'm going to...*Ah!*"

He watched in awe as Gracie flew for the second time that night. Her body clenched down on his, a rush of wet heat instantly covering his pulsing erection.

Hearing her cry out his name upon release, knowing he was the one who'd gotten her there, drove him over that same, magnificent edge.

"Gracelynn," he grunted out her full name. His muscles stiffened, and with one, final thrust, Nate erupted.

A shudder ran through him and his hands instinctively held hers a little tighter as his seed shot out forcefully, filling the end of the condom.

Several seconds later, Nate was still reeling from the longest, most intense orgasm of his life.

Though, he was on the verge of collapsing, he somehow was able to keep from crushing the goddess lying below him. He leaned in and kissed her softly, needing her to know it was more than just sex for him. That this wasn't just a casual one and done.

Somehow, in the short time he'd known her, Gracie had found a permanent place in his heart. His soul.

He may not be ready to say it out loud yet, but after what they'd just shared, Nate knew he was never letting her go.

* * *

Gracie watched as Nate left the room to take care of the condom, knowing she'd never get tired of that view. He was so fit, she could see his muscles flex with each movement.

His ass was a thing of beauty, its sides dipping slightly inward to form two perfectly defined globes.

Smiling, she sighed and rested her head back onto the bed. What she'd told him had been the truth. Before tonight, it had been over a year since Gracie had been with a man. And it was nothing like what she'd just experienced with Nate.

Her last boyfriend was a guy she'd dated for about six months. Gracie had thought maybe there was a future there, until he got a promotion that took him from Maryland to southern Florida. He accepted the position without even discussing it with her first.

It made her realize she'd never really meant that much to him. If she had, he would have at least taken her thoughts and feelings into consideration before deciding on a change that would affect them both.

Nate returned with a washcloth in his hand, all thoughts of the past vanishing as he walked toward her. Gracie rose up onto her elbows and reached for it, but rather than hand it over to her, he rested a knee onto the bed and pressed the damp material gently against her sex.

Inhaling deeply, she moaned as she laid back down, welcoming the cloth's soothing heat.

On the verge of falling asleep, Gracie didn't even realize he'd left the room again until he came back and began to pick her up. She opened her eyes and stared up at him sleepily.

"What are you doing?" she mumbled as she wrapped her arms around his neck.

"Putting you to bed."

After pulling back the covers on the side closest to them, Nate carefully laid her back down, positioning her head in the center of her pillow. He covered her back up then walked around the foot of the bed to the other side.

Crawling in beside her, Nate scooted across the mattress until they were touching. Then, wrapping one of his strong arms around her waist, he pulled so her back became flush with his front.

She wasn't certain, given his natural size, but Gracie could swear her bare bottom bumped against his growing erection.

"Already?" She teased, wiggling her cheeks against him. His hair there was rough, and Gracie found even that was a turn-on.

Nate's hand squeezed her hips, halting her movements.

"Told you before, it has a tendency to do that when you're around. Just ignore it."

"What if I don't want to ignore it?" She pressed back against him. Again, his hand halted her movements.

She felt the low rumble of his laugh against her back. "As much as I'd love to slide into your gorgeous body again, we both need to recharge."

As though he could see her pouty expression, Nate leaned over and used his fingers on her chin to turn her face toward his. He lowered his lips to hers, giving her one of the most loving, sensual kisses she'd ever had.

"Don't worry, baby." He brushed the tip of her nose with his. "This thing between us is just getting started."

Gracie took her own kiss. When she finally pulled away, she smiled up at him and said, "You bet your ass it is."

Chuckling, Nate pressed his lips to her forehead. "Get some sleep. I have a feeling we're both going to need it."

With his arms wrapped snuggly around her, Gracie laid her head back down and closed her eyes. She was still smiling when she fell asleep less than two minutes later.

The next morning, she woke to the aroma of something sweet and savory. She took a deep breath, inhaling the scent of bacon and brown sugar, and realized Nate was in the kitchen cooking them breakfast.

After a rushed shower to help wake herself up, Gracie threw on a pair of clean panties and her bra. Dressed in loose running shorts and a tank top, she put her hair up into a messy bun and brushed her teeth. Not bothering with makeup, she made her way to the front of the cabin.

Nate was standing at the stove with his back to her. He was shirtless and his hair was damp, as if he'd recently taken a shower, too.

The cargo shorts he wore hung loosely on his narrow hips, and she took a moment to appreciate the way his back muscles danced as he maneuvered the set of metal tongs over the hot pan full of sizzling bacon.

Gracie loved how the khaki material of his shorts was stretched taught over his rear. She thought of his powerful thrusts, her inner muscles flexing as she remembered how incredible it felt when he first pressed himself inside her.

"You gonna just stand there and stare, or come give me a proper good-morning kiss?"

Laughing, Gracie didn't bother to ask how he knew she was there. She started toward him, the area between her thighs already beginning to feel heavy.

Though, she'd only been watching him for a couple minutes, it was enough to cause her sex to swell and ache with need.

Careful not to get too close to the popping grease, she stepped up to his side. "Good morning."

He looked at her and smiled. "Mornin', beautiful."

Nate then leaned down and gave her the most fantastic greeting she'd ever had. Tasting of the same, minty toothpaste she'd used, Gracie took her time with the kiss.

A loud pop filled the air and she felt his body jerk in reaction. Breaking the kiss, she took a step back.

"Did it get you?"

He shrugged and rubbed a spot on his arm. "A little. Nothing major."

"Can I help with anything?"

"Nope. This is done, actually." He turned the burner off. "Just need to put it onto a plate."

Moving around her, he reached into one of the cabinets and pulled one out. After covering it with a couple layers of paper towels, Nate moved the strips of bacon from the pan onto the plate.

Turning around, he rested back against the counter behind him, his hands loosely gripping its edge at his sides. "There's French toast in the oven. It'll be ready in about fifteen minutes."

Fifteen minutes, huh?

Gracie knew exactly how she wanted to pass the time. Feeling bold, she said, "Perfect."

Nate's brows turned in. "Perfect? For what?"

"This."

Reaching for the button on his shorts, she yanked it free before grasping the metal tab at the top of his zipper and pulling it all the way down.

Nate gave her the sexiest grin she'd ever seen a man wear.

"I was going to ask if you had any regrets, but I guess this answers my question."

"There's only one thing I regret from last night."

She shoved his shorts and boxers down, stopping mid-thigh. What she had planned didn't require them to be completely off.

Concern flashed behind his eyes even as his solid spear of a cock bobbed between the magnificent V his muscles created.

"Wait, what do you regret?"

"Not having more time to do this."

Without giving him a chance to protest, Gracie bent over at the waist and took him into her mouth as far as he would go.

"Oh, shit!" Nate's hips instinctively moved forward. "Gracie, you don't have to..." he moaned loudly before being able to finish his thought. "Baby, you don't have to do this."

She released him with a quiet pop and looked up. "I know I don't have to." She licked her lips. "I want to."

Heat filled his eyes as one corner of his mouth rose. "Well, if you insist." He was still looking her in the eyes when she sucked the salty tip between her lips again.

Slowly, she took more of him in, then worked her way back up. Gracie licked before swirling her tongue around the hot, swollen head.

Deciding to take all she could while she had the chance, she began licking her way down to the base...and below.

Using a hand to assist, Gracie lifted his heavy sack and ran her tongue back and forth against it.

"Fuck, baby," Nate ground out. "Jesus, that feels amazing."

Smiling against his delicate skin, Gracie took things a step further when she opened her mouth wide and carefully sucked part of it into her mouth.

"Ah, God," Nate grunted breathlessly. "You're killing me, here."

Gracie almost stopped, but when she felt his hand resting on the top of her head, she knew he wanted more. Licking her way back up, she began sucking his shaft again.

Remembering how she nearly brought him to climax last night, Gracie added her fist, pumping him as she sucked. Putting a little twist in her grip as she moved, she felt him become impossibly harder beneath her palm.

Nate started to pant loudly, his breaths heaving in and out as she drew him closer and closer to orgasm. Gracie could feel her own moisture pooling inside her panties, her body aching for its own release.

God, there was nothing hotter than knowing she could affect him this way.

She opened her throat, preparing for the wave of hot semen. She'd never swallowed before, but Gracie couldn't wait to taste Nate's essence on her tongue.

Just when she thought it was going to happen, she felt herself being pulled up and away from the very thing she wanted most.

"What are you doing? You said I could—"

"Inside you," he growled. "Now."

He spun her around and guided them to the small kitchen table. The position of his shorts at his thighs constricted his stride, making his steps a bit jerky and awkward as they went.

At the table, he stopped in a space between two of the four chairs and proceeded to place her hands onto its flat surface. Nate yanked her shorts and panties down, hastily removing them from one ankle, but not bothering with the other.

With his hands on her hips, he pulled her backside

toward him. Knowing what he wanted, Gracie slid her arms forward and lifted her ass in the air.

He used a leg to spread hers wider, and she smiled when she felt his blunt tip pressing against her entrance. More than ready to feel him moving inside her again, Gracie braced herself for the glorious intrusion. Then, he stopped.

"Shit. Condom."

She felt him pull away and blurted, "I'm on the pill." With a little more control, she added, "To help regulate things."

She stood straight. From over her shoulder, she realized Nate had frozen in place from her words.

With almost a deer-in-the-headlights stare, he quickly said, "We get tested every six months. I've always come back clean and I haven't been with anyone since my last round."

He'd told her last night it had been a while for him. She believed him then, just as she did now.

To the roots of her soul, Gracie knew she could trust this man with her life.

"Okay," she smiled back at him.

"I've never gone bareback before."

One corner of Gracie's mouth rose. "Me, neither."

Nate blinked, then closed the short distance between them. He didn't go straight for it, like she'd expected. Instead, he leaned down and cupped one side of her face.

Caressing her cheek with his thumb, he locked eyes with her and vowed, "I'd never do anything to hurt you."

"I know," she whispered back. And in that very moment, Gracie gave him the rest of her heart.

After a sweet kiss, Nate moved his lips to her ear. In a low voice that screamed of sex, he commanded, "Put your hands back on the table."

She did as he asked and Nate stepped behind her once more. With a gentle hand against the middle of her back, he pushed her forward.

"Bend over."

This time, when Nate lined himself up, he didn't stop. In one, slow motion, he pushed himself all the way inside.

They both moaned in unison from the indescribable feeling of being skin-to-skin, but then Nate froze in place again.

"Ah, fuck."

"What's the matter?"

"I just need...a minute."

Smiling, Gracie took great satisfaction knowing he was already close to coming. She also decided to get even for him interrupting the best blow job she'd ever given.

Lifting onto her toes, she pressed her ass backward. His fingers dug into her hips and he inhaled sharply.

"Seriously, Gracie. Being bare like this, in this position, is going to turn me into a two-pump-chump if you don't quit that."

"Sounds like a challenge to me. Unless you're not *up* to it." She slid her body back and forth on his cock again.

Nate gave a half-laugh, half growl. "Oh, I'm up. Just not sure how long it's gonna stay that way."

She grinned at him from over her shoulder. "What do you say, we find out?"

He shook his head, but said, "Just remember, I warned you." Then, very slowly, he began pumping himself in and out of her body.

It was the best kind of torture. The position made her feel impossibly full and the angle with which he continued to enter her had his dick brushing up against a sweet spot she never believed existed.

It wouldn't take much to push her over the edge, but Gracie was afraid he might lose it before that could happen. Knowing he'd feel guilty if he climaxed first, she decided to help him get her there.

Steadying herself with her left hand, she slid her right one between her legs. Reaching down to where they were joined, Gracie coated her fingertips with her own arousal.

Nate's body jerked when her fingers brushed against his thrusting cock.

"Shit, Gracie. You're not helping."

"Yes, I am," she teased. Coating her swollen clit, Gracie began to rub it slowly.

Nate thrust harder. Faster. "God, yeah."

Knowing he was getting close, Gracie picked up her own pace. The pads of her fingers moved in small, tight circles until a glorious tingling began to build deep inside her belly.

"I'm close," Nate grunted behind her. His balls slapped against her ass. "Bring yourself there, baby. I need you to come. Now."

The combination of her fingers and his words set her off. Crying out, Gracie rode out the rest of her orgasm as he got himself there, too.

In a sudden and unexpected move, she felt him pull out at the last second and grunt loudly. Several spurts of hot liquid hit her lower back until his body was completely spent.

With loud, heaving breaths, he said, "Stay there."

Not trusting her legs just then, Gracie had no problem obeying the order. She laid her head on the flat surface and waited.

Within seconds, he was back. He first wiped her skin clean with a warm, wet cloth, and then dried her off with another.

Some women might have been offended by his primal act, but not Gracie. On a deeper level, she understood it had nothing to do with taking preventative measures, but was more like he'd staked his claim.

Nate had marked her as his. And she loved it.

After breakfast, they began discussing their afternoon

plans. She and Nate were trying to decide whether they should go fishing or hiking when his phone rang.

"Carter." There was a short pause as he listened to whoever was on the other end of the line. "Hey, Matt." Nate's eyes went back to hers. "Yeah, she's right here. Hang on a sec."

Nate lowered the phone and tapped the screen. "It's Matt. He asked me to put it on speaker so you could hear, too."

Nodding, Gracie said, "Hey, Matt."

"Hey, darlin'. How are ya? Hope my man Nate is treating you well."

Though, Matt couldn't see her, Gracie felt herself blush. "Uh, yeah. He's been really…nice."

Nate's jaw dropped, looking appalled by the sentiment. *Nice?* He silently mouthed.

She cringed, giving him an apologetic look as she shrugged and whispered, "Sorry."

He bit his lip to keep from laughing.

"Nice." Matt repeated. He waited a few beats before adding, "Okay, then. Good to know."

Shit. Was he suspicious? Thankfully, Nate changed the subject before she could find out.

"Tell me you found something."

"Oh, we found something, alright. Gracie, you said Craig never sent you anything, correct?"

For what felt like the billionth time, she tried not to sound as frustrated as she felt.

"No. I never received anything from Craig. Not in person or in any other fashion."

"See, that's interesting, because he said you did."

CHAPTER 13

Gracie's eyes flew to Nate's then back to the phone. Trying to make sense of what he'd just told them, she stammered, "I-I thought Craig was dead."

"He is."

Gracie's shoulder's fell a little. *Damn.* For a second there, she thought maybe they'd gotten the identification wrong or something. In a sweet, comforting gesture, Nate rubbed his free hand across her back a few times.

"You need to explain that, Turner."

"It's kind of a long story, but I'll try to keep it like Gracie. Short and sweet." Beside her, Nate rolled his eyes as his friend kept talking. "Basically, after all you guys left, Jake arranged for your mail to be forwarded to the office."

"Oh, crap!" Gracie exclaimed. "With everything going on, I didn't even think about my mail."

"Don't worry," Matt told her. "That's why Jake makes the big bucks."

Despite the reason for the phone call, Gracie smiled. "Sorry to have interrupted. You were saying?"

"Right. So, anyway, between the regular R.I.S.C. mail, Sarah's and Kole's, and yours, there was quite a bit."

"Thought you said you were making this short, Turner."

"I'm getting there, jackass. Jake was taking the mail back to his office when some of it fell out of his hand. He picked it up off the floor and noticed something on one of the envelopes addressed to Gracie."

"What about it?" Gracie asked, feeling as though she was on pins and needles.

"The name on the return address was Craig Wyatt."

She couldn't hold back her gasp. Her hand flew to her chest. "It was from Craig? H-how is that even possible?"

"That's the thing. There was a note scribbled on the back of the envelope. A nurse at the hospital Craig was in wrote you a short note explaining how Craig had asked her to mail the envelope to you the day after you left for Texas. It got mixed up with some other papers and she forgot all about it. Apparently, she found it a few days ago and went ahead and mailed it."

"What was in it?" Nate demanded.

His back was straight and his voice was tight. Focused. He was back in operative mode, just like that night in the alley.

"A letter addressed to Gracie."

Her heart raced. "What did it say?" she asked, not caring in the least that Jake had opened her mail.

"Basically, Wyatt was letting you know he sent you something important. Something other than the letter. Once he felt it was safe, he'd be in touch to retrieve it."

"Did he say what it was?"

"Not specifically, no. Just that he had evidence against Edric Yavuz that would change President Russell's mind about signing the treaty with Turkey. He didn't go into detail."

"That's why he was killed," Gracie whispered the obvious.

"Agreed," Matt said firmly.

"You don't know what the evidence was?" Nate asked again.

"Unfortunately, no. He purposely didn't go into detail for fear he'd be putting Gracie into danger."

Nate snorted. "Yeah, that turned out well for the asshole, didn't it?"

"Nate!" Gracie scolded, but she could tell he didn't feel a bit sorry for what he'd said.

Those sexy, fierce eyes locked with hers. "That letter is the reason you're in Yavuz' crosshairs. Sorry if I don't have much sympathy for the man who put you there."

"Maybe."

As if he'd just realized Matt was still on the phone, Nate cleared his throat. "What do you mean, maybe?"

"Unless Yavuz saw that letter, he found out about Gracie another way."

"Damn. You're right." The crinkles on Nate's worried forehead smoothed instantly. "Sonofabitch. You think Wyatt gave her up?"

"Wait. What are you talking about?" Gracie interrupted. She hated that they were having this discussion about her when she was standing right there.

Nate looked at her with a somber expression. "You saw the picture, Gracie. You know what was done to Craig. There's only one reason someone does that to a person."

Yeah. She knew. "To get information."

"Right."

Gracie shook her head. "No. Craig wouldn't do that. He wouldn't knowingly put me in danger like that." Hating the sympathy flashing in his eyes, she looked to the phone again. "Matt, you said yourself he didn't put any details in the letter for fear he'd be putting me in danger. Why would he be all covert about whatever it was he had on Yavuz, just to turn around and give me up to him anyway. No, I'm sorry. I don't believe he would do that. Not for a second."

The picture of Craig's mutilated body ran through her mind. She squeezed her eyes shut to make it stop, sending a tear she didn't even realize had formed down her cheek. Cursing, Nate squeezed her shoulder as he tried to comfort her.

Gracie opened her damp eyes and looked into his again. She pleaded with him to believe what she was saying about her friend.

"Craig was a good, kind man, Nate. He was funny and sweet. Most importantly, he was a Navy SEAL. Now, I may not have been in the military, but I understand what that means. What kind of training he had to go through. And, I know we weren't friends for all that long, but Craig never would have given my name to Yavuz or anyone else. No matter what. In my heart, I know that."

"I agree," Matt said through the phone's speaker. "I read Wyatt's record. He was as tough as they come. He would have known they'd kill him after he gave them the one thing they wanted anyway. Don't see a man like Wyatt giving Yavuz that much satisfaction."

Nate nodded. "It's possible Yavuz found out you and Craig spent time together and he assumed Craig gave you whatever evidence he had. A man like Yavuz would've grasped at any size straw to find something that important. With his money and resources, it's not really a stretch to think your name popped up as a possibility."

Gracie reached up and squeezed the hand still covering her shoulder. "Thank you." She wasn't sure why, but Nate's opinion of Craig mattered to her.

He took a deep breath and went back to Matt. "So, what's the plan?"

"We keep digging."

"Why not use Craig's letter?" Gracie asked both men. "We could take it to the authorities. Somehow get it to President Russell so he'd know not to sign that treaty. If that was Craig's goal in this whole thing then maybe, if we do that, Yavuz won't have a reason to come after me."

"Can't," was Matt's only response.

"Why not?"

Nate answered for him. "There's no proof. Right now, all we have is Craig's word that he had *something* on Yavuz."

"Nate's right, Gracie," Matt agreed. "We have no evidence of Yavuz doing anything illegal. Without knowing what it was Craig supposedly sent to you, we have to sit on this until we have tangible proof to take to President Russell."

"So, we're back to square one." She didn't even bother to hide her frustration.

"More like square two," Matt answered her. "At least we know now, with one hundred percent certainty, that what happened to both you and Wyatt are related. We also know that Edric Yavuz is definitely involved. So, really, we're at like square three."

Matt was trying to make her smile again, but it didn't work. Gracie wiped her eyes dry and asked, "What now? Do we just stay here?"

"That's what Gabe wants. For now, he's ordered the two of you to remain there and Sarah and Kole are continuing their pre-wedding whatever it is."

Resigned, she walked away. Standing by the sliding door, Gracie stared out at the water, wishing like hell she and Nate were out there swimming instead of in here, learning that her friend may very well have gotten her killed.

From behind her, Nate finished up the call with his teammate.

"Thanks, Turner. Appreciate the update. I'll try to keep looking on my end, though without knowing what it is I'm looking for, it's going to be the luck of the draw."

"I hear ya, man. I'll be in touch if and when we find something. Stay safe."

"You, too."

Nate's soft footsteps travelled closer before a set of strong, caring arms wrapped around her from behind. Pulling her back against his chest, Nate kissed the top of her head.

"It's going to be okay, Gracie."

"I hope you're right." She turned and wrapped her arms around him, resting the side of her face against his chiseled muscles. "I'm just ready to be home and past all this." His heart thumped heavily against her cheek.

"All of it?"

"Well," she pulled away just enough to look up at him. "I'm hoping *this* can continue on after we get back."

The loving expression in Nate's eyes was surprising as he leaned down and pressed his mouth to hers. His tongue breached her lips as he continued to ease her worry in the sweetest way possible.

When he ended the kiss, he tucked a few loose strands of hair behind her ear. With a low rumble said, "You're stuck with me, baby. Better get used to it."

* * *

Nate was torn. Part of him wanted to be home and have things back to normal. The other part—the bigger part— wanted to stay here. With Gracelynn.

He glanced up at her from over the top of his computer. She'd been a trooper throughout this whole thing, but he knew Matt's phone call yesterday had hit her pretty hard.

After dinner, they'd ended up taking a walk along one of the trails near their cabin. Gracie shared sweet stories of when she and Sarah were younger. He entertained her with tales of his and Scott's many youthful antics that often resulted in one or both of them being injured.

Their stroll was filled with both laughter and comfortable silence. Then, there were those moments Nate was fully aware Gracie was thinking of Craig. Not only his horrific death, but also how he'd inadvertently put a target on her back.

The night ended with them making love to the sound of the rain on the cabin's roof. Nate had purposely gone slower that time, determined to give her as much pleasure as he possibly could while at the same time, taking her mind off her unfortunate reality.

She fell asleep almost immediately afterward, but then tossed and turned throughout the night. Nate hated not being able to invade her dreams and make them better.

He'd spent most of today working every angle he could think of to try and figure out what the hell Craig could possibly have had on Yavuz. Unfortunately, that hadn't left much time for her.

Sitting by the cabin's small fireplace, where she'd been most of the afternoon, he saw her shiver beneath the thin throw they'd found in one of the bedroom closets. With all the rain they'd had lately, the temperature at the lake had dropped significantly.

Pulling the blanket more tightly around her shoulders, Gracie grabbed the poker and stoked the bigger of the two logs he'd put in there a few hours ago.

"You cold?" he asked.

She swiveled her head toward him and gave him a smile that didn't reach her eyes. "A little. It's okay, though."

"I'll go get some more wood."

"This was the last of it, remember?"

Shit. That's right.

"We can run to the campground store and grab another bundle."

"That's okay. Don't worry about it."

Nate stood and stretched his back. "I need to take a break, anyway." He walked to the door and began putting on his boots.

"You mind if I stay here?"

The question surprised him. "Uh, not a good idea."

"Come on, Nate," she said, giving him a look. Standing, she kept the blanket around her as she walked over to where he was. "No one other than Jake and your team knows we're here. There haven't been any other incidents or signs of the men who tried to take me before. I'm pretty sure I'll survive the ten minutes it'll take for you to drive down the road and back."

He finished tying the second boot and went to her. Rubbing his hands up and down her upper arms, he said, "I'm sure you would, but I don't want to risk it. I don't want to risk *you.*"

"It's ten minutes, Nate," she pleaded, then sighed. Unwrapping herself, she slid her arms around his waist and laid her head on his chest. "I'm sorry. I don't know what my problem is today. I'm just in a funk and thought a few minutes alone might help."

Hugging her back, Nate kissed the top of her head then rested his cheek there. "First, there'll be no apologies. I said before, this is a lot to take in, and I meant it. Second, you're probably exhausted. I know you didn't sleep well last night."

"No," she raised her head and looked up at him. "I didn't." Her brows creased. "I hope I didn't keep you up."

"I got plenty of sleep," he lied.

Almost nervously, she licked her lips and asked again, "Can I please stay here? I'll lock the door behind you and I promise to stay inside the entire time you're gone. I just need a few minutes to...I don't know. Regroup, I guess. It'll be easier to do that if you aren't here."

Nate got it. He really did. And she was right. Nothing else had happened and it was just a short trip down the road.

Even though his gut said otherwise, Nate looked back down into those gorgeous, pleading eyes and caved.

"Fine." He'd barely gotten the word out when she smiled wide.

"Thank you."

When did I become such a pushover?

Forcing a serious expression, he squeezed her a little tighter and said, "You know, I'm not sure I like the fact that my leaving makes you so happy."

She chuckled. It was the closest she'd come to laughing all day.

"That's not it. I love being here, with you."

He raised a brow. "You'd better."

Raising on her toes, she gave him a quick kiss. "I do. And I promise I'll be a new woman when you get back."

"Don't want a new woman, sweetheart. I like you just the way you are."

This made her smile grow even more. "Yeah? Well, you're not so bad yourself."

Unable to keep from it, Nate leaned down and put his mouth to hers. What was meant to be a quick kiss turned into something more.

Unfortunately for him, she pulled away before he was

ready. Although, he had a feeling when it came to this woman, he'd never be ready to say goodbye.

"Go. Get the firewood and come back. I think I'm going to run a bath. And who knows," she raised a brow. "Maybe I'll still be in there when you get back."

"I'm going," Nate blurted, making her laugh. "Right now. And I'm begging you, please...whatever you do...do *not* get out of that tub."

Still chuckling, she pushed a hand against his chest. "You'd better hurry, then. Don't want the water getting cold before you get back."

He turned to leave, spun back around and gave her a hard, fast kiss. "Lock the door and do not open it for anyone but me. No exceptions."

Using a finger, she crossed her heart. "No exceptions."

Taking her for her word, Nate grabbed his keys off the small, metal hook above the double light switch and walked out. He prayed lake security wouldn't be out this way, because thoughts of Gracie naked in a sea of bubbles had his foot pushing the gas pedal down as far as it would go.

Of course, his ten-minute trip took twice as long, thanks to a couple who'd messed up the registration paperwork and had to start over. This was followed by their four kids spending another five minutes deciding which snacks and drinks they wanted to buy.

After finally paying for the chopped wood—something that would have taken him less than five minutes to find and cut himself, had the resort allowed it—Nate double-timed it back to the cabin. The entire way there, he imagined Gracie, naked and waiting for him.

Though, he'd only been gone about thirty minutes, he hoped the alone time had done her good.

Back at the cabin, he parked the car and got out. Opening

the driver's rear door, Nate grabbed the thick plastic tie holding the split logs together and headed inside.

The minute he stepped onto the porch, he knew something was wrong.

The door she'd promised to keep locked was slightly ajar and the wood near the lock was splintered. Heart pounding, Nate bent down and silently set the bundle onto the porch's wooden slats.

His training instantly took over as he pulled his concealed pistol from his back waistband.

With his weapon gripped tightly in his right hand, Nate drew in a steadying breath and slowly pushed the door open with his left. He then entered the cabin like the operative he was.

Gun drawn, he checked the space behind the door, then expertly swept the rest of the open area. Nothing.

There were no obvious signs of a struggle. His computer set-up was as he'd left it and Gracie's purse was still hanging off one of the kitchen chairs, which told him they hadn't been robbed.

Fear for Gracie ratcheted through his system, but Nate pushed it back and continued further inside. He wanted so badly to call out for her, but he didn't dare make his presence known, in case the intruder was still in the cabin.

Doing his best to control his breathing, he headed toward the hallway. Nate had just made it past the living room area when the back bedroom door squeaked open and his nightmare unfolded.

Adrian Walker moved slowly toward him. With an arm wrapped around Gracie's waist, he held her tightly against his chest, his other hand pressing a gun to her head.

Nate's hatred toward the man skyrocketed when he noticed the skin on the side of her face was red, as if she'd been struck.

Fucking bastard.

He didn't dare look into Gracie's eyes for fear he'd lose his shit and get her killed. Speaking in a calm and collected voice right then was one of the hardest things Nate had ever had to do.

"Let her go."

Walker smiled. "Ah, good. The big, bad protector has finally arrived."

Seething, Nate held his gun steady as he spoke again, this time through clenched teeth. "I said, let her go!"

The other man ran the barrel of his gun along the side of Gracie's cheek. Stopping just below her chin, he leaned forward and brushed his bearded jaw against her temple, almost as a lover would.

Gracie whimpered, Nate's veins flooding with pure, murderous rage at the sound.

"Hurt her, and I swear to God it'll be the last thing you do."

The warning had no effect on the soulless bastard. Speaking softly in Gracie's ear, Walker said, "Such strong words from the man who left you all alone." Then, to Nate he taunted, "Too bad you didn't take longer. You interrupted our...playtime."

He's working you. Nate knew this. Had been trained for it. Hell, Gracie was still fully dressed.

Still, in that moment, Nate realized all the training in the world couldn't prepare him for the anguish those words caused.

The very idea that this man, this traitor, had touched his woman like that...Christ, he couldn't even think about it.

Blinking, he finally looked at Gracie. A tear had escaped the corner of her eye, ripping him open as it fell.

Nate held the weight of his gun with ease, but the fear and guilt reflected in her eyes nearly had the power to bring him to his knees. She was blaming herself for what was happening and terrified he'd get hurt because of it.

"You're okay, Gracie," he vowed, praying his words would bring her some comfort. "I promise, everything's going to be okay."

Making a clicking sound with his tongue, Walker brought the gun back up to the side of her head. "Shouldn't make promises you can't keep, Carter."

Schooling his expression, Nate nodded. "So, you do know who I am.

"I know everything about you, *Nathan.*"

"Good. That means you know what I do and who I work for."

Walker looked bored. "This interests me, how?"

"Think about it. If she had what Yavuz has been looking for, don't you think we would have used it to take him down by now?"

"And I'm just supposed to believe you know what it is he wants?"

"Craig Wyatt had dirt on Yavuz. Something that would destroy the relationship he's built with Russell, as well as the citizens of the country you once vowed to defend. Isn't that right, *Adrian?*"

The man smiled. "I see you've done your homework, as well."

"I have. I know a lot about you, too. For example, I know you're a very smart man. Otherwise, you would've been caught a long time ago."

Shrugging, Walker said, "Doesn't pay to get caught. And we both know I love my money."

"We do. Which is why we're going to make a deal."

The man's brows rose. "*You* are going to make a deal with me?" Chuckling, he whispered in Gracie's ear. "This should be good."

"Let her go right now, and you walk away free and clear."

Walker laughed. "Your deal is missing one very vital thing. I leave without her, and I don't get paid. To be honest, Nathan, I'm disappointed in you. I thought you were supposed to be the brains on Bravo Team."

It was Nate's turn to shrug. Continuing on with the seemingly casual conversation, he said, "Sure, you won't get any of Yavuz' money. But you'll be out there—" he tilted his head toward the cabin window— "and not stuck in a six by eight cell. Surely a man with your skills would have no problem finding another employer."

During a stretch of silence, Walker actually appeared to be considering Nate's proposal. Nate prayed with everything he had the man would make the smart choice and leave.

Please, God. Don't let him hurt her.

"Or," Walker countered. "I kill you, take the girl, and get paid a shitload of money by the man with the power to destroy your country." He looked down at Gracie. "What do you think, sweetheart? Doesn't that sound like a better plan?"

To her credit, Gracie kept her eyes on Nate, standing stoically, even though Nate knew she was terrified.

That's my girl.

The three of them stood there, waiting in silence while Walker decided to make his next move. When he finally spoke again, his words shocked the hell out of Nate.

"You know, Nathan. You actually make a good point. I think maybe I will take that deal, after all."

Nate forced himself not to react, but holy shit! He hadn't truly believed Walker would just leave them both there and vanish.

Thank you, God.

Those three words of praise had barely left his thoughts when the Walker gave him a feral smile and said, "On second thought…"

Moving faster than Nate had been prepared for, Adrian Walker pulled the gun from Gracie's head, pointed it at him. Then, he pulled the trigger.

The bullet felt like a Mark-50 torpedo as it slammed into Nate's chest. He could hear Gracie screaming his name as he fell, followed by another shot, just before everything went black.

CHAPTER 14

What the ever-loving fuck? It was the first thought Nate had as he slowly began to regain consciousness.

A dull ache was present in his left shoulder and it felt as though a drumline was performing in his head. He didn't know what he'd done the night before, but whatever it was, he and the guys must've had one hell of a time.

"Jesus Christ," he mumbled.

Why did his voice sound so rough? Nate swallowed, the soreness in his throat answering his internal question.

"The fuck did you guys do to me last night?"

Matt's voice reached his ears. "'Bout time you woke your lazy ass up. You gonna stay with us this time?"

This time? Nate forced his heavy eyes to open against the harsh lighting. Someone must have realized his struggle because the room suddenly dimmed. Even without the bright lights, his eyes felt like he'd been rubbing them with 60-grit sandpaper.

Blinking strongly, the room and everyone in it finally came into focus. It took a few seconds longer for Nate to realize he was in the hospital. *What the hell?*

Then, in one horrible, gut-wrenching moment, it all came rushing back.

The cabin…

Adrian Walker…

He looked down at his left hand and saw that the fake wedding ring was gone. Just like…

"Gracie!"

Nate blurted her name as he tried to sit up. Fire spread rapidly throughout his left shoulder and the throbbing in his head got exponentially worse.

"Whoa." Zade dropped the chair he'd been leaning back in and stood.

To Nate's right, Matt pushed against his uninjured shoulder. "Easy there, brother."

Standing on his left, Gabe held up a hand to stop him. "Calm down, Carter. You were shot. You're going to be fine, but you need to relax."

"Yeah, man," Zade tilted his chin toward the dark blue sling supporting Nate's left arm. "You took one to the shoulder and you have one hell of a concussion."

Well, that explains the fire and drums. Through the medicinal fog, Nate remembered moving to the right just as Walker pulled the trigger.

He'd wanted like hell to shoot back, but he couldn't without risking Gracie. So, he'd tried to jump out of the way.

Apparently, he didn't move fast enough.

"Where's Gracie? Is she okay?"

Matt and Zade both looked to Gabe, their faces full of trepidation. True to his character, their team leader didn't bother to sugarcoat it.

"We're still trying to find her."

Oh, God. "How long?"

Regret flashed across Gabe's eyes. "You've been in and out of consciousness for the last day and a half."

Sonofabitch. "I have to get out of here." Nate used his good arm to throw the sheet and blanket off his legs.

"You need to keep your ass exactly where it is." Matt spouted back.

Without turning to look at his teammate, Nate growled, "I have to find her."

"And we will," Gabe assured him.

Nate looked up to see his team leader's cool eyes zeroed in on his. As usual, he appeared calm and rational. *Fuck that.*

"Adrian Walker has her, Dawson. That murdering sono-fabitch has her."

"We know."

That took Nate by surprise. "How?"

"Larry Hays."

It took him a minute to place the name. "The man staying in the cabin next to ours?"

Gabe nodded. "The retired sheriff, yeah. He and his wife were inside watching T.V. when they heard the shots. Hays ran back to their bedroom and grabbed his rifle. Got outside just in time to see Walker put Gracie into a black SUV and speed off."

Nate's pulse spiked from the image Gabe's words created. He felt like he was going to puke.

Matt spoke up. "Hays said he didn't want to shoot for fear he'd hit Gracie, so he focused on helping you. Found you bleeding and unconscious and called it in. His wife kept pressure on your shoulder until EMS got there."

"You were taken to the local hospital first," Zade explained. "They stabilized you, and then Ryker's airlift team arrived a few minutes later to fly you here. Hays may very well have saved your life."

The 'here' Zade referred to was a private medical facility owned and operated by Homeland. Kept secret from the general public, the place was staffed by some of the best doctors and nurses in the country.

"How did Ryker know to send a chopper?"

Gabe gave him a look. "You're shittin' me, right? The guy heads up a covert unit for Homeland, Carter. He has eyes and ears everywhere. A member of R.I.S.C. gets shot, you'd better believe Jason Ryker's gonna know about it."

"There's something else." Zade looked as though he felt sorry for him. "They broke into your apartment the other night. Your neighbor was out of town when you left, but came back the day you were shot. She reported it to the landlord, who then called the police. Derek's brother got wind of it and gave Jake a heads up."

"We got your place secured," Matt assured him. "Jake got a guy to come fix the door and we installed a new system. Yours had been hacked and destroyed."

Shit. Walker and Akmar were better than Nate had given them credit for. "Thanks."

He appreciated what his team had done for him, but the only thing that mattered to him now was finding his woman.

Getting them all back on track, Nate spun around until his legs were dangling over the side of the mattress. "I need to be out there. We have to find Gracie. Christ, Gabe," he looked up at his friend and teammate. "You know what they'll do to her."

"We're going to find her before that happens, Nate," the other man vowed. "But you'll be no good to her if you're lying in a goddamn coma because you refused to follow doctor's orders."

"Fuck the doctors!" Nate yelled.

Didn't they get it? His soul was being ripped to shreds and they were worried about a damn bump on his head.

Sliding off the bed, the bottoms of his bare feet slapped against the cold-as-ice tiled floor. A wave of dizziness hit and his hand flew down to the mattress for support. *Fuck me.*

He stood there a moment, trying to steady himself.

"See, you stubborn ass?" Zade stepped a little closer to the bed. "That's exactly what we're talking about."

"I'm fine," he mumbled back, blinking rapidly. Okay, maybe *fine* was a stretch, but he sure as hell wasn't going to stay around here while Gracie was going through only God knows what.

Walking slower than he cared to, Nate shuffled his feet until he'd reached the plastic bag sitting on the floor, next to an empty chair. Careful not to move too quickly for fear his teammates would start nagging him again, he bent over to pick it up.

"Jesus, man." Matt exclaimed from behind him. "Cover that shit up, will ya? No one wants to see your ass and balls hanging out like that."

Not giving a flying fuck about the opening in his paper-thin gown, Nate stood up and sat the bag down into the chair. With his back still to his friends, he used his good hand to clumsily open its drawstring.

"Where are my clothes?" he grumbled.

"We had to cut them off."

The soft, feminine voice left him startled. Turning around, Nate saw that Olivia McQueen had entered the room.

Shit.

His boss's wife was dressed in a set of form-fitting, black scrubs and her brown hair was pulled back into a ponytail. With a tablet and stylus in her hands, she began tapping the screen.

Being the consummate professional she was, Olivia made no comment about seeing his bare ass—and everything else —on display. Instead, she gave him a sweet smile of relief.

"Hi, Nate."

Nate cleared his dry throat. "Hey, Olivia."

Matt coughed to keep from laughing and Zade was trying hard not smile, looking everywhere but Liv's direction.

Nate wanted to punch the shit-eatin' grins off both assholes' faces.

Olivia smiled bigger, deepening her dimples. "It's good to see you awake and alert."

Normally, he would have been embarrassed as hell by the situation, but there were much more important things to worry about right now.

"Uh, yeah. I'm feeling much better now, so if you could just bring me some scrubs or something, I'll get dressed and be out of your hair."

She took a step forward. "I know you're in a hurry to get out of here, Nate. I also know why. But, you really need to lie back down. Bullet wound aside, you hit your head really hard and you were in and out of consciousness for quite some time."

Clutching the bag containing his belongings—minus his clothes—Nate forced himself to use a softer tone.

"I appreciate the concern, Olivia. I do, but I'm fine. Really."

Concern filled her pretty, hazel eyes. "The tests were negative for any bleeds, but you still have a moderate concussion. If it's not treated properly, it could turn into something more life-threatening."

"All due respect, Olivia, it's not my life I'm worried about right now. So, if you could get me the discharge papers or whatever it is I need to get the hell out of here, I'd really appreciate it."

"Nate, I really think that—"

"I don't give a damn what you think!" The harsh words were out before he could stop them.

The adorable brunette blinked, clearly not expecting the undeserved outburst. Feeling like a total asshat, Nate rushed to make things right.

"Shit, Liv. I'm sorry. I didn't mean to—"

"Glad to see you upright again, Mr. Carter."

All heads turned toward the doorway as Jake stepped into the room. His eyes landed on Nate's, and from the way he was clenching his jaw, Nate knew his boss had heard everything.

Fucking hell.

Clearing his throat again, Nate said, "I'm good to go, Boss."

Nate's eyes slid to Olivia's and he prayed she could see his apology there. Without missing a beat, she went right back into nurse-mode.

"Okay, boys. I need to examine my patient and it's getting kind of crowded in here."

More than ready to be freed from the awkward situation, Matt and Zade made a quick escape. Olivia looked at Gabe and her husband expectantly, but Jake just shrugged.

"Need to talk to them, sweetheart. Promise I won't get in your way."

Though, Olivia looked like she wanted to say more, she simply sighed and turned back to Nate. "I need to take your vitals. It'll be easier if you're sitting on the bed."

Appeasing her, he went back to the bed and sat on the edge. He'd jump through whatever hoops he had to if it meant getting out of here sooner.

After undoing the tie behind his neck, Olivia carefully pulled the material down far enough to access the area above his heart. Beside the thick bandage covering his wound, she pressed the stethoscope's metal disc against his skin. Nate hissed in a breath from the frigid sensation.

"Sorry," Olivia gave him an apologetic smile.

The minute his wife was finished with what felt like a battery of tests, Jake turned to Olivia and said, "I need the room."

After giving her husband a nod, she squeezed Nate's hand. "I'm sorry this happened to you and Gracie. Jake and the others have been doing everything they can." She leaned in and gave him a careful hug, whispering softly, "You'll find her, Nate. I know you will."

Olivia walked to the foot of the bed and put a hand on Jake's arm. With soft, loving eyes, she told him, "You know what he's going through right now. Try to remember that, okay?" Then, leaning up onto her tip toes, she kissed him on the cheek, and left the room.

Gabe wasted no time laying in to him. "What the hell happened in that cabin, Carter?"

Feeling like he'd been sent to the principal's office, Nate went through everything he could remember, not leaving any detail out.

Okay, so maybe he left out a *few* things, but nothing pertinent to what had happened.

When he was finished, he turned to Jake. "You gotta get me out of here, Boss. Please. I have to find her. I have to get to her before—"

Jake interrupted him by ordering Dawson to wait for him outside.

Gabe's eyes slid to Nate's then back to their boss's. With a bob of his head, the big guy made his way to the door.

The space became incredibly uncomfortable during the long seconds it took for the other man to leave. It wasn't until the door had completely shut that Jake finally spoke again.

"It's just us, now, so no bullshit. How are you? Really?"

Surprised he didn't fire him on the spot, Nate told his boss the truth. "Shoulder hurts and I've got the headache from hell." He quickly added, "But, my vision's clear and there's nothing wrong with my shooting arm."

Jake started to shake his head, but Nate refused to be shot down on this.

"Look, I know I fucked up, Jake. So, let me make this right. Let me work with the team until we take down Yavuz and his crew. I need to bring Gracie home. I'll resign the second that happens, if that's what you want, but please. Don't cut me out. Not until I know she's safe."

"I'm not firing you, Carter." One of the man's dark brows rose. "Not yet, anyway."

It wasn't the response Nate expected, but he sure as hell wasn't going to argue. "Thank you. You should know, even if you had, I'd still be going after her."

"I know. It's one of the reasons you still have a job."

"Boss?"

"I'm not gonna have you running off half-cocked with no real plan or any backup."

"How'd you know that's what I'd do?"

Jake sighed and shoved his hands in his jeans pockets. "Because it's exactly what I would do, if the situation was reversed. Hell, I almost *did* do that last year when Liv was taken. Thankfully, I have a kick-ass team on my side who offered their support. And so do you."

Yeah, Nate thought. He did. He also had one hell of a boss.

Needing Jake to know, Nate said, "I didn't lie to you." When Jake's brows turned inward, he explained. "Before, when I told you Gracie and I weren't together. We weren't, then."

"But you are, now." It was a statement, rather than a question.

"Yes," Nate answered honestly. His heart ached. "I have to find her, Jake."

The other man tilted his chin. "I'll get you signed out of here, but before I do, we're going to get a few things straight."

Damn it, they were wasting so much time with this shit.

"Boss, I already told you I'm fine."

Jake put his hand palm-up. As hard as it was, Nate understood he needed to shut his mouth and listen.

"First, as Bravo's team leader, Gabe will decide how active a role you'll play in this."

"Meaning?"

"Meaning, if he doesn't feel you're up to it or he believes you're going to be a liability, either to yourself or your team, your ass sits on the sidelines while the others go in after her."

Nate clenched his jaw. No way in hell he'd sit back while his team risked their lives for his woman. Unfortunately, he wasn't really in the position to argue.

"Fine. What else?"

The other man's tense expression softened with a painful understanding. "What you're feeling? That fear and guilt swirling in your gut? The uncertainty of what's happening to Gracie? I get it."

Nate thought back to what Olivia said to Jake before leaving the room. As if reading his mind, Jake explained just how well he understood.

"You know about what happened to Liv last year, right?"

Nate's chest tightened. The idea of anyone as sweet and caring as Olivia going through what she had cut him deep. "I know she was taken by a drug lord, but your team found and rescued her."

Jake nodded. "That wasn't the end of it. What we didn't make public was what happened after we got her back home to the States." A haunted look came over the man's eyes. "Long story short, I fucked up and Olivia nearly died because of it."

"Damn."

Blinking away the terrible memories, his boss drew in a deep breath. "My point in telling you all this, Nate, is so you'll believe me when I say I do understand how you feel right now. You want Gracie back and you want to end the fuckers responsible."

Nate nodded. "Yes, sir. I do."

"You'll get that chance. I promise. We've been doing everything we can on our end, but, as you know, this sort of thing can take time."

"Gracie doesn't have time."

"Agreed. But we have to be smart about it, or we could end up putting her at an even greater risk. You hear what I'm saying?"

"Yeah, Boss. I hear you."

Looking pleased with that answer, Jake said, "Good. I'll have Liv bring you some scrubs and get the doctor to sign your discharge papers."

Because he was the kind of man who could get shit like that done.

"Thanks, Jake."

The other man turned and crossed the room toward the door. He was about to reach for the knob when he faced Nate again.

"Oh, and Carter?"

"Yeah, Boss?"

"You ever yell at my wife that way again, and losing your job will be the least of your concerns."

Fuck me. "Understood."

With a final nod, Jake left him alone in his room.

Running his good hand over his face, Nate clutched the muscles at the back of his neck. He closed his eyes and thought the words he wished Gracie could hear.

I'll find you, baby. I swear to God, I will.

CHAPTER 15

Gracelynn no longer felt any pain. Her raw, bloodied wrists no longer throbbed, and she barely noticed the many bruises Achim Akmar had left on her body that first day.

She couldn't even bring herself to cry anymore. Of course, that may have something to due to her being dehydrated.

When smacking her around hadn't gotten her to give up the file they thought she had, Yavuz had ordered her not to be fed again until she talked.

Not wanting her to die before that happened, he had allowed Akmar to bring her a glass of water each morning and night. That was all she'd consumed in the past three days.

At least, she thought that's how long it had been.

Three agonizing, torturous days since Nate had been gunned down right in front of her—*because* of her—and she'd been drugged and brought here, to what she assumed was one of Edric Yavuz' many homes.

As much as it broke her heart to admit it, Gracie had finally come to the conclusion that Nate had gotten off easy.

One bullet, then poof. Gone. *Just like that.*

Lying there, with her wrists chained to the room's beautiful, ornate bed, Gracie tried to snap her fingers with the thought. She giggled, her mind muddled and her movements sluggish, thanks to whatever chemicals she still had running through her veins.

Beating and starving her hadn't yielded the results Yavuz desired, so this morning he'd tried another method. A few hours ago, Achim had come back into her room. She'd tried to fight him off, but like all the other times, her efforts had been futile.

Gracie had been tossed into a chair in the middle of the room, her wrists and ankles tied. Then, the bastard had shoved a needle into a vein in her left arm. Some sort of truth serum, they'd told her.

Which, of course, hadn't worked, either. *You can't divulge what you don't know.*

Yavuz, the idiot, thought she was holding out on him in hopes of being released. Gracie snorted to herself. She knew better than to think this would end with anything other than her death.

She knew her fate. Had even accepted it. She'd be murdered, just as Craig had been. And Nate.

God, Nate. I'm so sorry.

Her eyes caught a glimpse of the gold band still shining on her finger. A tear escaped the corner of her eye, trickling down her temple onto the pillow below her head.

Huh. Guess I do have a few more left in there, after all.

Blinking against them, Gracie shook her head and tried to clear her mind. The drugs were starting wear off, but she still felt a bit loopy.

Part of her wanted to just give up, but she couldn't bring herself to. Nate wouldn't want that. She could practically hear him yelling at her to snap out of it and keep fighting.

So, she would. For him.

The door to the room opened, but instead of Achim Akmar standing there, it was Yavuz. The bastard smiled.

"You are awake. Excellent."

"No," Gracie glared back at him. "Excellent would be watching your head explode right off your shoulders."

She knew better than to provoke him, but those damn drugs made it even harder than normal for her to keep her big mouth shut.

Rather than yelling or striking out at her, as she'd thought he would, Yavuz threw his head back and laughed. The asshole *laughed.*

"The drugs are still working, I see. It is so refreshing to hear the truth fall from a woman's mouth for a change." He stepped farther inside the room. "It is not often I hear such honesty in my line of work."

"And which work would that be?" Gracie asked the madman. "Crooked politician or cold-blooded murderer?"

Yavuz laughed again. "Both, I suppose."

"Well, since you believe the drugs are working, that means you believe me when I say I don't know what it is you want from me. If Craig sent me something, and I'm not so sure he actually did, I obviously have no idea what it was or where it could be."

"You know, Miss McDaniels, I am starting to believe you. In fact, I think you're just an innocent pawn in all this."

Gracie laid her head back onto the pillow and muttered, "About fucking time."

Making a clicking sound with his tongue, Yavuz shook his head and scowled. "Now, that's no way for a lady to talk."

Was this guy serious?

"Sorry, Edric. My manners left about the same time your buddy Akmar punched me in the face and then put a gun to my head."

"Yes, well. He is very good at what he does. We all have certain things we have to do."

"And what is it you think you have to do, Mr. President?" Gracie spit the title out like it had left a bad taste in her mouth. "Protect something you clearly have no real threat of losing? Craig's secret died with him. You're free and clear to do whatever the hell it was you'd planned to do. So, why don't you just let me go?"

Faux sympathy crossed his face. "Oh, my dear Gracelynn. We both know it's too late for that."

Though, she'd known it was a ridiculous hope to carry, a tiny part of her had still held on to the idea he'd feel sorry for her and let her go back to her life. A life that no longer included Nathan Carter.

Another tear slipped from her eye. She hated the satisfaction it gave Yavuz when he saw it.

"Do not cry, Gracelynn. I have not come to kill you, yet."

"Then, why are you here?"

He smiled that sick, evil smile again. "You may not know where the evidence against me is hidden, but having you in my possession keeps me protected. No one would dare come after me to rescue you. If they did, they'd only be ensuring their deaths, as well as yours."

"So, what is your plan, then? To keep me here indefinitely?"

"Not indefinitely, no. Just for the next few weeks, until President Russell and I sign the treaty guaranteeing US protection for the people of my country."

Gracie snorted. "You don't give a shit about anyone but yourself. So, what's this treaty really about?"

Seemingly impressed, Yavuz grinned. "You're a very intelligent woman, Miss McDaniels." Shrugging, he said, "I suppose it won't hurt to tell you, since you're death has already been ordered to be carried out the minute your president and I have signed our names on the dotted line."

What an arrogant prick.

"That agreement puts me as an ally of your country. It will allow me to sit in on important meetings with your president. Meetings which will divulge high-level information. Information I can then bring back to my country to use against the United States. Eventually, I will gain enough trust within your government to infiltrate and destroy your precious country from the inside out."

Jesus. This guy wasn't just arrogant. He was insane.

Yavuz looked at his watch. "Oh, dear. I did not realize the time. I have a meeting I must attend. Actually, it is a conference call with President Russell, himself."

Gracie didn't bother to hide her sarcastic tone when she said, "Tell him I said hi."

Chuckling, Yavuz turned toward the door. "I'll do that," he told her from over his shoulder, just before shutting and locking the door behind him.

So, this was how she'd be spending the rest of her days. Chained to a bed in what should have been a gorgeous room. Alone.

If only she'd listened to Nate and gone with him to get that damn firewood. He'd still be alive, and she'd be with him instead of lying here, waiting to die, too.

She'd never forget the look on Nate's face when he realized Adrian Walker was about to shoot him. His eyes had grown so wide.

In that last second, he'd tried to move to the side, away from the bullet's trajectory, but he was too late.

Gracie had screamed, then. Over and over, she'd screamed his name, but Nate remained on the floor where he'd fallen. His body still and bleeding.

She remembered thinking if she could just get to him and

stop the bleeding, he'd be okay. Before she had the chance, Walker had stuck a needle in her neck, whatever chemicals the syringe had been filled with causing her to lose consciousness almost immediately.

She was taken and Nate was left in the cabin to die alone.

"I'm sorry, Nate," she whispered to him. Eyes closed, more tears fell as she pictured his beautifully handsome face smiling back at her. "I'm so, so sorry."

Unable to handle the grief festering up inside, Gracie gave into her worn down body's need for rest and the remnants of the drugs she'd been given.

Within minutes, she was unconscious once again.

* * *

"Goddamnit!"

Nate slammed his laptop closed and stood from Jake's couch. Ignoring the pain and pull in his shoulder, he linked his fingers on the top of his head and began to pace the room.

There had to be *something* they'd missed that would lead them to Gracie. For the life of him, he just didn't know what.

That was the most frustrating part. He was supposed to be the brainiac of the team, yet every lead he thought they had was nothing more than a dead end. Every. Single. One.

Maybe I'm in the wrong profession.

"Fuck!" he shouted out at no one in particular.

From the corner of his eye, he saw Sarah jump a little. She'd been curled up in one of Jake's recliners, her phone clutched tightly in her fist.

His heart broke at the site of her sitting like that, as if she expected Gracie to simply call her up and say hello.

"That really necessary?" Kole glared up at him from across the room.

He was sitting at Jake's dining room table going through the files Ryker had given them. They contained copies of pretty much everything Homeland had on Edric Yavuz., Achim Akmar, and Adrian Walker.

Kole was his best friend, but right now, Nate was pretty sure the guy would give him a second bullet hole if he thought he'd get away with it.

Ignoring Kole's death stare, Nate addressed the group. "We're wasting our time with this shit. It's been three fucking days and we're no closer to finding Gracie now than when we started."

"He's right," Jake and Gabe entered the room together. "Which is why Gabe and I decided to bring in some help. Another team."

"Who?" Nate asked their boss, clearly not liking the idea.

"They're good, Carter," Gabe stated with confidence. "And, they're already positioned near Turkey, which is where we believe Yavuz took Gracie."

"You know where she is?" Nate took three long steps toward Gabe. "Then, why the hell are we still here?"

Jake raised his palm. "We don't have an exact location, yet, but we hope to, soon. King," he looked to Zade. "Why don't you and Nate run into town and grab some pizzas? Put them on the company card. In the meantime, Gabe and I will be in the war room on a conference call with Ryker. He's helping coordinate our meeting with the guys from the other team."

Nate wanted to start yelling again. "All due respect, Jake, I don't want to go to town for fucking pizza. I need to be here. Helping."

"You need a break, Carter." Nate opened his mouth to argue, but Jake stopped him cold. "That's an order."

Jake and Gabe disappeared down the hallway to the back of the house. Zade stood from his seat at the end of the couch and said, "Come on, Nate. Sooner we get the food, the sooner we can get back to work."

"Take Turner with you. I'm staying here."

Matt, who was sitting in the chair across from Kole, looked at Zade, then over to Nate.

"Uh, Carter? Boss said it was an—"

"Order," Nate finished for him. "Yeah, I got that. Listen, we don't need some other guys coming in and telling us what to do on this. We can find her on our own. *I* can find her. But I won't if I'm playing fucking pizza delivery boy instead of being here, where I'm needed."

Kole looked as though he was about to say something, but pressed his lips together and kept silent.

"What?" Nate held his arms out to his side, opening himself up to whatever his friend wanted to throw at him.

Kole shook his head and mumbled, "Nothing," before turning back to the file in his hand.

Fuck that.

From across the room, Nate hollered out, "You got something to say, Jameson? Say it."

"Kole, don't," Sarah sat up a little straighter in her chair.

"It's okay, Sarah," Nate assured her. "Really. I mean, I already know what your fiancé is thinking. I just want to hear him say it." He looked back over at Kole. "You've been keeping that shit in ever since you got back, so go ahead. Spit it out."

"Come on, guys," Zade tried to keep the peace amongst the two friends. "This isn't helping."

"No, he's right." Kole stood from his chair and slowly began walking toward the living room. "You want to know what I'm thinking? Fine. You had one job, Nathan. One. Fucking. Job. And you're gonna stand there and whine because Jake has someone who might be able to help us get Gracie back faster? Seriously?"

"We know nothing about these guys, Kole." Nate took a couple steps closer. "You really want to risk her life by trusting some other team we've never worked with? Guys we've never even met before?"

"Well, we wouldn't have to, if you'd just—"

"Kole!" Sarah reprimanded her fiancé, but it was too late. The damage was already done.

"If I'd what, Kole?" Nate brought himself nearly toe-to-toe with his friend. "Say it. We wouldn't be asking for help if I'd just what?"

Kole had never looked at him the way he was now. Like he was the enemy, rather than his friend and teammate.

"Been thinking with your brain instead of your dick."

And there it was.

"Don't," Nate warned Kole.

"Don't what? Call you out on your fuck-up? Just admit it, Nate. You were so busy trying to get into her pants, you forgot why you were even at that fucking cabin to begin with. Shit, you dropped the ball before you and Gracie even left town."

"What the hell are you talking about?"

"The picture, Nate!" Kole yelled in his face. "You left that fucking picture of you and your brother in your apartment for them to find. You may as well have drawn them a goddamn road map."

"Fuck you, Kole. You have no idea what happened at that cabin, and you sure as hell don't know that picture had anything to do with them finding us."

Nate wasn't about to admit to the jackass that he'd already been beating himself up about the picture of him and Scott. It had been on his mantle for so long, he hadn't given it a second thought.

"No, fuck you, Nate. This is Gracie we're talking about. She's my fiancée's sister! She's going to be *my* sister!"

"And she's my—" He stopped himself short. Christ, he'd almost said *wife*. No, she'd only been pretending to be. And Nate had loved every single minute of it.

"She's what, Nate?" Kole kept on with his rant. "Your newest fuck-buddy?"

Nate's fist was flying through the air before he even realized he'd moved. His knuckles slammed into the side of Kole's jaw, causing the mouthy bastard to fall down to the wooden floor.

"Kole!" Sara leapt from the chair and ran over to his side.

Blood dripped from the split Nate put in his friend's bottom lip. Hovering over him, Nate spoke low and deadly.

"You have no fucking clue what went on with me and Gracie, and frankly, it's none of your goddamn business."

Surprising both Kole and Sarah, Nate held out his hand to help Kole up. Once the other man was back on his feet, Nate kept his grip tight.

"I love you like a brother, Kole. You know that. But you ever disrespect Gracie like that again, and you and I? We're done."

Not waiting for a response, Nate turned and walked over to the sliding doors leading to Jake's back patio. Without another word to anyone, he went outside, closing the door behind him.

He wasn't sure how long he stood out there, looking up at the night sky. His mind was so completely filled with thoughts of Gracie, Nate became oblivious of the passing of time.

He thought about that first night they met. How desperate he'd been to simply talk to her.

A corner of his mouth curved up slightly, remembering the nervous text she'd sent to Sarah when they'd decided to take their food to his apartment. The raw, emotional look in her eyes the first time they made love.

237

At some point, Nate found himself wondering if he and Gracie were staring at the exact same stars at this exact same moment. The possibility eased his pain slightly, making him feel as though they were somehow still connected.

Then, he remembered what Jake had said about Yavuz possibly being back in Turkey. If that was really the case, it meant Gracie was eight time zones away from him.

For her, it was already tomorrow morning. If she was even still alive.

Nate shook his head. He would *not* give up on her. Not ever.

The door behind him slid open, but he didn't bother turning around. He was surprised to see it was Kole who'd stepped up beside him. The other man was carrying two paper plates stacked with slices of meat-covered pizza.

"Thanks, but I'm not really hungry."

Kole set both plates onto the glass table behind them, and then turned to Nate. "Look, man. About what I said in there. I would never intentionally disrespect Gracie. She's like my little sister. And what went down at the cabin," Kole paused. "That shit could've happened to any one of us. It wasn't your fault and I never should have implied that it was. I don't blame you, Nate. No one does."

I do. Nate would never forgive himself for leaving her alone the way he had.

When he saw Nate wasn't going to say anything, Kole added, "Seriously, man. I know you never would have left that cabin if you didn't think she was safe. I only said those things to you because I'm pissed and scared and, I don't know. I just want her back."

"You think I don't?" Nate looked at his friend incredulously.

Kole studied him a moment. Then, very slowly, the

corners of his mouth raised. "You really care about her, don't' you?"

Rather than answer the question, Nate responded with one of his own. "Is that really so hard for you to believe?"

Kole's immediate reaction was to shake his head and say, "No, man." Then, the truth came out. "Well, maybe a little bit. Yeah."

"Right." Nate clenched his jaw and shook his head before looking away.

"Oh, come on, Nate. Can you honestly blame me? The entire time I've known you, you've had no desire to settle down. Hell, even the night you and Gracie met you were spouting off bullshit about how love isn't for you and all that crap. So, yeah. If I'm being completely honest, it does surprise me. But, I see it now."

Nate's brows crunched together. "What do you see?"

"The way you are when you talk about her. And you've got that same look in your eye now that I'm sure I had the night that asshole tried to hurt Sarah."

"What look is that?"

Kole smirked. "Like you're ready to kill anyone who dared hurt your woman." He rubbed his fat lip. "Or knock the shit out of someone stupid enough to run their mouth about her."

Nate gave him a half-smile. "I'd say I'm sorry, but I'd be lying."

Kole chuckled. "I know."

A moment of silence passed between the two men before Nate began speaking again. "I get that Gracie and I haven't known each other all that long. And yeah, I know the list of serious relationships I've had in the past is, well, non-existent. But I think I might be…" he paused, swallowing hard. "I *know* I'm in…"

He didn't say the words, terrified of what they meant for him.

With a knowing smile, Kole gave him a nudge. "Just say it, man."

Nate looked his friend in the eyes and admitted, "I'm in love with her, Kole. Ah, Jesus."

Sucking in a breath, Nate bent over at the waist and rested his hands on his knees. Feeling as though he were going to puke all over Jake's concrete slab, he forced himself to take several slow, deep breaths.

Kole barked out a laugh and slapped the back of Nate's good shoulder. "Welcome to the club, my friend."

"God." Nate stood up straight again. "What the fuck am I going to do, Kole? I can't lose her, man. I can't."

All signs of humor gone, Kole looked him square in the eye and vowed, "You won't."

CHAPTER 16

Two days later...

Sweat trickled down Nate's back in a steady stream. A heavy, protective vest covered his thin tee, which was becoming more and more soaked as the minutes passed by.

From behind his dark lenses, he kept watch out the abandoned home's cracked window and inwardly cursed Turkey's sweltering heat.

Fucking shithole country. If he never stepped foot in it again, it would be too soon.

After landing at a private air strip not far from their current location, one of Homeland's local assets picked them up and drove them here. To the middle of fucking nowhere.

Using the structure's thick, stone wall as a shield, Nate kept himself hidden from the outside while maintaining a decent view of the immediate area out front. So far, he'd seen no sign of the men they were waiting to meet.

"They're late," he grumbled.

"They'll be here."

Nate looked at Gabe. The powerful man was leaning against the wall to his right, legs casually crossed at his ankles. If it wasn't for the M16 resting in his hands, Gabe would look like he was just hanging with his buddies.

"If these guys can't be trusted to show up on time, how the hell are we supposed to believe they'll have our backs?"

Gabe glanced at his watch then to Nate. "They're two minutes late, Carter. They'll be here."

"Seriously, dude," Matt sided with Gabe. "We may not know these guys, but McQueen does."

"He's right," Zade chimed in from the window at the back. "Jake said he and the one guy...what was it he called him?" He looked to Matt for the answer.

"Ghost."

"Right. Jake said he and Ghost worked some ops together back when Jake was still Delta. Said these guys are the best."

"Well," Matt smirked. "Aside from us."

Zade wore a smug grin. "Duh."

Both men snickered, but Nate wasn't in the laughing mood. This was the most important mission of his life, and they were getting into bed with a team they'd never worked with. Plus, they were a man down.

Kole had chosen to stay behind to ensure Sarah's safety. It was just a precaution and Nate got it, but right now he couldn't help but wish his best friend was here. With him.

"I don't give a shit how good these guys are," Nate looked at Matt. "If their intel on Yavuz' location isn't solid, all we're doing is wasting time."

Gabe pushed himself off the wall and walked over to him. "We're all worried about her, Carter. But, you know as well as I do, Jake wouldn't have sent us all this fucking way if he wasn't certain these guys could help us bring her home."

With a loud sigh, Nate turned to his team leader again. "I know. Logically, I know you're right. I just wish we were doing something besides sweating our asses off in this crackerjack box."

It was nothing more than a one-room clay structure on the outskirts of Gaziantep. The city itself was quite large, but where they'd been sent to wait was isolated.

With the exception of the occasional tree here and there, the land around them was all but baron. They were like sitting ducks in a very small pond, which did nothing to help Nate's already hyped-up anxiety.

"You know how Delta guys are. They're as secretive as they come."

Zade smiled. "Unlike you SEALS."

Gabe raised a brow at the former Marine. "Yeah? What are you implying, King?"

With an incredulous expression, Zade provoked the formidable man. "You're kidding, right? I mean, you do know how to tell whether a group of guys are SEALs, don't ya, Dawson?" When Gabe remained silent, Zade teased, "Wait long enough, and they'll tell ya."

"You're a real funny guy," Matt smarted off, sticking up for his fellow Navy serviceman. "For a jarhead."

"I'll take being a jarhead over a frogman any day," Zade spouted back.

Gabe gave Zade an evil smile. "Keep it up, King. You'll joke your way right into an extra week's worth of training."

"Oh, come on, Boss," Zade looked to Gabe. "You know I love you and your sexy frog legs." He kissed the air, and then waggled his brows a few times, making Matt laugh.

"Christ," Gabe groaned. "It's like working with a bunch of twelve year olds."

Nate started to smile, too, but something outside caught his eye. It took him a few seconds to realize there were two black jeeps with tinted windows coming down the dirt road.

"Look alive, boys," he announced to the others. "We've got company."

Instantly on alert, the men positioned themselves on either side of the door. Nate and Matt took the left, while Gabe and Zade covered the right.

With guns in their hands, the men of Bravo Team watched and waited to see who would step out of those two vehicles. Parking a few feet from the building, the drivers and passengers began exiting the jeeps.

Four men approached them. Three wore matching desert camo and vests much like what Nate and his team had on. Also like Bravo, their long guns were secured in straps running diagonally across their chests.

All three were tall, the one bringing up the rear standing well over six feet. That guy had short, dark hair and was darker complected than the other two. Like Gabe, he was also built like a fucking brick house.

The man to Nate's left appeared to be right at six feet—still tall, but definitely shorter than the human tower in the back—and also had brown hair. Though, not by much, he looked to be a bit older than the other two and walked with an air of confidence that made Nate think he was the one in charge.

To his right was a third member of the team. Also standing over six feet, the man's hair was a bit longer than regulation and his arms were covered in bright ink. Of course, Delta came with its own set of rules, so it didn't really come as much of a shock.

Much shorter than the others, the man walking in front was dressed in worn jeans, a light blue button-up, and ball cap.

With his head hung low, it was hard to make out his features, but when one of the Delta guys put a hand on his shoulder and gave him a slight nudge, Nate caught a glimpse of the all-too-familiar face.

He was looking at Baron Karos, Ryker's useless prick of an informant.

"Barry?" he growled. Nate looked over at Matt. "What the hell?"

If Barry was here, it was because he had intel that could lead them to Gracie. It also meant he'd most likely held out on them when they were trying to track down Achim.

"So help me, if he knew something that could have prevented all this..." Nate didn't finish the sentence, but his unspoken words were clear.

I'll fucking kill him.

Not waiting for Gabe's okay, Nate walked around Matt and swung open the wooden door.

"What the fuck is he doing here?"

Hearing his sharp tone, the Delta men stopped their forward progress and began to reach for their guns. When they saw Nate's gaze was honed in solely on Barry, they relaxed a little.

Hiding his head—Nate wasn't sure if it was in fear or shame, nor did he give a flying fuck which—Barry took a couple steps backward, bumping into one of the other guy's chests.

"Watch it," grumbled the man he'd hit.

"You Carter?" The man to Nate's left asked.

Nate gave him a single tilt of his head. "You are?"

"Ghost." He stepped forward and held out his gloved hand for Nate to take. "Good to meet you, though I wish it were under better circumstances."

Nate shook his hand and muttered, "Thanks for coming."

"No problem. Always happy to help our brothers out, active duty or otherwise. Especially if it means rescuing an innocent woman from the clutches of a couple shitfucks like Akmar and Yavuz."

Damn. The guy actually seemed okay.

"This is Fletch," Ghost pointed to his teammate on Nate's right. "The big guy back there is Coach, and from the sounds of it, you already know our new friend, Barry."

"Yeah," Nate bit out. "We fuckin' know him." The chicken-ass bastard was still focused on the dirt at his feet. "Not sure why you bothered bringing him here, though. This guy doesn't know shit about shit. Isn't that right, Barry?"

"Actually," Fletch came forward. "I think you'll be surprised to hear what good ole' Barry knows."

Ready to kick the pipsqueak's ass, Nate started to take a step forward. A strong hand on his shoulder stopped him.

"Gabe Dawson." Reaching around Nate, he held his hand out for Ghost. "Bravo Team Leader. This is Matt, our medic, and Zade's one of our snipers. Appreciate the assist. Come on in."

Nate stepped aside to let the four men enter the small space. It took everything he had not to grab ahold of Barry as he passed by and squeeze his scrawny little neck.

"Well," Ghost spoke as they all chose a spot to stand inside. "McQueen and I may not have been on the exact same team back in the day, but we worked enough joint ops for me to know the kind of man he is. So, when our commander called to fill me in on the situation with your office manager, I didn't hesitate to offer my help."

"She's a hell of a lot more than that." Nate didn't elaborate, but then again, he didn't need to.

Ghost nodded. "Jake filled me in on that part, as well. Don't worry, Carter. My team and I have been where you are. We won't stop until we have your woman back in your arms, safe and sound."

"No offense," Matt spoke up, "but we were expecting a few more guys than this."

Fletch responded. "Not everyone could come. We've been over the border in Syria finishing up an op. The rest of the team stayed back to tie things up on that end while we came here."

Better than nothing, I guess.

"I'm assuming you want to get on this ASAP, so we'll fill you in on what we've learned and go from there." Ghost looked to Gabe for approval.

Gabe nodded. "Share away."

Looking down at Barry, Ghost prompted him, "Go on, Barry. Tell them what you told us."

Jaw clenched, Nate and the others stood quietly as Barry shared what he came to say.

"Akmar brought the woman you are searching for to a farm not far from here."

Nate's pulse spiked. "How close?"

"About a forty minute drive."

Motherfucker. All this time, they'd been waiting for these guys to show, and Gracie was less than an hour away from them? Nate's patience was wearing dangerously thin.

"You know this, how?" Gabe asked Barry.

"My cousin, Rasat, is a guard for Edric Yavuz. Has been for the past two years. He said the woman was taken there a few days ago."

"Is she okay?" Nate stepped forward, unable to keep from asking. "Did your cousin say whether or not Gracie had been hurt?"

Please say no. God, please say no.

"Rasat stands guard outside the house. He has seen the woman a few times through the window, but that is all."

"What did he see? Did Rasat tell you what condition she was in? What exactly did he see, Barry?"

"Carter." Sensing he was dangerously close to losing his shit, Gabe had said his name in a low, even tone.

Nate whipped his head around. "I need to know if she's okay, Gabe. We need to know whether or not she's able to…" Nate swallowed. "If she can walk herself out of there once we get to her."

"My cousin says he watched through the window her first day here."

Barry's tone was full of regret, sending Nate's heart into his throat. "Tell me," he ordered the nervous man. When Barry hesitated to answer, Nate yelled, "What the fuck did he see?"

"Achim was beating the woman. Hitting and kicking her. Rasat did not watch long for fear *he* would be discovered and beaten for becoming distracted while guarding the property. I am sorry."

Nate sucked in a breath. The thought of Achim using his fists on Gracie was worse than any direct hit he'd ever taken.

"Sonofabitch," Zade hissed from behind him.

Matt was just as upset. "Swear to Christ, I want to rip that motherfucker's head clear off his shoulders."

Even Gabe, who remained calm in even the most intense situations, was clearly fuming. "Don't worry. Achim will get what's coming to him."

"I am sorry I do not know more about the woman."

Nate snapped. "You're *sorry?*" Grabbing the front of Barry's shirt, he shoved the other man's back against the nearest wall. "You lying piece of shit! You said you didn't know anything about Achim. You could've asked your cousin where to find him the first time we came here. If you had, Gracie wouldn't be with him now!"

"I-I did not know Rasat was working for Yavuz until now. I swear it!"

"Bullshit!" Nate got into his face. "You expect us to believe this cousin of yours just happened to come to you out of the blue and tell you who he works for and what he saw? Do we look that fucking stupid to you?"

"I tell you the truth. Rasat came to me earlier this week and told me everything."

"Why?" Gabe asked from beside Nate. "Why now?"

"Rasat, h-he wants out. He does not like what Yavuz has become."

"What Yavuz has become, Barry," Nate growled, "is a lying, murdering sonofabitch."

"I know," Barry bobbed his head. "It is why my cousin wants to leave his job. But he is too afraid. No one leaves a position like that alive."

"Of course they don't," Ghost spoke up. "They know too much."

"Precisely," Barry agreed.

"I still don't get it." Nate shoved the other man free and stepped back. "Surely this isn't the first time Rasat has witnessed Yavuz and his men hurting an innocent person. What changed?"

Barry's eyes slid from Nate's to Ghost's, which pissed Nate off even more. "Don't look at him, asshole. I asked the question. What makes this time different?"

Shame crossed over the man's face. "The Navy SEAL. The one you asked about when you were here before."

"Craig Walker. What about him?"

"His unit was supposed to meet with me the day they were hit with the bomb. I was supposed to give them information on a weapons dealer who has since been apprehended."

"Get to the point, Barry," Gabe ordered.

"Rasat was there. Standing guard outside when Yavuz and Achim killed him. My cousin came to me because he knows I have worked with the Americans in the past. He has agreed to testify against Yavuz and Achim in exchange for asylum."

"Holy shit," Matt exclaimed excitedly. "We've got him. Rasat is a witness. We've fucking got both Yavuz and Achim."

"We do," Ghost concurred. "We've been ordered to bring them both back to the States."

"Hold up," Nate raised a hand, skepticism written all over his face. "Our government gave us extradition rights for Edric Yavuz and Achim Akmar solely based on a statement by a man who is cousins with a guy who works for Yavuz? The same guy, by the way, who sat by while an American hero was tortured to death? Seriously?"

"Well, that, and we also have this."

Ripping open the Velcro flap from one of the pockets at his thigh, Ghost pulled out a phone and tapped the screen. He held it up for Nate and the others to see.

It was small and grainy, but the picture appeared to be of two men talking in a middle-eastern alleyway. Nate leaned in closer, his murderous rage returning when he recognized one of the men.

"Is that Yavuz?"

Ghost nodded. "Yeah. And if you look closely enough, standing guard in the background is a guy who looks an awful lot like Achim Akmar."

"Who's the other one? The man Yavuz is shaking hands with?"

"Shamir Nazari. He's a known arms dealer from Syria who acquires and sells specialized weaponry."

"Such as?"

"Bombs. Bioweapons." Matt jumped in, shaking his head in disbelief. "Most recently, there's been chatter that he's opened his sales to nuclear weapons."

Nate shot him a questioning glance, so Matt explained. "First heard about this bastard when I was working with

FAST. We were always keeping an eye out for him or any of his known associates. Like Adrian Walker, Nazari's a slick bastard. Always manages to make his escape."

Nate turned back to Ghost. "Where did you get this picture?"

"Miss McDaniel's phone."

The deep answer came from his left. Nate turned his head in that direction. The tall guy named Coach was staring right at him.

"The hell you say," Nate retorted back. He could tell by the look on the guy's face he didn't much appreciate being called a liar. *Isn't that too damn bad.* "I looked at her phone myself. There were no emails, texts, or documents sent to her containing that pic."

A muscle in Coach's chiseled jaw bulged, but he kept his tone even. "It was hidden within one of the selfies Craig Wyatt sent to your girl."

"Yeah? How the fuck did you guys get it, then?" Nate challenged.

He knew he was being a Class-A jerk, but couldn't seem to stop. If he did, he'd have to admit he'd missed a vital piece of information. One that could have locked Yavuz' ass up before he ever had the chance to touch his Gracelynn.

Coach exhaled loudly, keeping his cool as he explained. "McQueen called us on our way here. Said he'd been racking his brain trying to figure out where Walker would have managed to hide a file so Gracie would know nothing about it. He had a guy named Derek West take a second look at her busted phone. Said West was part of R.I.S.C.'s Alpha Team and is some sort of genius when it comes to computers."

Mumbles of agreement came from some of the other Bravo guys. Coach glanced their direction then back to Nate.

"From what I understand, you are too. But since you've had your hands full and the assignment West had previously been on was finished, McQueen figured it was worth a shot to let the other guy have a crack at it so you could focus on what needed to be done here."

Okay, so that…actually made sense. *Well, shit.*

"Apparently—" Coach continued on— "West noticed something off about one of the pictures. A missing pixel or something. Hell, I don't know. All that tech shit is Harl's—my wife's—territory. Not mine." The guy waved it off. "Anyway, when West downloaded the selfies, the one with the missing pixel disappeared and this one materialized in its place."

About a billion thoughts hit Nate all at once. "Why did Jake send this information to you guys and not us?"

"I asked him the same thing," Ghost answered for Coach. "McQueen said he tried, but couldn't get it to go through on your phones. Must've been sending it while you were traveling through a dead spot."

"Got a lot of those around here," Fletch muttered from where he stood.

Nate ran a frustrated hand over the scruff of his jaw. "I can't believe I fucking missed it. Encryptions like that are like goddamn child's play for me and I fucking missed it."

"Quit beating yourself up, Carter," Gabe ordered. "No one thought about checking her picture album for a missing file. We were all focused on trying to find some sort of document or folder of some sort. This is on all of us, not just you."

"He's right," Matt gave him a solid nod. "What matters is we now have irrefutable evidence that Edric Yavuz has been in contact with a known nuclear arms dealer. Put that with Rasat's eyewitness testimony, and the guy's toast."

Coach spoke up again. "Once we're home, both Yavuz and Akmar will be formally charged with the murder of Petty Officer Third Class Craig Michael Wyatt, as well as the kidnapping and assault of a civilian, Gracelynn McDaniels."

"President Russell has already been informed of the

charges and the evidence collected up to this point. Though, it has not been made public, Ryker assured us that Russell and his people are already working on a statement to announce the cancellation of the treaty."

"Halle-fucking-luja," Matt threw his arms up in praise.

"That is good news," Gabe remarked, "but that's only half of it."

"Yeah," Zade agreed. "The easy half."

"He's right," Coach chimed in. "That piece of shit treaty may have gone up in smoke, but before we can ensure Yavuz and Achim pay for their crimes, we have to get to them."

"Which brings us to the fun part," Fletch quipped.

Ghost did something on his phone as he came closer to Gabe and Nate. Matt and Zade hovered around them to get as good a view as they could.

Tapping the screen, Ghost located and enlarged the picture.

"This is a satellite image of the property where we believe Gracie is being held. Like Barry said, it's a farm about forty minutes south of here. It's isolated and secured. When Yavuz is present, there are armed guards watching the grounds twenty-four seven."

"No fence or wall along the perimeter," Zade noted. "Makes our job a bit easier."

"Absolutely."

"I'm surprised there isn't some sort of barrier, given the shit going on behind closed doors there."

"It's not one of Yavuz' regular go-to spots," Fletch explained. "The property belonged to a relative of his mother. It's still listed under the relative's last name, which I'm guessing is why it didn't pop up in any of your original searches."

"Shit," Nate reprimanded himself. Jesus, he'd been

screwing this whole thing up from the beginning. "I should've looked deeper."

"Stop." Gabe ordered sharply. "No way you could've known Yavuz had access to a farm that belonged to a relative of a relative of a relative. So, knock that shit off and stay focused. Otherwise you're going to be of no use to us or Gracie."

Gabe was right. Nate had to get his head out of his ass and focus on this like any other mission. Gracie's life depended on it.

With a tilt of his chin, Nate obeyed his team leader's command and moved on. "Okay, so we know where he is, and we know the security's pretty basic around the perimeter. What about the inside?"

"If I may?" Barry intervened. "My cousin said no one else has been allowed inside the house other than Yavuz, Achim, and one other man. An American."

"Adrian Walker."

"Yes!" Barry's face lit up as if he were excited to contribute. "That is it. Rasat said a man named Walker was there. He escorted the woman into the house and since then, he has aided the other men in their security details. I do not know any more about him than that."

"That's all we need to know," Matt assured him.

Nate took a few seconds to study his friend. Of one thing, he was certain; if Matt ever got his hands on Adrian Walker, things would end very badly for the Patriot-turned-traitor. Speaking of traitors...

"What's your cut in all this?" he asked Barry.

Looking confused, he asked, "What do you mean by 'cut'?"

Nate rolled his eyes. "What do you get out of this? Because as sure as I'm standing here, I know you didn't just walk up to these fine gentlemen and offer all this intel out of the goodness of your heart."

"Ah, cut. I see, now." Barry bobbed his head, but it was Ghost who answered the question.

"Our commander used a few connections he has to make arrangements for both Barry and his cousin to be transported safely to the States once the mission is complete."

"Then, what?" Zade asked. "Those two go into Witness Protection or something?"

"Or something," Coach's deep voice rumbled.

"Fine by me," Matt shrugged.

"I don't give two fucks where this asshole and his cousin end up. I just want to go in, take care of Yavuz, Achim, and Walker, and get Gracie the hell out of here."

A smile spread across Ghost's face. "That's the plan, Carter."

"Alright, then." Nate looked at the men crowded in the tiny space. "Let's get to it."

CHAPTER 17

An hour later, after mapping out their plan of attack, Nate and the others were riding down a long, dirt road.

Ghost was driving the jeep he, Gabe, and Coach were in. Fletch, Matt, and Zade were in the one following them.

Nate had to admit, it was somewhat amusing seeing someone as tall and large as Coach sitting in the vehicle's front seat. It was an average-size Jeep, but Coach was definitely not an average-size man. The dude also had one hell of a memory.

During the drive, Nate made the four men go back over their plan again. He had to be sure they were ready. Gracie's life—his life—depended on it.

When Gabe asked a question about the farm home's layout, Coach spit out the building's floor plan with so much detail, you would've thought the man designed the place himself.

Afterward, they found out Coach had an eidetic memory, which explained everything. It also made Nate a little jealous of the big guy.

Between working intelligence for the Navy and now as

Bravo's technical analysis expert, the ability to remember everything he read and saw sure would've come in handy.

Soon, Ghost was pulling off the road and into a smattering of trees. Fletch followed their tracks. Once they were too far off the road to be seen by anyone driving by, they stopped and the men got out.

After a final weapons and com check, Ghost led them through the trees to the backside of the property Yavuz was supposedly at. Nate's heart pounded harder and harder with each step.

He didn't know what condition they'd find Gracie in, but no matter what, he would get her out of there. Even if it was the last thing he did.

Walking beside Gabe, Nate began to silently pray. He'd been doing that a lot, lately. More than he had in a very long time. He just hoped, for her sake, God was listening.

As they reached the edge of the tree line, Ghost held up a fist to signal to the men they needed to stop. Nate glanced through the limbs at the large, white house before them.

From their position, he could see two men dressed in black pacing back and forth along the south wall. Another did the same along the east side. They assumed a fourth man was to the west, as well as two more in the front.

So far, everything lined up with what Barry had told them.

One of the two guys in back matched the description Barry had given them of his cousin. Their informant hadn't wanted to stay at the tiny shack of a house alone, but there was no room for him in their vehicles. Even if there was, he just would've been another distraction.

"Ready?" Ghost whispered over his shoulder.

"Hell, yes."

Nate and the Delta badass shared a look before Ghost said, "Remember the plan. We go out just enough to cover

Zade, retrieve Rasat, then regroup back here before heading into the house. On my count."

Using the same fist as before, he silently counted down from three. On one, the men raised their guns and made their way through the trees, spanning out on either side of Zade to provide cover, if needed.

Using his modified HK G28 automatic sniper rifle, Zade showed off his sniping skills by effortlessly taking out one of the back guards, followed by the one to the east.

Both men were dead within a second of each other.

The other guard, the one they believed to be Barry's cousin, looked startled and a little lost. He raised his own weapon and began moving it about from side-to-side wildly, clearly unsure of where the two silent shots had come from.

Rasat was not made aware of the exact day or time Delta would be arriving, but per Ghost, Barry had assured him he would know when it was safe to surrender.

Confident in their identification of the man, Ghost risked becoming a target and made his presence known. Stepping away from the cover the trees and foliage provided, the well-trained man waved an arm in the air to get Rasat's attention.

When the other man finally spotted him, Ghost motioned for him to come to them. Rasat looked over his shoulder to make sure no one was watching.

After a few seconds of hesitation, the man began sprinting across the few yards spanning between him and the trees.

The second he was within arm's reach, Ghost grabbed hold of Rasat's arm and yanked him into the trees with the rest of them.

"You are Ghost?" the terrified man asked, his heavy accent matching his cousins.

"I am. What's the code word?"

"Snickerdoodle."

Matt snorted. "Snickerdoodle? Really?"

"What?" Ghost asked, his tone defensive. "It's one of my wife's favorite cookies."

Several of the men chuckled, but Nate's chest tightened when he realized he didn't know what Gracie's favorite cookie was. Or her favorite color.

God, there was so much he still needed to know about her. He just prayed he got the chance to learn it all.

"Thank you. I was beginning to think you were not coming."

"I don't go back on my word."

Rasat took Ghost's free hand in his and repeated, "Thank you."

"Don't thank me, yet. This deal hinges on us getting Yavuz and Achim into custody and getting the woman out alive."

"Yes. I understand. The woman is—"

"Gracie," Nate growled.

They needed to move their asses, but what he had to say was important. Looking at each man, including his own team, Nate made sure they knew who they were going after.

"Her name is Gracie. She's smart and funny. The most beautiful, compassionate woman I've ever known. She's not some nameless, faceless hostage. Gracie is someone's sister. Someone's daughter." Then, because he had to, he added, "And she's mine."

The others remained silent for a moment before Ghost spoke again. "He's right." He looked at Nate. "I said before we've been where you are. In my case, I didn't even realize my woman was a hostage until I walked into an op and found her chained to a bed about to be raped by a kid trying to become a man. Fletch's woman was taken as a pawn in some sick fuck's plan of revenge against our unit. And Coach, here...hell, his woman vanished without a trace for four days. To make matters worse, the police called him in 'cause they thought *he'd* done something to her."

Jesus. Nate looked up at Coach. A pained expression flashed across the intimidating man's face.

"Longest ninety-eight hours of my entire fucking life."

"What happened?" Nate couldn't help but ask.

"Her car. Harley had gone off the road and down into a ravine where no one could see her."

"Shit, man," Zade remarked. "It's a miracle she survived."

"It's a miracle any of them survived," Coach mused.

"Thankfully, we had God and our training on our side." Ghost's focus landed on Nate again. "Same as you. So, what do you say, Carter? Ready to go in there and get Gracie back where she belongs?"

He could feel his heart rate rising in anticipation. "Fuck, yeah, I am."

"Whoa." Rasat looked at them all cautiously.

"What?" Gabe asked.

"I think women should stay clear of you men. Much better for them and you."

This made every man's shoulders shake. Especially Matt's. "Rasat, I believe that's the smartest thing I've heard all day. I am one hundred percent with you on that."

"Yeah," Nate muttered to his friend as he got ready to head out. "Until about three weeks ago, I would've been, too." His gaze slid to the house again. "Kole warned me, and I blew him off, just like you're gonna blow off what I'm saying now. But mark my words, Turner. There will come a time when a woman slips past that wall of yours. One day, you're gonna wake up and realize she's become your entire world."

A strange look flashed behind Matt's dark eyes, but it was gone before Nate could decipher what it was.

It would have to wait. Right now, Nate's world was somewhere in that house and he was more than ready to take back what was his.

"The woma…" Rasat's nervous eyes flew up to Nate's. "Your Gracie—" he corrected himself— "is being held in a room on the first floor. Far, northwest corner."

Gabe gave Rasat a nod and his thanks before addressing the group. Per his and Ghost's agreement, he would be in charge of the op from this point on.

"Alright, gentlemen. It's go time. Rasat, you wait for us here. The rest of you, just like before. On three."

Like a finely-choreographed dance, the two teams worked together as one. Fluid in their movements, they made their way into position around the outside of the house. The remaining guards were neutralized without incident.

Through the coms, Ghost relayed a quiet, "Perimeter is secure, boys. Hooah."

One corner of Nate's mouth turned up. Despite his earlier qualms, he was really starting to like that guy.

Repositioning, Nate and the others waited for the green light from Gabe. When it was given, the men breached the house simultaneously.

As planned, Nate moved into the hallway to his right with Matt on his six while the others spread throughout the house to check for any potential threat.

It was an older home, so the hallway was long and narrow. There were three doors to the right and two on the left.

One by one, Nate and Matt cleared each room with silence and efficiency. As expected, they were all empty.

The closer they got to the room at the end of the hall, the harder Nate's heart began to pound inside his chest. His fingertips began to tingle, the level of adrenaline flowing through his veins at an all-time high.

He and Matt were only a few inches away from the final room's door when a man's angry words bellowed out from the other side, followed by a woman's equally loud voice.

Gracie.

Nate's heart stopped.

She was yelling back, her words muffled behind the thick walls. Nate didn't need to hear them to know she was pissed. He smiled.

Hearing her yell meant she was still alive. The fact that there was still a bite to her tone meant Gracie's strong spirit hadn't been broken.

That's my girl.

"Get her under control and let's go!"

Yavuz' words were clear that time, confirming one of their three targets was in that room. His elation was short-lived, however, when he heard the sound of flesh hitting flesh and Gracie crying out.

Motherfucker. Knowing she'd just been hit nearly undid him. He started to take a step forward, but somehow, his training forced its way through.

Nate wanted nothing more than to storm into that room, take out Yavuz and anyone else standing between him and Gracie. But he had to keep his head clear.

They didn't know exactly what they'd be walking into and he refused to do anything that would put Gracie—or Matt—at an even greater risk.

Holding his gun in his right hand, Nate made a motion with his left. The pain from his bullet wound was beginning to flare up again, but he ignored it. With his fingers, he silently told Matt to take the other side of the doorway.

Locked and loaded, both men raised their guns and waited.

* * *

Gracie picked herself up off the floor. Raising a hand to her cheek, her fingertips met the hot, tender flesh where Achim had just backhanded her.

Still a bit stunned from the blow, she tried to make sense of what was happening.

One minute, she'd been lying there, chained to the bed. The next, Yavuz and Achim were storming into the room with Adrian Walker hot on their tails.

The conversation that took place just moments ago had given her more hope than she'd felt in days...

"How the fuck did they find us?" Yavuz yelled.

"No idea, but unless you want to spend the rest of your life in an American prison, we need to get our asses out of here. Now."

"Shut the door," Yavuz ordered Walker.

"Did you not hear what I just said? We have to leave."

"I heard what you said," Yavuz spit back, nodding to Achim to unlock the metal clasp around her wrists.

A confused look crossed over Walker's face. "Forget the woman. Leave her here and let's go."

It was the first and only time Gracie had agreed with the man.

"No. She comes with us."

Achim continued to release her. The men were so busy panicking and trying to figure out what to do next, they'd completely underestimated her will to survive.

The second Gracie's wrists were free, she'd grabbed one of the chains a few inches from the bracelet and swung it at Achim's head. It hit with surprising force, knocking the man off his feet and onto the mattress beside her.

Gracie then tried to run for the door, but Walker was in the way.

She hadn't exactly thought the plan through all the way, but it wasn't like she'd had a lot of time. Walker had grabbed her around the waist and spun her around so his arms could pull her back tightly against his chest.

Gracie kicked and yelled, praying whoever had come would hear her and bust the door down. Instead of a white knight, she got white-hot pain when Yavuz ordered Achim to get her under control. The asshole was more than happy to oblige.

Now, she was being held in place by Walker while Yavuz hurried over to his desk. The man rushed to find something in one of the drawers, a smirk forming on his evil face when he found whatever it was he needed.

Gracie fully expected him to pull out a gun. Instead, his hand came back empty. Even more shocking was the fact that the wall behind the room's antique dresser had just begun to open.

A secret passageway.

In another time and place, she would have thought it fascinating. Today, it was terrifying.

Gracie opened her mouth to scream, determined to let the men outside know about the tunnel. Unfortunately, Walker anticipated this.

With a hand pressed roughly against her mouth, he moved her toward the tunnel's entrance, her call for help silenced behind his palm.

They followed Yavuz and Achim down a set of concrete stairs into a darkened tunnel. With a flip of a switch, Yavuz illuminated the long corridor, allowing them to see where they were going.

The tunnel stopped several yards from where it began. From what Gracie could see, there was another tunnel, leading to the left.

She tried to squirm out of Walker's grasp, but just like in the cabin, his strength over powered her.

A musty, basement-type smell filled the damp air and, because the tunnel was dug deep below the earth's surface, it was much cooler than the room she'd been kept in.

By the time they'd turned into the next section, Gracie was covered in goose bumps.

Must be what it feels like to be buried.

Shaking off the morbid thought, Gracie tried to remember every detail she could. If by some miracle she made it out of this alive, she wanted to be able to do everything she could to help the authorities nail these bastards to the wall.

What felt like hours later, they finally reached the end of the tunnel. Instead of another section, there was a metal door with an electronic keypad.

Gracie's heart sank. Even if whoever was up there came this way, they'd never get past this point without the code.

Nate could have.

Despite her best efforts, a tear fell down her cheek, landing on Walker's hand.

"Don't cry, love," he crooned. As if he could tell exactly what she'd been thinking, he whispered into her ear, "Looks like your boyfriend survived my bullet after all."

What? Gracie's heart flew into her throat. Shaking her head, she fought to break her mouth free.

Turns out, she didn't need to fight. Walker simply lifted his hand away from her lips.

"What are you saying? Nate's alive?"

"Alive and, from what I saw on the security monitors in this place, he's more than a little pissed at me for taking you away from him. Of course, it might also have something to do with my having shot him."

"Shut up," Yavuz ordered.

Gracie noticed the man was so nervous, he kept pressing the wrong number for the door's code. Each time he did, he had to start over.

"I can't hear myself think."

Like she gave a shit about that. In fact, maybe if she kept

265

talking, it would distract him enough to buy Nate time to get to her.

Is he really alive?

"Tell me what you saw," she begged Walker. "Was it really him? Is his team here, too?"

"Oh, yeah. Plus a few extra, from the looks of things."

"I said shut up!" Yavuz yelled over his shoulder.

Gracie's eyes slid to the lock. She smiled when she saw him hit the button that read 'clear' and start over again.

"He's going to kill you all. You know that, don't you?"

Yavuz paid her no attention, but fear sparked in Achim's eyes. He tried to cover it, but it was too late. She'd already seen it.

Playing on that, Gracie continued to taunt him. "You're going to die today, Achim. And for what? Money? Who gets it all when you're gone, hmm? Do you have a family? Someone who will miss you?"

"Shut the fuck up."

"Surely, you have no children. Not with your kind of work. A mother, perhaps?"

Rage filled his features then, the vein on his forehead bulging as he put the barrel of his pistol to her head and yelled, "I said. Shut. Up."

Bingo. She'd definitely touched a nerve with that one. It was probably sad she felt so much enjoyment from that, but at this point, it was all she had.

That and the possibility that Nate hadn't been killed after all.

Please, God. Let him still be alive.

"Both of you shut up!" Yavuz turned, his face as red as Achim's. Pulling his own weapon, he shocked the hell out of Gracie when he pointed it at Achim's head, and not hers.

"Whoa, Edric. Easy with that, man." Walker spoke calmly

from behind her. "Let's just all take a deep breath and calm down."

"There's no time to calm down. I keep messing up because this imbecile can't handle one weak female who is clearly trying to upset him and distract me."

"Let me shoot her, Yavuz," Achim spoke through clenched teeth. "You don't need her anymore. She's useless to you now and will only slow us down."

"She's my insurance, you idiot. She's the only thing standing between me and those men's bullets if they catch up to us. You, on the other hand, have outlived your usefulness."

Gracie watched with horror as the man's eyes grew wide with the realization of what was about to happen. Achim slid the barrel of his gun away from her head in an attempt to shoot Yavuz first, but he was too late.

"Edric, no!"

They were the last two words Achim Akmar would ever speak.

The sound of Yavuz' gun blast was deafening as it bounced off the concrete walls. Blood splattered those same walls as the bullet ripped through the center of the Achim's forehead, his lifeless body dropping to the ground where he stood.

"Oh, my God!" Gracie exclaimed, unable to hide the utter terror and disgust vibrating throughout her entire system.

She'd just watched a man die. Witnessed him being murdered in cold blood less than a foot away from her.

Later, when the shock of it all wore off, she'd probably feel bad for Achim. For now, though, all she could think was that was one less threat she and the others had to worry about.

What sounded like someone yelling reached her ears then, and she knew deep down inside, it was Nate.

"Nate!" she screamed back as loudly as she could. "Nathan, I'm here! I'm here!"

Yavuz pointed his gun toward her, then. "I know what I said to him, but I will put a bullet through your brain next if you do not shut your mouth and stay quiet. Then, I will wait here for your boyfriend and his friends. Trust me when I say, he will not survive a second time."

Shit, shit, shit.

When she only had to worry about her own life, Gracie had felt bold and brave. Now, she was scared to death she would inadvertently do something to bring more harm to Nate.

The man had already been shot once because of her. She refused to do anything that may put him in even more danger.

Never again, Nate. I promise you. Never again.

Gracie pressed her lips together and remained quiet while Yavuz finally got the code entered correctly and the door began to open.

"Let's go."

Yavuz grabbed her arm and pushed her into a large, underground garage. Walker followed behind her and was pulling the door closed when she heard Nate's voice.

"Gracie!"

Her head whipped around to the sound of Nate screaming her name just as the lock on the door clicked back into place.

CHAPTER 18

Every ounce of hope Gracie had left was destroyed with that damn door.

Nate was smart. She knew this, but the chances of him being able to hack into that lock's system in time to save her were slim to freaking none.

Her mind raced as she tried to think of how she could get away, but Yavuz' grip was surprisingly strong and she was still too weak to overpower him.

He pushed her toward one of two compact cars parked a few feet in front of them.

"This is where we part ways," Walker pulled a fob from his pocket and started one of the cars. "Good thing I had you transfer the money before the shit hit the fan. Man, Edric. Looks like you'd better take a cue from my playbook and vanish to someplace far away from here."

"Just go!" Yavuz told the man angrily as he pointed his gun at Walker. "Go, now, before you end up like Achim."

Adrian Walker laughed. "Oh, Edric. I do think I'm going to miss you a little bit." When he turned to Gracie, his smile dimmed. "Good luck, Miss McDaniels."

Yeah, right. "Fuck you," Gracie shot back, making Walker's smile grow wide again.

"I hope you make it out of this, Gracelynn. I mean that."

Oddly, he actually sounded as though he did.

Two minutes later, Gracie watched as Adrian Walker drove his car up the wide exit ramp and disappeared into the sunlight.

"Get in."

Yavuz pushed her again before walking around to the driver's side of the car. She stumbled, nearly falling to her knees in the process.

Once she'd regained her footing, Gracie stopped and looked at the black car.

If you get in there, you're dead.

It was the same thought she'd had the day Achim and Walker had tried to abduct her in front of the office. It rang true then, and the probability was even higher, today.

Raising her chin, she looked Yavuz in the eye and said, "No."

He pointed the gun at her again, enunciating every word as he spoke through his teeth. "Get. In. The. Car."

Though, she was beyond frightened, Gracie stood her ground. Taking in a deep breath, she exhaled slowly before repeating, "No."

For the second time in only a few minutes, Edric Yavuz pulled the trigger.

"Ah!"

Gracie cried out, her right hand immediately going to the wound on her upper left arm. Blood seeped through her fingers and began to drip onto the concrete floor next to where she stood.

"The next one goes into your head. Now, get in the fucking car."

Someone pounded on the door they'd just come through. Though it was muffled, she could hear Nate yelling her name. At least, she told herself it was him.

Gracie wanted to fight. Could picture herself either running back toward the door or up the ramp leading out into the open. Either way, she knew exactly what would happen.

If she ran, Yavuz would shoot her in the back and take off. When Nate finally did make his way into the garage, he'd find her lying on the ground. Dead.

No way could she do that to him. Nor, would she give up that easily.

Gracie reached for the door handle.

Slick with blood, her fingers slipped on the first try. Fearful he'd shoot her again if she took much longer, she got the best grip she could and tried again.

The door opened that time and Gracie slid into the passenger seat. Feeling a bit lightheaded she shook her head to clear it. She had to stay focused if she had any chance of making it out of this alive.

Now that she was seated and actually had time to think, her adrenaline rush was beginning to subside and pain unlike any she'd ever known began to burn through her arm.

She inspected the wound as best she could, thankful the bullet only grazed her. But, holy shit, it hurt.

The car tilted to her left as Yavuz sat down in the driver's seat. He quickly closed his door and pushed the button to start the car's engine.

Shifting into reverse, the monster shot the car backward. Tires squealed and Gracie was thrown back against the head-rest as he threw it in drive and sped toward the ramp.

Just then, Gracie thought she heard someone yelling at them, again. Believing it to be wishful thinking, she ignored it. It was a waste of time to daydream, and she was definitely short on time.

She heard it again.

Blinking against the slight dizziness, she spun around in her seat, unable to believe what she saw.

Nate was running toward her as fast as he could with Matt following closely behind. They'd somehow managed to get past Yavuz' secure door and now Nate was chasing after her as if his life depended on it.

Her heart swelled to the point she thought it would burst. Gracie hated knowing he was risking his life for her again, but at the same time, she fell in love with him even more because of it.

She tried opening the door, ready to jump out, but it remained closed.

"Child locks," Yavuz smirked beside her.

Damn. She was trapped.

Desperate to get as close to him as she could, Gracie clawed her way to the back seat and pressed the palm of her good hand against the back windshield's cool glass.

She knew the minute he saw her. His steps faltered, but only for a fraction of a second. He sped up then, clearly determined to catch up to her, even though Gracie knew it was an impossible feat.

The blood on her hand smeared across the clear surface, but all Gracie saw was Nate. She could tell he was favoring his right arm, and she hated herself once again for being the cause of his pain.

She screamed his name as loudly as she could. Again and again, she called for him, but it was no use.

Yavuz had picked up speed and daylight filled the car as they exited the garage. Dust and gravel spewed out from the tires as they went from the smooth surface onto a dirt road leading away from the tunnel.

Looking up, Gracie realized they'd come much farther from the house than she'd originally thought.

Then, seemingly out of nowhere, Zade, Gabe, and a man she'd never seen before came running across the grass toward them. They were carrying very large guns, the one she didn't recognize halting his forward progress in order to get a good shot.

Yavuz saw this, too, and lowered his window. He stuck his pistol out the open space and fired wildly, splitting his attention between the road in front of them and the deadly threats to their side.

The stranger returned fire.

Glass from the driver's side mirror shattered when one of the bullets slammed into it. Gracie screamed and ducked.

The shooting stopped, then. Through the back window she watched Nate running with all his might, still trying to catch up to them. But even from a distance, she could see the anger and fear in his eyes as he realized what she already knew.

It was too late. There was no way for him and the other men to catch up to her. And once Yavuz was far enough away, he'd kill her.

The thought of just sitting and waiting for this heartless beast to ruthlessly execute her—especially when she still had no idea why—angered Gracie beyond description. But what could she do?

She'd been beaten and damn near starved. They'd given her some type of drug and she'd been shot, for Christ's sake. She held back a hysterical laugh, thinking the odds most definitely did not seem to be in her favor.

Gracie glanced down at her throbbing arm. She thought maybe the bleeding was slowing, but was so light-headed now, she was having a hard time focusing.

Maybe I'll pass out before the end comes.

She shook her head, unwilling to give up now. She'd come too far and fought too damn hard to just sit back and wait to die.

Gracie made a decision, then. If these were to be her last moments on this earth, she refused to spend them willingly surrendering her life to this man. A life she'd never get to have with Nate.

She looked out the front windshield. The road they were travelling on was leading them to what looked to be a river or lake.

There was a narrow, wooden bridge they had to cross in order to get to the other side. Neither the bridge nor the body of water was overly large, but they'd work for what she had in mind.

She damn near smiled at the idea that had formed. Gracie glanced at Yavuz, whose attention was split between what was in front of the car and the road behind them.

Perfect.

Her plan became clearer the closer they got to the bridge. Eyeing both it and its distance to the water below, she sat back and waited.

She would do everything in her power to survive this, but if she was going to die today—and it was looking like she would—at least she'd die knowing she fought to the end.

* * *

"No!"

Nate ran toward the car, but it was too late. *He* was too late. It had taken too long to hack into that goddamn lock, and Yavuz had slipped right through his fingers. With his Gracie.

Stopping in the middle of the road, his chest heaved and his heart broke. He could barely see the back of the car, now.

With his hands on his hips, Nate hung his head between his shoulders and squeezed his eyes shut, trying to fight against the helplessness threatening to take over.

After a few deep breaths, he stood straight again and stared at the empty, dust-covered road. His mind was a melting pot of swirling thoughts and numbers. He worked to calculate Yavuz' speed and the distance he'd already travelled.

Nate then figured up the time it would take to run back to their vehicles so the two teams could catch up to the car.

He was still trying to come up with a plan of action—one that didn't end with him losing the best thing in his life—when one of the two Jeeps pulled up next to him.

"Get in!"

Nate's head swung up and around. Behind a cloud of dust, he saw Ghost behind the wheel and Gabe and Matt sitting in he back.

A rush of hope flourished once more as Nate jumped up into the passenger side. Ghost took off down the road, his booted foot slamming the gas pedal down to the floor before Nate's ass even hit the leather seat.

"Go! Go! Go!" Nate yelled, slamming the palm of his hand onto the dashboard. Renewed hope billowed throughout his veins as the four men sped down the dirt road.

Ghost glanced over at him, and Nate instinctively knew he was assessing his mental status.

"I'm good. We'll get her," Nate told the other man, his determination clear.

"Fuck, yeah, we will," Matt exclaimed from the back.

Gabe agreed. "Didn't come all this way to lose her now."

Nate was never more appreciative of his teammates as he was right then. They were ready, willing to fight to the death to help him get Gracie to safety.

Hang on, baby. We're coming.

Until now, Nate hadn't allowed himself to think about it,

but he'd seen the blood. He hated that she'd been hurt, but at least she was alive.

Nate damn near lost his shit when they'd come up on Achim Akmar's dead body. At first, he'd thought it was Gracie lying there in that tunnel.

Then, his heart shattered into a million pieces seeing her in the back seat of the car like that, with her bloody hand pushed against the glass, neck strained from screaming his name.

In the end, it was the look in her eyes that really got to him. The fading hope spreading over her face as she got farther and farther away had cut him deep into his soul.

Nate didn't know how he'd go on if he lost her.

"There they are!" Gabe pointed toward them from the back seat.

That spark of hope he'd been holding on to erupted as Ghost sped to close the gap between the two vehicles.

Nate saw a bridge up ahead, but knew they'd never make it in time to keep Yavuz from crossing it. They'd have to wait until they got to the other side to intervene.

That was fine. They were covering a lot of ground and getting closer by the second.

Ghost drove like a NASCAR driver, expertly weaving back and forth over the dirt road to avoid the many potholes. The entire time, the man never took his eyes off their target.

Like Ghost, Nate's gaze remained glued to the car in front of them. They were about fifty yards away from Yavuz, but Nate was confident they'd be able to stop him once they'd crossed the lake.

The car drove onto the low-lying, wooden bridge. It appeared to be about fifteen feet from the water's surface. He just prayed the damn thing would hold the weight of both vehicles.

Nate was mentally planning for what needed to happen

once they'd crossed, when Yavuz' car suddenly veered sharply to the left.

"What the hell?" Ghost muttered, gripping his steering wheel a little tighter.

The four men watched as the car then shot to the right just as forcefully, nearly hitting the protective railing on that side of the bridge.

Nate's heart slammed against his ribs. "What the fuck is he doing?"

"Oh, shit," Gabe called out from the back. "It's not him. It's her."

"What?" Nate asked from over his shoulder.

Having positioned himself in the center of the bench seat, Gabe was using his tactical binoculars to watch the car in front of them.

"What's happening?" Nate demanded an answer.

Gabe lowered the binoculars. "Gracie's fighting for control of the car."

Nate grabbed the binos from his team leader's hands and looked through the circular lenses. What he saw left ice running through his veins.

With her body hanging over the seat, Gracie was fighting Yavuz off as she grabbed for the steering wheel.

"What the hell is she trying to do?"

Several curses filled their vehicle as the car shot to the left again.

"I get the need to fight." Ghost shook his head. "But if Gracie's not careful, she's gonna end up driving that thing right off the fucking bridge."

Nate focused on her movements again. Fear clutched his soul when he finally realized what was really going on.

"Oh, God." He lowered the binoculars, not wanting to believe what he was seeing.

"What?" Gabe sounded alarmed. "What's wrong?"

Yavuz' car continued to weave back and forth over the structure. Nate looked at his team leader, his voice turning flat with disbelief and fear.

"That's exactly what she's trying to do."

Ghost's brows arched. "What? Are you sure? Maybe she's just—"

The other man's thought was cut short when the car swerved to the left one last time. Its front end hit the wooden railing, the boards there splitting apart on impact.

Nate was forced to just sit there and watch as the car—and Gracie—flew over the edge of the bridge, falling nose-first into the water below.

"No!"

The word of denial was ripped from his throat as the car splashed against the water, the front end already beginning to sink.

Ghost slammed on the breaks, the tires skidding a few inches before coming to a stop well before the point of impact.

There was no way to tell just how much of the bridge's structural support had been compromised. The last thing they needed was for it to collapse with them on it.

Unable to prevent it, Nate's analytical mind began to whirl with possible outcomes as he opened his door and jumped out.

Running toward the railing's gaping hole, he thought about how strong a swimmer Gracie was. That helped her odds of survival, for sure. Unfortunately, his brain also considered all the things that could happen to make that fact irrelevant.

She could have been knocked out by the impact, her head already submerged. Yavuz was still in the car. He had a gun. The bastard could be hurting her. He could...

Gracie screamed.

A gunshot rang out from inside the car.

"Gracelynn!"

He ran faster.

"Nate!" she screamed back.

Oh, thank God. "Hang on!" He began stripping off his vest, and then untying his boots to make swimming much easier and safer for them both. "I'm coming!" he bellowed down to her.

"Damn it, Carter. Wait up!" Gabe ordered from behind.

Ignoring him, Nate kicked off his boots and jumped feet-first into the water below. The water was unexpectedly cold, stealing his breath as he went under.

Pushing with his arms and legs, Nate paid no attention to the pain in his left shoulder as he broke through the surface and began swimming to Gracie's side of the car.

She must have either climbed into the front seat or was thrown there when the car went over.

He made it to her closed window, the water's surface sitting a few inches below the bottom of the glass. On a glance, Nate was relieved to see Yavuz' head flung forward, his body unmoving.

Wide, terrified eyes met his from behind the glass. The water inside the car was already at her waist and rising steadily. Nate reached for the door and pulled, but it didn't budge. He tried again with no success.

Fuck! The water must have fried the car's electrical system, which meant the locks were permanently stuck. Of course, even if they weren't, the pressure from the surrounding water would most likely prevent him from opening it, anyway.

Not wanting to risk her being cut if he busted out her window, Nate quickly made his way around the car to Yavuz' open window.

He reached in and pulled the other man out. As he did,

Yavuz' head fell back, revealing a newly formed bullet hole at the base of his neck.

Nate tried not to react, but, Jesus. On top of everything else, she'd just been forced to kill a man.

Knowing they'd have to deal with that later, Nate pushed the dead man's body through the water and out of the way to make room for himself.

"Hang on, baby. I'm going to get you out of there."

Using the open window's metal frame, Nate pulled himself far enough inside the car to reach her.

First things first.

With his feet dangling out the window, Nate grabbed hold of her face and planted a hard, short kiss on her lips.

"Hi."

"H-hi." Gracie smiled, but he knew she was fighting the urge to break down.

"Come on." He grabbed her hands and pulled "Keep ahold of my hands and I'll pull you through the window with me."

"I can't," she shook her head.

The water inside the car had already gotten much higher. It was almost chest-level and the bottom few inches of her hair were floating around in it.

"Sure you can. Just don't let go."

"No," she pulled back on his hands. "I mean I *can't*. My foot's stuck." They both looked down to the floorboard near the center of the car. "I was thrown forward when we hit the water. My foot got jammed up in there. I can't get out."

Nate wanted to howl with frustration, mentally cursing the fact that they faced yet another road block in getting her to safety.

Pushing it back, he made his way fully into the car and forced himself to sound calm.

"Okay. Here's what we're going to do. I'm going to go under and get your foot unstuck." He glanced back at the open window's edge. The water only a few centimeters away now. "In the meantime, if you see the water is going to get above your head before I'm back up, I want you to take the deepest breath you can and hold it. Just like that day at the cliff."

"Nate, please. Just go." Her bottom lip quivered and a tear fell down her cheek. "There's no reason for us both to die today."

"Gracie, listen to me. No one else is dying today, you hear me? You can do this."

Nate leaned up and kissed her one more time before dipping his head beneath the water. He saw where her left foot was trapped, but try as he might, he couldn't get her loose.

Unwilling to give up, he continued his attempts to work her free until he saw black dots flashing before his eyes. Knowing he'd be no use to her if he passed out, Nate shot back up for another quick breath.

Terror gripped him when he realized the water was about to come into the car from the window. Once that started, it would only take a few seconds before the entire car became completely submerged.

"Nate!" Gracie shouted his name. Her fear was palpable as she looked at him with wide, panicked eyes.

Water poured in through the driver's window. Because Nate was free to move about, he was able to get his head up next to the car's ceiling. With Gracie being stuck, hers was at the same level as the seat's headrest.

Gracie tilted her head as far back as she could, but it made very little difference. The water was already hitting the bottom of her chin.

"Take a deep breath!" he ordered from above her, his eyes fixated on the rapidly rising water.

"I don't know if I can!" Tears fell from her eyes. "I feel so weak."

"Goddamn it, Gracelynn, just do it!"

"I love you, Nate!"

His eyes flew to hers as she inhaled deeply then closed her eyes and mouth.

"Gracie!" he shouted back. "I love you, too!"

But water was already above her head. She hadn't heard his precious words.

They were words he swore he'd never say to any woman, his mother the only exception. Now, as the interior of the car became flooded and they began to sink at a much faster rate, Nate found himself praying for the chance to say them to her again.

Ignoring the yelling coming from outside the car, Nate filled his lungs, and went back to work trying to pull the plastic panel trapping her foot free.

It moved an inch or two, but Nate lost his grip on the damn thing when the car jolted, coming to a rest on the lake's shallow bottom.

He started to pull again when he felt something tapping him on his shoulder. Looking up, Nate realized Gracie was waving her arms through the water, trying to get his attention.

Not really having the time to do so, he pushed himself up closer in order to see her face more clearly. The love in her eyes both filled his heart and shattered it, all at the same time.

She shook her head back and forth. Her hair swirling around her face, but he could still make out what she was trying to tell him.

Silently, through dark water, he read Gracie's lips.

I'm sorry.

Panic filled Nate to his core. Before he could think of a way to respond, she took his face into her hands and mouthed the words, *I love you.*

And there, surrounded by water, Gracie pressed her lips to his and kissed him goodbye.

For a fraction of a second, Nate kissed her back before pushing her away and furiously shaking his head.

Praying she could see what he was trying to tell her, Nate mouthed back, *I'm not leaving you!*

Please. Her eyes begged him to go. To save himself.

Didn't she know? If he lost her now, he may as well be dead, too. Well, fuck that. Their story wasn't ending today. Not like this.

With his finger, Nate told her to hold on a little longer. He raced back down to where she was stuck and tried again. He was still pulling when a second set of hands came into view.

Startled, he looked through the water to his left, grateful to see Gabe at his side.

Nate swallowed against the need to breathe—a trick he learned in the Navy. It fooled your brain into thinking you were able to breathe and could buy him an extra twenty, thirty seconds underwater. He needed those extra seconds, now.

Both men pulled as hard as they could. They repeated their efforts a second time. Finally, blessedly, on their third try, the plastic snapped and Gracie's foot floated free.

Through the dark, murky water Gabe used his hands to let him know he was going out first and would help him pull Gracie from the car. Nate understood and nodded in agreement.

Once Gabe was out of the way, Nate made his way back up to Gracie. A feeling of profound relief hit when he saw

Gabe reaching beneath her arms to pull her out of the driver's window.

That relief was replaced with devastation when Nate realized her head had slumped forward and her arms were floating motionless at her sides.

CHAPTER 19

Refusing to believe she was already gone, Nate pushed against Gracie's hips and legs to help Gabe get her out faster. Kicking as hard as he could, his thigh muscles burned as they made their way through the cool water.

Nate's lungs felt as though they were on fire as they screamed for some much-needed oxygen. His vision blurred and darkened around the edges just as his head broke through the surface. He opened his mouth wide and gasped, filling his lungs over and over again.

Struggling to catch his breath, Nate helped Gabe swim an unconscious Gracie to the nearest shoreline. It was only a few feet away, but felt like the length of twelve football fields as the two men fought to get her there.

Having arrived in the second Jeep with Fletch, Zade yelled something at him as they made their way down to the rocky bank.

Nate didn't listen. His entire focus was on getting Gracie to shore.

Gabe reached the rocks first. Nate held on to Gracie while the other man got out of the water and secured his footing. As soon as he was steady, he grabbed beneath her arms and slid her back with him.

Laying her down onto a large, flat rock, a dripping Gabe stepped back as Nate climbed up onto the rock and made his way beside her.

He fell to his knees and followed his training, laying his head onto her chest even though he already knew she wasn't breathing.

Raising back up, he pressed two fingers to the side of her neck. A feeling of despair washed over him when he didn't find a pulse.

"Ah, God."

With his fingers beneath her chin, he tilted her head back to open her airway and made a tight seal with his lips and hers. Blowing two, strong breaths, Nate then crossed his palms over each other in the proper area of her chest and locked his elbows.

He began the compressions.

Remembering to push to the beat of the song he'd been taught during his initial military training, Nate kept his pace at one hundred beats per minute, counting to thirty as he went.

Don't leave me, baby. Please don't leave me.

Those same thoughts repeated themselves over and over in his head as he got to thirty, stopped to give two more breaths, and started the chest compressions again.

"She won't," Ghost assured him from somewhere to his right. "You got this, buddy."

Shit. Nate hadn't meant to say the words aloud. Not that he gave a rat's ass.

"Come on!" Nate growled, the muscles in his arms burning.

The pain in his injured shoulder worsened with each compression, but he didn't stop. He wouldn't stop.

Another thirty in, he filled her lungs again and went right back to pumping her heart.

"Come on, sweetheart," he pleaded. "Don't give up on me now."

He'd made it to fifteen compressions during the fourth round when he felt a hand on his shoulder.

"Nate, man." It was Matt. "I-I think she's gone."

"No!" Nate shook him off and continued pressing. "Gracie can hold her breath for a really long time. She showed me when we were at the lake together. She's going to be fine."

His words were strong, but the weight on his heart was crushing. He continued fighting for her, refusing to accept what he already knew.

"Goddamn, Gracie!" he yelled as he finished that cycle. "Breathe! You will *not* leave me today, you hear me? You have to breathe, baby. Fucking *breathe!*"

Two more breaths, thirty more compressions.

"She was put through hell, Nate," Zade tried to reason with him. "She looks really worn down."

"Shut the fuck up!" Nate yelled at his teammate.

"Come on, Carter," Gabe grabbed his bicep. "At least let me take over for a bit."

Nate threw the other man's hand off. "No one else is touching her."

Beads of water and sweat dripped from his hair and the tip of his nose as he kept pushing against her chest. It would take a team of wild horses—or every man here—to pull him away from her now.

He'd keep pumping her heart until it either started again or his own heart stopped. Nate ignored the statistical numbers running through his head telling him if she didn't have a pulse by now, chances were, she'd never have one again.

Giving in to the visceral need to feel the life flowing through her body once more, Nate stopped the compressions. He reached up, pushing the pads of his shaking fingers to the delicate skin covering her carotid.

His shoulders fell, his soul dying a little more with each second that passed.

"I'm sorry, brother," Ghost spoke solemnly from beside him. "You did all you could. Her body just couldn't hold out."

"Wait!" Nate's own pulse spiked. "I think I feel something."

Praying his mind wasn't playing tricks on him, Nate pressed against her neck with a little more force and waited. He felt it, then.

A slight, rhythmic thump.

"She has a pulse!" He announced loudly, blinking back tears. "It's faint, but it's there. I can feel it."

Whoops and hollers surrounded him, but they'd only won half the battle. Her heart was beating again—*thank you, God!* —but, she still wasn't breathing.

Tilting her head back again, Nate pressed his lips to hers and began breathing life back into her.

It took several tries, but eventually, the function in her starved lungs returned. Gracie coughed and sputtered, Nate turning her head to the side so the water she'd inhaled could be expelled.

"That's it, baby." He almost cried with relief. "Let it all out."

"I'll be damned," Matt exclaimed. "You did it, man. You fucking did it."

Several other at-a-boys were spoken and Nate received a few pats on the back, but his concern for Gracie wasn't over.

She'd been without a pulse for a while, and her brain had been deprived of precious oxygen for several minutes. She was breathing on her own again, but her eyes remained closed and her only response to his voice was a mumble and slight squeeze of his hand.

"You're going to be okay, Gracie. You hear me? I'm here, and you're going to be okay."

"The rest of my guys are en route via chopper," Ghost told him. "I contacted them the minute the car went under. They'll take Gracie and your team to a jet that will be waiting at a private air strip not far from here. There will be medical equipment on board, and with Matt's background, he'll be able to monitor her until you're back home. McQueen's already made arrangements for Gracie to be transported to Homeland's private medical facility after you land in Texas."

"What about Rasat and Barry?"

"Let me worry about them."

Nate was taken aback by it all. Not only had Ghost, Fletch, and Coach helped with getting Gracie back, they'd clearly been busy while he'd been working to keep Gracie with them.

In addition to that, Ghost's other men—men Nate had never even met before—were dropping everything to help get her back home.

He was damn near speechless, which was saying a lot for him.

"I-I don't know what to say." Nate looked up at the Delta leader. "Thank you."

Ghost grinned. "You can thank us by taking good care of your girl."

And that's exactly what he did.

Before long, three more members of Ghost's Delta Team —their nicknames Beatle, Truck, and Hollywood—arrived with the chopper. They landed it in a large, open area just on the other side of the bridge.

Handing an unconscious Gracelynn off to Gabe, Nate climbed up into the bird then helped Gabe load her onto the pallet of blankets Ghost's men had made for her. Gabe, Matt, and Zade all piled in behind them. After making rushed introductions to Ghost's guys, the chopper took off.

Feeling like he could breathe for the first time in days, Nate sat on the floor next to Gracie. Gabe, and Zade each took one of the small cargo seats while Matt remained on the chopper's floor opposite him.

The former corpsman gave her a shot of antibiotics to fight off possible infection from the lake's murky water. Then, using the other supplies Ghost's team had provided, Matt began cleaning and dressing the bullet wound he'd found on her arm.

Once again, Nate was beyond grateful for Ghost and his men. They'd stepped up in a huge way, and he knew he'd never forget everything they'd done to help.

Nate's own men remained quiet, but Nate was fully aware each one was there for him. No matter what happened.

They were his team. His family. His brothers.

Glancing down at Gracie, Nate used a finger to gently wipe away the damp strands of hair that were sticking to her beautiful face. Unable to keep from it, he leaned in and kissed her softly before settling himself back down onto the metal floor.

With her hand in his, Nate stayed like that the entire way to the airport. He absentmindedly rubbed the gold band still on her left hand as he kept vigil over her. Though it wasn't a real symbol of their love, he couldn't bring himself to remove it.

For the first time since finding her, Nate allowed himself to really look at her. His eyes swept over her body, taking in every injury he could see.

Fierce outrage raced through his system as he studied her bruised and battered face. He cringed, his teeth grinding together when he noticed the raw, torn skin on her wrists.

Back at Yavuz' farmhouse, he and Matt had realized something was off and finally busted into the room where she'd been held. His teammate had stopped him from tearing the place apart when he saw the metal cuffs and chains attached to the bed's headboard.

The bastards had kept her bound, but she'd fought hard to try break free.

His eyes rested on the rise and fall of her chest. Nate found he was terrified to look away for fear she'd stopped breathing again.

Squatted across from him, Matt assured Nate, "She'll make it, brother. You got her out and got her breathing."

He tore his eyes from her and looked up at his friend. "I almost didn't."

"But you did. And she's strong. A fighter." Matt looked down at Gracie's unmoving form. "Wouldn't have made it this far if she wasn't."

From their seats, both Gabe and Zade muttered words of agreement, and Nate realized they were right.

Glancing back down at the woman he never wanted to live without, he reflected on the strength and wit it had taken for her to stay in hiding after her apartment had been broken into.

He thought of that night in the alley and her unwillingness to put her sister in harm's way, despite the fact that Gracie would've been safer if she had.

There was no doubt Gracelynn McDaniels was a fighter. More fierce and brave than any woman he'd ever known.

She'd kept it together, even when she believed there was no way out of that sinking car. Had looked at him with calm, clear eyes when she'd kissed him goodbye, begging him to save himself.

Tears welled in his eyes and his nose began to burn, but

Nate pushed it all back. He had to remain strong. For Gracie's sake.

Between the short trip on the chopper, a fourteen-hour flight into Dallas, and then getting Gracie from that airport to Homeland's medical center, the last few hours had passed by in a blur.

And Nate never left her side. Until now.

The doctors and nurses assigned to Gracie had been waiting at the doors for them. Before letting her go, Nate had given her a kiss on her forehead, whispering his promise to be back with her as soon as he could.

That seemed like forever ago.

Logically, he knew there were several tests that had to be completed before he'd be allowed to see her again. The emotional side of him wanted to scream with the need to be with her. To touch her.

"She's gonna be okay."

Nate turned to find Gabe standing next to him. He was holding out a paper cup, steam escaping through the plastic lid's tiny opening.

The other man gave him a half-smile. "Thought you could use some coffee."

"Thanks." Nate took the cup.

The heat against his palm had a bit of a bite, but he welcomed it. That pain meant he was alive. And so, by some miracle, was Gracie.

"You did good, Carter. You never gave up."

Nate took a sip, the bitter liquid nearly burning his lips.

Swallowing, he shook his head. "I thought I'd lost her, Gabe. Hell, I *did* lose her."

"But you got her back. You followed your training, listened to your instincts, and stuck with her even when the rest of us probably would have given up. Gracie's alive because of you, Nate. You should be proud of yourself. I know I am."

Any other time, Nate would have jumped at the chance to give Kole a hard time about their team leader bragging on him. Today, he just wanted to be able to look his friend in the eye and tell him Gracie was going to be okay.

"Any word from Kole?"

"He and Sarah are on their way with Jake. They should be here any minute."

Nate looked Gabe square in the eye. "I never thanked you. For helping me get her out of that car."

"Never have to thank me for that, Carter. You're part of Bravo and, as far as I'm concerned, so is Gracie. We take care of our own." When Nate gave him a nod, Gabe went on to say, "I filled McQueen in on what happened and how every-thing went down. He'll need a full report from us all later, but that's nothing you need to worry about right now."

Thoughts of official reports led him to ask, "What's happening with Yavuz? And Rasat and Barry?"

"Ghost and Fletch recovered Yavuz' body. They drove it back to the guy's property and met up with Coach who'd stayed behind with Rasat. Beatle, Hollywood, and Truck went back for Barry. Last I heard, Ryker was sending people in to deal with Yavuz' and Akmar's bodies, and Delta team all met back up and were preparing to escort Barry and Rasat to the States."

Nate thought a moment. Achim Akmar and Edric Yavuz had been taken care of, but there was still one more guy Nate needed to know about.

"What about Walker? Any sign of him?"

"Unfortunately, no. Adrian Walker's in the wind again. I suspect he'll stay that way for a while."

"Hopefully for fucking ever," Matt scowled from the other side of the room.

Nate agreed, though he didn't think Walker was a threat to Gracie anymore. The gun for hire had been paid to bring her to Yavuz, which he had. There was no reason for him or anyone else to come after Gracie again.

The door to the private waiting room opened. They all glanced up to see Sarah rushing in, closely followed by Kole and Jake.

"Nate!" She rushed over and hugged him tightly. "Where's Gracie? She's going to be okay, right? Jake said she was going to be okay."

"Take a breath, babe." Kole pulled Sarah to his side. "I'm sure she's going to be fine." He gave Nate a look that said he hoped he'd just told his fiancée the truth.

Nate didn't want to give her false hope, in case the unthinkable happened. "The doctors are still with her."

"What happened? Jake told us the car she was in went over the side of a bridge and into a lake?" Sarah sounded horrified just saying the words.

"Um, yeah," he nodded, trying his damnedest not to think about those terrifying moments. "She, uh...she went under, but Gabe and I...we got her back up." His eyes went to Kole's, as he struggled to share the worst of it. "She wasn't...her pulse. She didn't..."

Jesus, what was the matter with him? It was as if he'd lost the ability to speak in complete sentences, for fuck's sake.

"Nate saved your sister's life, Sarah," Matt stepped up beside him. "That's all you need to focus on right now."

With a grateful glance, Nate shared a look with his teammate, who gave him a wink and a pat on his back before heading over to the cushioned chair in the corner of the room.

"So, what now?" Sarah turned to Nate for the answer.

He gave her the only one he had. "We wait."

The waiting was the worst. Nate felt as though he was

being ripped apart from the inside out with the need to see Gracie again. To touch her and be able to tell her how he felt.

An hour and sixteen minutes later, he finally got that chance.

"I'm assuming you are all here for Gracelynn McDaniels?"

Nate's head snapped up. Standing in the doorway was Gracie's doctor. He was an older gentleman with nearly snow white hair, but his eyes told Nate he was as sharp as a tack.

"I am," he shot out of his chair. Remembering the others in the room, he added, "We are."

"I'm Doctor Callahan." The man shook Nate's hand. "I've been taking care of Gracelynn."

"Nate. I'm Gracie's...we're..." Shit. He wasn't sure what to even call himself.

"Nate and Gracie are together, Doctor." Sarah stepped forward.

Kole stood behind her, his hands resting on her shoulders. "How is Gracie?"

"She's stable and resting comfortably."

"Oh, thank God." Sarah's watery praise of relief mimicked Nate's silent one.

"Can we see her?" Nate asked, not caring how desperate he sounded.

"You may. But only one at a time, for now."

God, Nate wanted to be the one to go in there, but Sarah was Gracie's sister. He should let her go first.

"You go." Sarah offered before he could, surprising the hell out of him.

"You sure?"

She smiled. "Yeah. Trust me, she'll want to see you first."

Nate prayed her sister was right. "Thank you."

Sarah grabbed hold of him again and gave him a tight

hug. "No, Nate. Thank *you*. You brought my sister back home to me. I'll never forget that."

Nate fought against the sudden onslaught of emotions and stepped back. "I'll let her know you all are here."

"Take your time," Kole smiled.

Nate followed the doctor down the long, white hallway to Gracie's room. Before he went in, Dr. Callahan filled him in on the extent of her injuries.

"She's going to be weak for a few days due to the lack of nutrients and dehydration."

"Lack of nutrients?"

The doctor nodded. "It appears as though Miss McDaniels hasn't eaten in several days. She was also severely dehydrated."

Several days?

Nate flashed back to that moment in the car. She was trying to tell him she was too weak to hold her breath, but he'd been so busy trying to keep her from dying that he hadn't paid much attention to her physical appearance.

A renewed rage toward Yavuz made Nate wish the man was still alive, just so he could kill him all over again.

"What else?"

"She lost quite a bit of blood from the gunshot wound, but not enough to cause any major concern. We cleaned and bandaged the tears to her wrists and one of her ribs was cracked. Thankfully, the location of the fracture prevented it from breaking any further during the administration of CPR."

During the plane ride here, Matt had triaged Gracie before hooking her up to an I.V. Nate thought his heart would stop when he realized she'd been shot. To find out her rib was broken, too?

All that time he'd been pushing on her chest...it was a wonder he hadn't punctured her lung.

"Jesus."

"She's going to be fine, Nate," the doctor assured him. "She'll be sore for the next week or two, but thanks to whoever got her blood pumping again, I see no reason she won't make a complete recovery."

"Thanks, Doc," Nate shook the man's hand.

He didn't bother to taking credit for the save. It had been a team effort. He couldn't have done it alone.

"I took the liberty of giving her some pain medication to help with the rib. Between that and the trauma she's endured, I suspect she'll remain sleeping for at least the next few hours."

"Thank you," Nate said again.

Dr. Callahan nodded his head. "I'll go fill your friends in on what I just shared with you. You're welcome to stay as long as you'd like."

Nate watched as the kind man turned and walked back toward the waiting room. Taking a deep breath, he then pushed the door to Gracie's room open and stepped inside.

Every ounce of air he'd just drawn in escaped with a loud rush.

There, looking so fragile he thought she might break if he touched her, lay Gracie. Her hands were at her sides and she was hooked up to several monitors. One in particular beeped with every glorious beat of her heart.

It was a sound he could listen to forever.

Stepping closer, Nate grabbed one of the plastic chairs, dragging it to the side of the bed without the I.V. stand. Before he sat down, he leaned over the metal railing and pressed his lips to her forehead.

After letting them linger there a few seconds, he rested his forehead against hers and whispered, "I'm here, Gracie. There's something I need to tell you. Something really important, but you have to be awake to hear it. So, I'm going to stay right here until you wake up."

Both emotionally and physically exhausted, Nate kissed her lips before settling into the chair. Reaching between the railings, he took her hand in his and let out a slow, steady breath.

She was okay. Gracie was alive and breathing, and she was going to be okay.

Something happened, then.

One minute, he was just sitting there, watching Gracie's chest move up and down with each magical breath she took. The next, Nate found himself replaying the horrific scene of that fucking car going over the bridge, along with everything else that had happened.

Him waking up in the hospital, only to be told she was missing.

The guilt and shame from finding out she'd been chained to a fucking bed and starved while he and the guys were all sitting around at Jake's eating pizza.

Her telling him she loved him when she thought she was going to die.

Pulling her lifeless body through the water.

Pushing against her chest, begging her not to leave him.

Again and again, Nate was hit with the same terror he'd experienced when he thought he'd lost her forever. It played over and over in his mind, ending with the profound relief he'd felt only moments ago when the doctor had assured him she would be fine.

Then, it started all over again.

Somewhere in the middle of the vicious, heartbreaking cycle, it happened. Sitting there, with Gracie's limp hand held tightly between both of his, Nathan Carter broke.

He tried to fight it at first, but it was no use. Tears fell down both cheeks as he hung his head and wept.

His broad shoulders shook with silent sobs while he thanked God for not taking her away from him.

When he finally got himself under control, Nate sat up straight. Using the clean shirt he'd changed into on the plane ride here, he dried his damp eyes.

Once he'd regained his composure, Nate gave in to his need to be nearer to her and carefully lowered the bed's railing. He scooted the chair as close to her as he could.

Resting his head on the mattress near her shoulder, Nate gently draped his arm across her waist and closed his eyes. A few minutes later, while holding the most treasured gift he'd ever been given, Nate drifted off to sleep.

Throughout the night, Sarah, Kole, and each member of Bravo and Jake took turns coming in to check on both him and Gracie. After vowing to not leave her side and promising to call if there were any changes, Nate eventually convinced them all to go home and get some rest.

Several hours later, a small, delicate hand began playing with his hair. Suddenly awake, he lifted his head, tears forming again when he saw two gorgeous, sleepy eyes staring back at him.

"H-hi," she smiled, her voice dry and cracking.

"Hi," Nate smiled back, quickly swiping the moisture from his eyes.

"We...made it." Her speech was slow and broken, but the light shining in her eyes let Nate know she truly was going to be okay.

"Yeah, baby," he leaned up and kissed her forehead, then cupped the side of her face with his hand. "We made it."

"You stayed."

Nate didn't care for the surprise he heard in her soft voice. "Of course, I stayed." He reached over to the pink pitcher on the mobile tray and poured her a glass of water.

Placing the bendable straw between her dry lips, he told her, "I've been here all night."

After drinking half the contents in the cup, Gracie looked back at him. "No." She shook her head slowly, her hair making a swishing sound against the stark white pillowcase. "In the car. You stayed with me…in the car."

Squeezing her hand, Nate prayed she could see how serious he was when he said, "I would have died before leaving you there alone."

Her cute brows turned inward. "Why?"

Why? "Gracie, do you remember what you said to me? Just before the water covered your face?"

Gracie licked her lips and nodded. "I remember."

"Did you mean it?"

Her brows scrunched together. "Of course, I meant it."

"Say it again."

She blinked at the somewhat harsh order. "What?"

"Say it again, Gracelynn." He took her face between both hands then. "I need to hear you say the words again. Here. Now. Not because you feel the need to make some sort of dying declaration, but because you want to." He leaned down and gently pressed his lips against hers. "Say it again, baby," he whispered. "Please."

"I love you, Nate."

He smiled wide and kissed her again. "God, Gracie. I love you, too."

"Really?"

Nate chuckled. "Yes, really."

Her smile grew even bigger, even as her eyes drew closed and her words slurred. "That's good."

"Yeah, baby," he agreed. "It sure as hell is."

EPILOGUE

Three weeks later...

Gracie stretched her muscles, relieved when she felt not even the slightest twinge of pain in her rib. She was getting stronger with each day that passed.

Not that she had much of a choice with Nate around.

The man had been so sweet and attentive, but she couldn't so much as fix herself a sandwich without him harping on her to go sit back down and let him do it.

Although, after hearing the story of everything that happened after she'd passed out in the car, she had a better understanding of why he was being so overprotective.

After she'd been discharged from the hospital, Nate had insisted he stay at her apartment while she recovered. Thanks to Jake, the mess from her break-in had been completely cleaned up.

Climbing out of bed, she headed to the bathroom for a quick shower. When she was finished, she decided to put on Nate's favorite shirt...sans panties.

He'd been taking care of every single need she'd had since coming home from the hospital. With the exception of one.

The frustratingly caring man was still so worried about her physical recovery, he was afraid to touch her romantically for fear he'd hurt her.

The only thing hurting her now was the constant ache between her legs.

Determined to remedy that situation, Gracie headed out to the living room where Nate was typing away on his computer.

"What are you working on?" she asked nonchalantly.

Practically slamming his laptop shut, his eyes shot to hers. "Nothing. Do you need something? I can get it for you."

Okay...that was odd.

He started to stand, but Gracie pushed down on his shoulder. Stepping between his open legs, she leaned down and nibbled his earlobe. "As a matter of fact," she whispered. "There is one thing you can help me with."

"Gracie," Nate started to warn her away.

Nope. Not this time.

"I'm fine, Nate." She kissed his cheek. "I've been cleared by the doctor and everything."

He put his hands on her hips. "I get that, but you're still sore. I don't want to hurt you."

Gracie pressed her lips against his neck. "The only thing hurting me is not being able to touch you." She ran the tip of her tongue along his pulse point, smiling when he tilted his head to give her better access. "Not feeling your touch."

"I don't know," he whispered, but even as he said the words, Nate's hands began to move lower.

Reaching the shirt's hem, his fingertips slid beneath the grey fabric. He sucked in a breath. "Jesus," he moved his lips to hers. "You're not wearing any panties."

"Nope," she smiled.

Gracie kissed him like she'd been wanting to for over a week. She knew she'd finally won the battle of the wills when his hands moved around to cover her bare cheeks. He gave them both a squeeze.

"Please, Nate," Gracie begged shamelessly. "It's been ages. I need you."

"God, Gracie," he bit her bottom lip. He shook his head, but then said, "Damn it, I need you, too."

In less than a minute, Nate's belt was undone and his jeans and boxers were pushed down around his ankles. Gracie smiled greedily at the way his long, full shaft stood at attention.

And it was all for her.

Straddling his lap, Gracie took the pulsating erection in her hand and positioned herself above it. With their gazes locked, she slid her body down over his.

Nate's hips pushed upward, determined to get as close to her as was physically possible. Feeling magnificently full, Gracie lifted herself up before coming back down again.

With her hands on his shoulders, she repeated the slow torture again. And again.

Finding the perfect rhythm, their bodies began moving at a faster pace. Reaching between them, Nate's fingers began rubbing her clit, knowing it wouldn't take long to get her there.

"Oh, God, Nate. I'm so close."

Beneath her, he began to thrust harder. Faster. Then, moving his fingertips in tight circles over her swollen bundle of nerves, Nate quickly pushed her over the edge.

"Nate!"

Gracie threw her hands out, grabbing the back of the couch for support. Keeping them there, she held on and rode out her orgasm in a way she knew Nate would love.

Her hips slid back and forth, the hair on his thighs rubbing against her own legs' smooth, sensitive skin.

"Ah, fuck, yeah. Ride me, baby. Just like that."

It only took a couple more thrusts before Nate began filling her womb with his hot seed.

Growling her name loudly, his entire body stiffened beneath hers as his climax hit with full force. She smiled smugly, loving the way he said her name like that when he came.

Letting go of the couch, Gracie took his handsome face between her hands and gave him a long, luscious kiss.

"I love you, Nathan."

"Love you, too, baby."

The smile he gave her made Gracie feel like the luckiest woman in the world. She was about to tell him that when his phone rang from behind her.

"Ignore it," he whispered, staring at her intently. His fingertip gently caressed the side of her face as he brushed a few wild strands behind her ear.

Recognizing Kole's ringtone, she sighed. "It might be work related."

With a scowl, Nate wrapped an arm around her back to keep her from falling and reached for the phone.

Sounding superbly grumpy, he answered with, "Swear to God, if this isn't important, I'll—"

Nate stopped talking to listen to whatever it was Kole was saying. The fingers still gripping her hips held her a bit tighter and Gracie wondered if he even realized he'd done it.

"He did?"

Nate waited as Kole said something else. A funny, almost nervous look flashed across Nate's face, but it was gone before she could be sure.

"Now?" he blinked a couple times. "Uh, yeah. Sure. Give me five to clean up and I'll be there."

Gracie eased herself off his lap, enjoying the groan he almost held in as their bodies separated. Nate narrowed his eyes at whatever Kole was saying now and responded with,

"Keep laughing, asshole. Not like you and Sarah have any room to talk."

Snickering as she walked past, Gracie yelped when Nate's hand landed on her bare cheek. It didn't really hurt, of course, which made her laugh even harder as she went back into the bedroom to change.

Donning a comfy pair of yoga pants and a sports bra and tank, Gracie found Nate by the door, lacing his boots. Her chest tightened.

Nate hadn't been back out on an op since they'd brought her to the hospital. None of the guys had. According to Nate, Alpha Team was back, so Jake had given Bravo this time off, along with her.

She knew Nate would have to go back out into the field at some point, and she trusted every single guy on his team to protect him while they were gone. Still, Gracie worried.

With her heart in her throat, she did her best to sound casual when asking, "Do you know when you'll be back?"

Nate finished tying the last boot and stood to grab his keys. "Half an hour. Hour tops."

"Oh." Yeah, no way could he miss the relief in her voice.

With a lopsided grin, he walked over and rested his hands on her hips. "I'm just meeting Kole for something. Did you think we'd been called out for a job?"

Embarrassed, Gracie shrugged a shoulder. "I wasn't sure."

Nate pulled her to him so her breasts were pressing up against his chest. "Bravo isn't officially available for another big job until Monday, so you don't have to worry about that for a few days yet. But," his brow furrowed. "I will get called out at some point. Is that something you'll be able to handle?"

She realized he was asking if she could be with a man whose job took him away as his would.

Leaning up, she pressed her lips to his. "Of course I can. I mean, I'll worry every minute until you get back, but I trust the guys to keep you safe. And I trust you."

Relief filled his eyes. Taking her mouth in his, Nate gave her the sweetest, softest kiss. "I'll worry about you, too, you know. But just remember, my one goal, aside from keeping my team safe, will always be to come back to you."

"Good." She smiled, knowing in her heart of hearts, he meant it. "Now, go," she shooed him with her hands. "Take care of whatever you need to with Kole and I'll cook us up some dinner while you're gone."

"Sounds good."

He gave her a sweet kiss on the tip of her nose then her lips before heading out the door.

Gracie turned to head to the kitchen, and began an easy meal of spaghetti and meatballs. While the sauce was simmering and the meatballs were baking, she decided to go freshen up a bit before Nate got back home.

She started past the living room toward the hallway, but Nate's closed computer caught the corner of her eye. She stopped.

He'd acted so strangely when she'd first come in to the room earlier. Almost as though he hadn't wanted her to see what he'd been doing.

Gracie glanced at her watch. He'd been gone nearly forty-five minutes. She looked at the door and then back to the computer.

"I really shouldn't," she whispered to herself. It would be a major violation of his privacy. Still...

He's hiding something from you.

Biting her lip, she waited two more seconds before giving in and rushing over to the couch. Sitting down, she took a deep breath and nervously opened the lap top and waited.

When the screen came back to life, Gracie was confused and hurt by what she saw.

Houses. Nate had been looking at a real estate site, and the last page he'd looked at was for a listing nearly an hour out of the city.

Gracie's heart sank. For the past few days she'd been imagining what it would be like if they lived together for real. During that same time, he'd apparently been considering moving farther away from her.

For a second she thought maybe he was thinking of asking her to move in with him, but they'd spent nearly every minute together for the past three weeks and he'd said nothing.

An old, familiar pain filled her chest.

Though it was only an hour away this time, she felt even worse than she had when her ex had told her he was moving to Florida without her. She was still sitting there, dumbfounded when she heard the jingle of Nate's keys in the locks.

Hurrying, Gracie closed his computer and shot up from the couch. She was half a second too late.

Already through the door, Nate's gaze moved from hers, to his computer, then back again. Disappointment shadowed his expression.

He quietly turned and closed the door, re-engaging the locks before setting his keys onto the small table next to him. With a deep sigh, he faced her.

"What were you doing?" he tipped his chin toward his computer.

"Nothing," she lied, a reflexive response she instantly wished she could take back.

He remained quiet, a raised eyebrow his only reaction.

Not quite sure why she felt guilty when he was the one who'd been keeping things from her, Gracie stumbled to find a plausible explanation.

"I-I was just checking my email."

Nate frowned. "Why didn't you use your own computer?"

Shit. "Um…I-I forgot to charge it. Battery's dead."

Studying her a moment, Nate surprised her when the corners of his mouth slowly began to curve upward. "I just realized something else you and your sister have in common."

Gracie didn't even try to guess. "What's that?"

He walked over to her in almost a predatory manor and wrapped his arms around her waist. Leaning in closely, he whispered in her ear.

"You're both terrible liars."

Gracie hid her embarrassment at being caught snooping by addressing the reason she'd felt compelled to do so in the first place. Pushing against his chest, she worked her way loose from his embrace and took a step back.

Arms crossed, she lifted her chin and said, "Well, at least I'm not keeping secrets from you." She let out a frustrated breath. "You're moving?"

Nate closed his eyes for a few seconds before looking at her again with a resolved expression.

"I *might* be. And I was going to tell you."

"When?" She turned toward the kitchen, only then remembering she still had food on the stove and in the oven.

"Soon. I promise. I was just waiting for the right time."

Head in the oven, Gracie pulled the tray of meatballs out and set them on the cooling rack.

"And when would that have been?" she asked without looking at him. "At your open house party?"

Gracie cringed inwardly, not liking herself very much at the moment. Yeah, he should have said something sooner, but that didn't mean she needed to be a total bitch about it.

Unfortunately, her mouth had other thoughts.

"You know, Nate. When you said you loved me, I thought

that meant we were going to give this thing between us a real try."

She grabbed the spatula and began scooping the meatballs off the pan and placing them onto a plate.

"And we are," he stated with certainty from somewhere behind her.

"Then why are you looking at houses almost an hour away from here? And why haven't you said something before now? It's not like there weren't plenty of opportunities."

Still refusing to look at him, she began stirring the sauce with a little more gusto than was necessary.

"I mean, I get that you've probably just been staying here because you feel responsible for what happened to me. Which, by the way, I've made clear on several occasions that it was not necessary for you to do so, nor was anything that Yavuz and his goon did to me your fault in any way."

"I do feel responsible for what happened to you, sweetheart. I always will. But that's not why I've been staying with you."

Still unable to look at him for fear she'd break down into a blubbering mess, Gracie began straining the pasta over the sink.

"I just don't understand," she tried to explain her feelings. "If you want to move away from here, that's fine. But why didn't you tell me that?"

"Like I said, I'd planned to. I just really wanted to talk to you about something else, first."

"What?" She poured the drained noodles back into the large pot.

Nate's voice softened. "This."

Feeling frustrated and hurt, Gracie practically slammed the pot down onto the stove and spun around.

Inhaling sharply, her knees began to shake so suddenly, she had to grab onto the counter's edge to keep from falling.

Nate was in the middle of her living room. And he was down on one knee.

In one of his hands was something small and shiny. She didn't have to see it clearly to know what it was.

"Oh, my God." Her hands flew to her mouth as his image began to blur.

"I didn't tell you about my thoughts on moving yet because I wanted you to have this first." Looking adorably nervous, he gave a little shrug and said, "Kole knows this jeweler who designs one-of-a-kind rings. That's where I went just now. Kole called to tell me the ring I'd had made for you was finished."

And here she'd been ranting on and on about him keeping secrets from her. Gracie was speechless.

"I was trying to plan something really special," he said, still kneeling before her. "I wanted the proposal to be perfect for you. And just so we're clear," he smirked. "This isn't a façade like our last marriage. This is a real engagement ring and I'm really proposing."

"It is perfect," she managed to whisper from behind her trembling fingers. "It's absolutely perfect. Nate, I-I..."

Gracie was so stunned, so full of love and excitement, she could barely speak.

He looked up at her and smiled. "I never believed in love, Gracie. Not really. Then, I met you. You were sunshine and happiness and love, all rolled into one. I couldn't get enough of you." He shrugged. "Never will."

Nate stood then and came to her. Wrapping his fingers around her wrists, he gently pulled her hands from her mouth and kissed her knuckles.

"From the moment I first laid eyes on you, I knew my world would never be the same."

Gracie thought back to that day at Kole and Sarah's. It

seemed a lifetime ago, but she remembered it as if it were yesterday.

Nate was sitting there with that ball cap, looking at her behind those mirrored Aviators and wearing that cocky smile.

Despite having tried to pretend otherwise, deep down she'd known right then that this was a man she needed in her life. She just hadn't realized how much.

Releasing one of her wrists, Nate cupped the side of her face, his thumb caressing her in the most gentlest of touches. Tears welled in his eyes, his words filling her with more love than she'd ever thought possible.

"I can't imagine my life without you, baby. You're everything I never even knew I needed."

Tears poured down her cheeks as he slid the most beautiful ring she'd ever seen onto her finger.

The round stone in the middle was the color of honey and it was surrounded by several small diamonds. It had a vintage feel and it was perfect. Just like him.

"Oh, Nate. It's beautiful."

"I picked that color stone because it matches your hair." He looked down at her with a soul-consuming love and asked, "Gracelynn McDaniels, will you please make me the happiest man in the world and be my wife?"

More tears of joy escaped as she grabbed his face and kissed him. And she kept kissing him until Nate pulled away long enough to ask, "So, is that a yes?"

Laughing and crying all at the same time, Gracie stared back at her future and whispered, "Yes."

* * *

Matt Turner sipped his beer as he watched the couple in the middle of the dance floor.

He was happy for Kole and Sarah, glad they'd finally tied the knot. The pair actually seemed ridiculously perfect for each other.

Though, they only had eyes for each other, he raised his glass to them anyway, silently wishing them nothing but the best in their future.

Matt glanced over at Nate and Gracie, who were also engaged to be married. That one had shocked him a little, considering the recent trials and tribulations those two had been through.

He'd even mentioned his concerns to Nate last month when he'd announced their engagement to the team while shooting at Jake's private range. Of course, being a man 'in love', Nate had simply smiled and patted him on the back, giving Matt a speech that still haunted him, all these weeks later.

Life's short, Matt. When you find the woman you want to spend it with, you need to grab on tight and never let her go. Even if you have to stand and fight death, itself, for her. Because when you truly love someone, you'll realize she's worth every drop of sweat and every tear that may fall. You'll also figure out pretty damn quick that, without her in your life, everything else seems meaningless.

Earlier tonight, after Sarah and Kole had vowed to love one another forever, Matt received one final piece of Nathan Carter wisdom.

Trust me, Turner. Your time is coming.

Matt looked back over at Nate and his fiancée. The two were snuggled up at a table in the corner, laughing about who knows what.

He shook his head and swallowed the last of his beer.

Normally, he would've spent the night trolling the crowd for a hot bridesmaid to give him a night of empty, meaningless sex. Tonight, Matt surprised even himself by wanting to get as far away from the scene as possible.

Standing, he made his way to the reception hall's exit. Nate's damning words were still rolling through his mind as he left without so much as a goodbye to anyone.

He understood Nate had meant well with his little talk a few weeks back, but what Matt's buddy didn't know was that he'd already found the perfect woman.

She was soft and sweet. Funny and cute. And smart. God, she'd been so fucking smart.

It had blown him away when he found out she had a crush on him, too. From that point on, Matt had been on cloud nine and before long, he was planning his own happily ever after.

But that was all before.

After, Matt had vowed never to give that much power to another woman again. Now, he had rules when it came to the fairer sex. The first and foremost being to never, ever, let it become serious.

If he did, he'd risk dropping his guard down. Maybe even find someone he could really care about.

Fuck that. He already knew how that turned out.

Now, Matt got in and out, and then he moved on. Never again would he let his guard down. Not for *any* woman.

Because Matthew Turner wasn't someone who made the same mistake twice.

* * *

Want to read more from Ms. Blakely's R.I.S.C. Series? *See how it all started with Jake and the rest of Alpha Team by clicking below:*

Book 1: **Taking a Risk, Part One** (Jake & Olivia's HFN)
Book 2: **Taking a Risk, Part Two** (Jake & Olivia's HEA)

Book 3: **Beautiful Risk** (Trevor & Lexi)

Coming Soon:
Book 4: **Intentional Risk** (Derek & Charlotte "Charlie")
Book 5: **Unpredictable Risk** (Grant & Brynnon)

Want to read Kole & Sarah's story for FREE?
Click below to sign up for Anna Blakely's newsletter and receive your *FREE copy* of *Unexpected Risk-A Bravo Team Novella*
https://dl.bookfunnel.com/u3zicn7yhu
*Unexpected Risk was originally released as part of the Because He's Perfect charity anthology. It is now only available through this link, and brings you Kole & Sarah's trying experience while dealing with shocking news and a malevolent stalker.

ABOUT THE AUTHOR

Author Anna Blakely brings you stories of love, action, and edge-of-your-seat suspense. As an avid reader of romantic suspense herself, Anna's dream is to create stories her readers will enjoy and characters they'll fall in love with as much as she has. She believes in true love and happily-ever-after, and that's what she will always bring to you.

Anna lives in rural Missouri with her husband, children, and several rescued animals. When she's not writing, Anna enjoys reading, watching action and horror movies (the scarier the better), and spending time with her amazing husband, four wonderful children, and her adorable granddaughter.

FB Author Page: facebook.com/annablakely.author.7
Blakely's Bunch (reader group): https://www.facebook.com/groups/354218335396441/
Instagram: https://instagram.com/annablakely
BookBub: https//www.bookbub.com/authors/anna-blakely
Amazon: amazon.com/author/annablakely
Twitter: @ablakelyauthor
Goodreads: https://www.goodreads.com/author/show/18650841.Anna_Blakely

facebook.com/annablakely.author.7

twitter.com/ablakelyauthor

instagram.com/annablakely

amazon.com/author/annablakely

There are many more books in this fan fiction world than listed here, for an up-to-date list go to www.AcesPress.com

You can also visit our Amazon page at: http://www.amazon.com/author/operationalpha

Special Forces: Operation Alpha World

Denise Agnew: Dangerous to Hold
Shauna Allen: Awakening Aubrey
Shauna Allen: Defending Danielle
Shauna Allen: Rescuing Rebekah
Shauna Allen: Saving Scarlett
Shauna Allen: Saving Grace
Brynne Asher: Blackburn
Jennifer Becker: Hiding Catherine
Julia Bright: Saving Lorelei
Julia Bright: Rescuing Amy
Victoria Bright: Surviving Savage
Victoria Bright: Going Ghost
Victoria Bright: Jostling Joker
Cara Carnes: Protecting Mari
Kendra Mei Chailyn: Beast
Kendra Mei Chailyn: Barbie
Kendra Mei Chailyn : Pitbull
Melissa Kay Clarke: Rescuing Annabeth
Melissa Kay Clarke: Safeguarding Miley
Samantha A. Cole: Handling Haven
Samantha A. Cole: Cheating the Devil
Sue Coletta: Hacked
Melissa Combs: Gallant
KaLyn Cooper: Rescuing Melina
Liz Crowe: Marking Mariah
Jordan Dane: Redemption for Avery

Margaret Madigan: Jungle Buck
Margaret Madigan: December Chill
Rachel McNeely: The SEAL's Surprise Baby
Rachel McNeely: The SEAL's Surprise Bride
Rachel McNeely: The SEAL's Surprise Twin
KD Michaels: Saving Laura
KD Michaels: Protecting Shane
KD Michaels: Avenging Angels
Wren Michaels: The Fox & The Hound
Wren Michaels: The Fox & The Hound 2
Wren Michaels: Shadow of Doubt
Wren Michaels: Shift of Fate
Wren Michaels: Steeling His Heart
Kat Mizera: Protecting Bobbi
Mary B Moore: Force Protection
LeTeisha Newton: Protecting Butterfly
LeTeisha Newton: Protecting Goddess
LeTeisha Newton: Protecting Vixen
LeTeisha Newton: Protecting Heartbeat
MJ Nightingale: Protecting Beauty
MJ Nightingale: Betting on Benny
MJ Nightingale: Protecting Secrets
Sarah O'Rourke: Saving Liberty
Debra Parmley: Protecting Pippa
Debra Parmley: Split Screen Scream
Lainey Reese: Protecting New York
Jenika Snow: Protecting Lily
Jen Talty: Burning Desire
Jen Talty: Burning Kiss
Jen Talty: Burning Skies
Jen Talty: Burning Lies
Jen Talty: Burning Heart
Megan Vernon: Protecting Us
Megan Vernon: Protecting Earth

As you know, this book included at least one character from Susan Stoker's books. To check out more, see below.

SEAL of Protection: Legacy Series
Securing Caite
Securing Brenae (novella)
Securing Sidney
Securing Piper
Securing Zoey (Jan 2020)
Securing Avery (May 2020)
Securing Kalee (Sept 2020)

Delta Team Two Series
Shielding Gillian (Apr 2020)
Shielding Kinley (Aug 2020)
Shielding Aspen (Oct 2020)
Shielding Riley (TBA)
Shielding Devyn (TBA)
Shielding Ember (TBA)
Shielding Sierra (TBA)

Delta Force Heroes Series
Rescuing Rayne (FREE!)
Rescuing Aimee (novella)
Rescuing Emily
Rescuing Harley
Marrying Emily (novella)
Rescuing Kassie
Rescuing Bryn
Rescuing Casey
Rescuing Sadie (novella)
Rescuing Wendy
Rescuing Mary

Rescuing Macie (Novella)

Badge of Honor: Texas Heroes Series

Justice for Mackenzie (FREE!)
Justice for Mickie
Justice for Corrie
Justice for Laine (novella)
Shelter for Elizabeth
Justice for Boone
Shelter for Adeline
Shelter for Sophie
Justice for Erin
Justice for Milena
Shelter for Blythe
Justice for Hope
Shelter for Quinn
Shelter for Koren
Shelter for Penelope

SEAL of Protection Series

Protecting Caroline (FREE!)
Protecting Alabama
Protecting Fiona
Marrying Caroline (novella)
Protecting Summer
Protecting Cheyenne
Protecting Jessyka
Protecting Julie (novella)
Protecting Melody
Protecting the Future
Protecting Kiera (novella)
Protecting Alabama's Kids (novella)
Protecting Dakota

New York Times, *USA Today* and *Wall Street Journal* Bestselling Author Susan Stoker has a heart as big as the state of Tennessee where she lives, but this all American girl has also spent the last fourteen years living in Missouri, California, Colorado, Indiana, and Texas. She's married to a retired Army man who now gets to follow *her* around the country.

www.stokeraces.com
www.AcesPress.com
susan@stokeraces.com

Made in United States
Cleveland, OH
15 July 2025

18580930R00184